The
Tamago
Stories

Owning Our Asian American Stories

By Vincent Yee

ISBN-13: 978-0-9859320-1-5

Second Edition

DEDICATION

Dedicated to Dr. Susumu "Sus" Ito, First Lientenant, FA NB, 442ⁿᵈ who was the only person who knew the name of this short story collection before his passing in 2015. With respect to his patriotic service to our country, in celebration of his life, and in remembrance of all the Japanese food we had together at GARI.

Dedicated to the next generation of Asian Americans who will yearn for stories where they are the heroes and heroines.

STORIES

ENGAGEMENT

I remember that dash to the restaurant well after I had luckily spotted a parking spot that early autumn evening. I was already late, but I was eager to meet the celebrity chef whom I respected and had gotten to meet in person some time back. Her first cookbook had just come out, and I wanted one autographed by her. She was in Boston only for that day, as she was scheduled to leave the next day for a national book tour, so time was pressing.

I entered the restaurant that started her career and asked the hostess about the book signing. The hostess, a brunette with hair elaborately tied up to suit the gourmet ambiance, turned her expression from cheery to disappointed. When she said, "I'm sorry, sir, the book signing for Kristi K. Shen ended about 30 minutes ago," my heart sank.

Suddenly, I heard "Andrew!" and I looked past the hostess in that direction to the familiar voice of Kristi. She waved me over to the private area in the back that must have been cordoned off for the book signing, and the hostess smiled and gestured in that direction.

Kristi was looking sharp in all-black slacks and a blouse. Her demeanor was always fresh and friendly, and I embraced her whole-heartedly. No one else was in the private dining area aside from two staffers who were cleaning up.

"It's about time!" she said teasingly.

"You know this Boston traffic," I said. "But I totally lucked out on the parking. As soon as I had the green light, I made a U-turn, parked and ran over here!"

"Well, you're in luck, I saved you the last cookbook!"

I smiled and extended my hands excitedly toward her. With a smile, she turned toward the nearby table and picked up the last cookbook. I received it with admiration and lauded Kristi by saying, "Congratulations! This is so exciting!"

"I know! It's so surreal! Who would have thought that a lowly sous chef would go on to win a top cooking show and to write a cookbook?" asked Kristi rhetorically.

I carefully flipped through a menu of culinary photos that started to pique my culinary aspirations. I got to the first few blank pages and said, "It's not autographed yet."

"Of course not! I thought you'd like to get a picture of me autographing it for you," said Kristi.

"You know my photo life too well," I said with some embarrassment.

Kristi plucked a sharpie from her front pant pocket, when all of a sudden, a voice interrupted us. "Oh no, is that the last cookbook?"

I turned around to see who had spoken when I was awestruck by the young woman behind me. Despite the beautiful black hair that framed her angelic face, she had a distraught expression. She wasn't even looking at me, but at Kristi, and I could only surmise that she was another culinary fan.

This beautiful woman, donned in a bluish wool coat that covered her black-skirt-and-ivory-blouse ensemble, literally walked past me until she was facing Kristi. She looked at my cookbook and then back at Kristi.

"I'm afraid it is…" said Kristi.

"I can't believe this. I saw this parking spot, but this car made a U-turn and got it before I could get to it. I had to circle the block to find another parking spot," I remember her saying. This made me feel entirely guilty because it was me that made that U-turn and took that parking spot.

"I'm so sorry to hear that, but you can always buy the book on Amazon," said Kristi reassuringly.

"But I so wanted to get a photo of you autographing it for me for my Instagram. My friends would have been so impressed," she said disappointedly.

It was either the guilt of me taking her parking spot with my aggressive Boston driving or the immense disappointment on her face that made me do the unthinkable.

"Here, you can have my copy," I said to her with a smile.

Finally she took notice of me and looked up. Her eyes turned into wonderment, and I felt a sense of Pope-like benevolence.

She didn't hesitate to grasp for the book, but her eagerness gave way to a sense of courtesy as she asked me, "Are you sure?"

I remembered smiling back, trying to be nonchalant, even though I really wanted that cookbook. But I very much wanted to meet this woman, so I said, "On one condition."

The young woman cocked her head a bit and teasingly said, "OK, what's the one condition?"

"Only if I can cook one of those recipes for you," I said confidently as I glanced at the cookbook. I'm not sure where the courage came from, but right there and then, as she and I held onto the cookbook together and our eyes locked, I just knew something was stirring.

As if on cue, our favorite chef Kristi interjected, "You should, Andrew is a great chef himself!" From there on, I knew Kristi was my wing woman, and I turned to her in appreciation for the good word, though she had never tasted any of my cooking before.

With a bit of confidence, courage, and chivalry, I was introduced to the ever-grateful and beautiful Melissa that fateful night.

She took me up on dinner a couple of weeks later, and of course, she chose the most complicated recipe in the cookbook. But I was prepared, and with Kristi giving me some inside tips, I cooked a glorious dinner that night, and soon we were doing everything together. The restaurant-hopping, the autumn walks at night, enjoying the theater, and just cuddling up on the sofa watching the latest series on Netflix along with take out had enriched my life. She also taught this poor soul how to salsa as we took classes during the winter. Her presence provided that missing piece in my life, which made me serious about asking her to marry me. There was no mistake that we intuitively understood one another, and we complemented each other very well.

I remember going to Tiffany's, wanting to buy that special engagement ring. I took the liberty of educating myself on the three Cs of diamonds (cut, clarity and carat). Though, of course, seeing the prices, I truly believed that one of the three Cs should have stood for cost. But this was one time where cost was not going to be a factor. This time, the ring would symbolize my love for her and the commitment that I wanted to have between us. Funny how commitment wasn't one of the three Cs. Though the sales lady was more than helpful that day, I decided not to purchase a ring just yet. There was so many to choose from. I wanted the time to think and choose carefully. Anyway, my lunch hour was about over, and I had to return to the office.

After work that day, I was supposed to go my parents' house for dinner. It was also an opportunity for me to tell my parents about my tentative plans. My parents knew of Melissa, but not too much. They just knew that she was the woman that I was seeing. My parents had tried to arrange dates for me in the past, which never worked out, especially when they started to name women who I went to elementary school with. Their amusing reasons like, "and she just lives down the street," was always laughable. But that night, I was going to tell them how I had found my perfect match, and that their dreams of having grandkids may soon be a reality.

My younger sister was out of town, so it was just my parents and me. Dinner went well; my mother made fish, the regular tofu dish, along with *bok choi*. Being in my early thirties, I'm sure that my telling them that I wanted to finally settle down would make them happy. They, of course, asked me about Melissa and I deferred the questioning until after dinner. My parents were curious; they'd only seen a few pictures of her and heard my wonderful accolades about her. After I helped my mother clear the table, I told my parents that I had some interesting news to tell them. I could see that they were eager to hear what I had to say. I told my parents that everything was going very well with Melissa, and even though we'd gone out for less than a year, I wanted to ask her to marry me. My announcement garnered the anticipated response, and I could see their elation. Their son was going to get married. It was at this point that my parents wanted to know more about Melissa and her family.

Melissa was an account executive at a large Boston advertising firm. She shared many of the Chinese values that Chinese parents could only wish for in a daughter-in-law, and was contemporary as well. I told them that I had not asked Melissa to marry me yet because I had not bought the ring. Of course, my parents admonished me by saying that I shouldn't spend my entire life savings on an engagement ring, and that a smart wife to be would understand that. My parents were clueless. I conveyed to them that having Melissa in my life had made me very happy. The conversation seemed to be going fine until

I started to tell my parents about Melissa's parents.

Melissa's parents emigrated from Taiwan when she was seven years old. My father's once happy expression turned serious. "She's Taiwanese?" he asked. To my astonishment, I said, "Yes." He pressed on, "And you never mentioned this?" and I responded by saying, "Should it matter?"

My father was stern, steeped in old politics from a generation ago. He was very strict when my sister and I were young. Always making sure that we did our homework and studied, even when we didn't have too. Even during summer vacations, my father and my mother would bring us to the library to read more books. We even had to go to school on Chinese New Year. He frowned on my sister and me taking up sports in high school, but he tolerated it as long as we brought home the grades. In college, sports were not even a consideration. My parents saved up their hard-earned money to send my sister and me to top colleges and paid the tuition entirely in cash because they did not want my sister and me to be burdened with debt after graduation. My parents took great pride in, and the credit for, my academic and financial success. It gave them joy to tell their friends that their son was an investment banker and that my sister was studying to be a doctor.

Because my father was born in China before moving to Hong Kong, he held onto a strong sense of pride in being Chinese. To him, the Taiwanese were traitors. My father's serious tone took hold, my mother looked concerned as well, but probably not for the same reasons as my father. She seemed more concerned about the brewing situation at hand. My father quickly silenced me despite my objections, and my father went on to lecture me.

"You know how I feel about the Taiwanese. They are really Chinese, but they are acting liked spoiled children, and they are making China look weak. Until they reunite with China, we should never associate with them, and definitely no son of mine will marry a Taiwanese!" he said firmly.

At this point I got up. I was furious, and my parents could see my face, distorted in frustration and anger. I did not know what to think at that time. I have met the woman of my dreams, the woman who I wanted to share my life with. I could see our wedding in my head, from the; the groomsmen behind me, the bridesmaids, the flower girl, the ring boy, and Melissa in some beautiful wedding gown. She would be the woman who I wanted to have children with and now my father was forbidding it? This was supposed to be a happy occasion for me, a time I wanted to share with my parents.

But my life was mine, and so too should my choice on who to marry. I tried to inject reason into my father that his politics were not mine, but he fired back. He stood up, pointed his finger in my face and with his stern look stammered, "You will not marry a Taiwanese!" Even though my father was several inches shorter than me, he was still a very imposing man. The mental control that he held over me was still there, and I felt myself stepping back, my spine turning to gelatin, holding myself in check. I looked to my mother, who was visibly shaken by the turn of events. She watched on as the two most important men in her life were arguing, or rather, one being lectured relentlessly.

I pleaded silently for her help, but she wouldn't lend it. She'd known of his political views for too long. She was going to take my father's side on the matter. I continued to tell my father about Melissa's virtues, and that if he would just meet her, he would accept her. He vehemently said that that was out of the question. He continued his berating of me, telling me that if I married a Taiwanese that he would disown me. He told me that I would be a disgrace to everything that he stood for.

I didn't know what to do. Every bit of my gut instinct told me that I wanted Melissa, but something in the back of my mind began to slowly ensnare me, telling me to listen to my father. I was so close to agreeing with my father that my chest began to tighten up in twisted knots. My heart was pounding furiously, beating against my head like the pounding of large Chinese New Year lion dancing drums. I felt the tears in my eyes begin to seep in, and I was about to give in when something happened. My fists tightened like steel clamps, and I muttered my answer: "No."

My father looked at me surprised, but his surprise was quickly replaced by disappointed anger. His hand came out of nowhere as it slapped me hard against my left cheek. The sound was intensely percussive. My mother let out a gasp. I could feel the sting upon my face, spreading outward and the blood in my cheeks swelling, filling every capillary there was. Without warning, a deep intense emotion swelled up from within me, it enveloped me and hunkered back deep within me like a cowered animal. But soon, this feeling had nowhere to turn as it felt cornered. An overwhelming fiery sense from whence unknown began to stir within. My head was still cocked to the side. I slowly turned my head back to face my father. I could see something different in his expression. My eyes met his, and I was no longer afraid. With my right hand, I grabbed him by the right shoulder collar and threw my forearm up against his neck, under his chin. My left hand grabbed his clothing at his mid torso. I began to push furiously. My father's bracing steps failed against my onslaught as I rammed him up against the wall, hitting him with such force the pictures on the fireplace mantle shook, and the breath in him was knocked out. I lifted him a few inches off the hardwood floor. His angry countenance was replaced by one of struggle and fear. His eyes began to bulge, his face turned a deep red, and the blood vessels on the side of his neck began to swell. But I had not noticed as the wrath in me took hold. I was physically stronger than my father and had been for many years.

I looked at the man who had held me hostage for so many years and unleashed myself at him.

"No! No! No! I have always done what you wanted of me, *Ba-ba*. I have always listened to you. I was always here when you needed me. I did everything you asked. I got good grades. I got into a great college. I studied my ass off and I got a good job! I did everything you told me to, and I became a success because of it, but you know what *Ba-ba*? Do you know that I was unhappy too! Yes! I was unhappy! I cried on many occasions because I couldn't hang out with my friends or I couldn't go to that party or stay out late on a school night. And every time when I did not listen to you, I did what you told me in the end. I took your punishment and your lectures but… I will not take them anymore! I am a grown man, and I will make decisions for myself. Even, even if we do not speak to each other again, I will still be there when you need me because that is the kind of son I am! But I will not listen to you! Not anymore! I will marry Melissa because I love her, *Ba-ba*!"

It was at this point that I felt my mother clutching my arms, trying to free her husband. I turned to meet her, and I could see the tears streaming down her face, and her screams pleading with me to let go of her husband, my father. She was shaking uncontrollably as she tried to use her body weight to break me free of my father, but to no avail. I looked at my father, and I could see he was choking with my forearm against his neck. He couldn't breathe. A sense of reality ripped into me, making me realize my horrible actions. I stepped back and released my grip upon my father. He slumped onto his knees with a thud, his hand rushing to his neck as he began to cough loudly. My mother quickly knelt beside him, tending to him, asking him if he was okay through her choked-backed tears.

I stared at my parents on the floor in front of me, and I asked myself what I had done. The emotion that possessed me just then vanished as quickly as it had appeared. I didn't know what to do. I roughly slid my fingers from my temples through my hair, let out a frustrated primal groan, and raced for the door. I heard my mother calling after me as I threw the door open. I looked back and I saw my mother with one arm outstretched to me, pleading with me to come back. But I couldn't, I just couldn't, so I went through the door, to escape the nightmare that I had just been a part of.

The next morning I awoke, still dressed in the previous night's clothes. I found myself on the couch as I straightened myself to a sitting position. I placed my elbows on my knees and let my face rest in my cupped hands as I tried to recollect what had happened the previous night. Everything was still vividly clear, but it was more like a flash. I rubbed my face into my hands and then through my hair. Despite what happened last night with my parents, I knew what I had to do. I called in to work and told them I would be a few hours late, which they found surprising, since I was always punctual. I told them that a personal matter had come up that I had to tend to.

I showered, got dressed, and left my condo. I found myself at Tiffany's once more and glanced down at the display case. The sales lady who helped me before came over and welcomed me back. I acknowledged her, and without a second's hesitation, I pointed to it. She looked up at me and asked "Are you sure?" I placed my American Express Black Card on the glass counter, and I said, "Yes, no need to bag it."

I arrived at Melissa's office; every minute in the elevator seemed like an eternity. The receptionist asked if she could help. I merely told her that I could find my way, which is when she started to say "Sir?!" repeatedly, which I conveniently ignored. I walked down a hall when I saw Melissa in her office. The door was wide open. She saw me as well and gave an astonished look. I quickly entered her office and closed the door when she asked me what happened to my face. I gently took her hand away from my cheek and I told her not to worry about it. A concerned look came over her angelic face. I took both her hands in mine and kissed them gently. I motioned to the couch in her office and sat her down. I knelt down in front of her and looked up at her.

With the same courage that I had to ask her to let me cook dinner for, I said, "Melissa, you know that I love you. So I have only one simple question: Would you marry me?"

Flawless that moment in every detail except, that the ring was not yet on the finger of the most beautiful woman to me. She let out a quick gasp as her right hand went quickly to her mouth. I could see the excitement in her eyes and with the same determination, I removed the ring from its case and slipped it onto Melissa's finger. I looked up once more and asked, "Will you?"

She threw her hands around me as she lunged forward, knocking me flat on my back. Her hug was vise-like as she said, "Yes!" numerous times in a gleeful voice. At that moment, the greatest burden in me was lifted, and joy rushed in to fill its void. We hugged and shared a joyful laugh as we held each other on the floor of her office. She sat on top of me, her smile beaming. I pushed back her hair to reveal her face when she reaffirmed in that confident voice of hers, "Yes, I will marry you." With my hand on her cheek, I drew her close until the lips were against mine and engaged in one of the most passionate kisses ever between us.

Much as I did not want the kiss to end, I told her I had to leave. There was a knock at the door, and I could hear the receptionist asking Melissa if everything was okay. Melissa, giggling, replied by saying nothing could be better. I held Melissa in my arms, indulging myself in that moment. I looked deeply into those eyes of hers and found happiness. I told her that I needed to go do something, and I promised her that I would see her at dinner.

I approached my parents' house. I looked about house, the grass that I helped my father mow and from which I removed the stubborn weeds when I was a kid, the tree that my sister and I used to climb, which usually resulted in my mother yelling at us to get off before we fell and broke our legs. I walked up the path and came to the front door. I did not know what to expect. This was one time where I did not know where I stood with my parents, but I knew I had to reconcile with them after the previous night's incident. I stood there not knowing how much time had passed. I let out a sigh to calm myself as I rang the doorbell. It seemed like hours until I heard the unmistakable steps of my mother. A sound of surprise came from her as she unlocked the door.

She stood there in the front doorway. A rush of guilt raced through me as I choked back the word, "Ma-ma." I stepped toward her cautiously, and she quickly embraced me and surprisingly told me there was nothing to worry about. She reassuringly patted me on the back as she led me into the house. "Where's *Ba-ba*?" I asked, to which she replied "In the study. Go, go see him. We didn't expect to see you until later today. I called your phone, but you didn't pick up. It's OK now. Go, go see your father." With a reassuring smile, she ushered me into the study where my father was sitting behind his desk.

He seemed surprised to see me, and I was glad that I did not leave any visible damage upon him. He raised himself from his seat and told me to seat myself at the couch. There was no hug, no handshake, but he did not seem to be mad, and I did not know what he was going to say. At this point, I did not care if he did not approve of my wanting to marry Melissa. If he was going to convince me otherwise, I was going to tell him that it was too late, that I had already proposed to her. My father looked at me, though his stare was stern, there was something new in his eyes.

He simply said, "You're a man now who can make his own decisions, I respect that." He reached out for my hand. His simple gesture was so confusing and I took his hand with mixed feelings. He held my hand, like a father to a son, looked at me once more and said, "Make sure you and Melissa give your mother and me grandchildren."

To this day, that day with my father is still one of the strangest days in my life. I still cannot fully comprehend what transpired, and perhaps it shall always remain so. I tried to come up with several reasons for my father's odd response, and could only reason the following possibility. In that moment of unbridled hatred, frustration, and anger I showed my father a side of myself that I've never allowed him to see. Perhaps what scared him the most was in that moment of anger, he saw himself through me. And strangely enough, it may have been that one moment in life that my father gave me the one thing I always wanted but never seemed to be able to achieve: respect. I had always done everything he asked without question, and when I finally stood up to him, I achieved what I wanted not by listening to him, but by demanding it of him.

It wasn't until few years later that my mother told me that after I left following that horrible physical engagement with my father, she knelt by my father until he could finally breathe normally again. She helped him to the couch, where he sat for some time, head leaning back facing the ceiling, in deep perplexed thought. She brought out a couple things out later that night: a cup of tea and the old copy of the U.S. Naturalization handbook that they had studied with years earlier. As he drank the tea, she reminded him that one of the reasons why he came to America was to be free from China's politics at that time, despite his pride in still being Chinese. After he understood her message, they spent the entire night reminiscing about their own journey in America.

As for grandchildren, my parents have two that keep them very engaged.

B A – B A

She gently gathered up the sheer black stocking and slowly pulled it over her foot. The stocking sensually clung to her smooth skin and glided over her toned calves and then her thighs. She slipped her crimson polished fingernails beneath the top of her thigh-high and made sure it was snug. Gently, Maya stretched out her legs, side by side, and compared the evenness of her thigh-highs.

Her black eyelash extensions undulated as she blinked a couple of times, playing in concert with her black eyeliner that she had expertly applied. Her lips were a vibrant glistening red, an invitation to be kissed.

She drew her right leg inward as her full wavy black hair dangled about her and she reached for the shiny black high heels that she was going to wear for the night. She slipped into them and leaned back as her red satin robe fell to her sides, showing her black lacy bustier and panties hugging her toned body. She clutched her hands together and placed them on her knees and let out a tired sigh under her breath.

A knock came at the door and she looked up. She asked for a moment as she pulled her robe together with the satin sash around her waist.

"Come in," she said.

The door opened and with his burly hand still holding the doorknob, he couldn't help but cast an eye on the beauty sitting on the bench before him. He was a middle-aged white man, with grayish hair cropped close to his sides and scalp. His face was leathered and his eyes were a dull blue, a sea of gritty life experiences. His denim shirt was loose, showing a hint of a beer belly, and his faded jeans were frayed at the hems that crumpled over his brown leather boots. A holstered black gun clung to the right side of his weathered brown belt.

She couldn't help but feel that he was undressing her with his eyes and to break the moment, she politely asked, "Do we finally have a customer tonight?"

The man's momentary distraction was broken, and he replied firmly, "Yah, we got one. You're going to like this one, a dirty old Asian man for you," he said with a smirk. "And he asked for our youngest girl."

"Oh, great," she thought. Her previous customers had usually been white men looking for their submissive Geisha fantasy, but now, an Asian man was going to be her customer. It had to happen eventually, men were men who needed to satisfy their sexual needs. "OK, let's get this over with."

"OK, I'll get him in here. We'll be listening next door, don't forget your earpiece and just give the word, OK?" he asked.

"Will do," she said as he nodded and closed the door.

Maya stood up, and with her 3-inch high heels, she stood at 5 feet, 6 inches. With her delicate fingers, she gathered up the ends of the sash and drew them snugly against her waist as her robe slithered down to her mid thigh. She looked down and teased apart her robe a bit just to show a glimpse of her lacy bra along with a bit of cleavage. The ends of her black silky hair dangled past her shoulders as she brought her hand to her right ear to check her earpiece. She then looked up when the knock came.

"Come in," she said gently along with a fake seductive smile.

The door slowly opened, and a middle-aged Asian man cautiously entered the room. With his slight frame, he wore a pair of jeans along with a wrinkled white-collared shirt that was covered in a worn-out navy jacket. He turned away from Maya momentarily as he closed the door behind him before turning back to look at her. He had some wisps of gray in his hair, which was otherwise neatly parted from the side. But wariness filled the bags underneath his eyes, and time had etched wrinkles around his mouth.

In her mind, Maya was disgusted, but she also felt a sense of pity for him. What was his deal? she wondered. Was he a restaurant worker just getting off his late shift and wanted to get a masseuse to pleasure him, and then maybe a little more? But she shook off that thought and got back to business.

"Hello there. What are you in the mood for tonight? A little party?" Maya said convincingly with a seductiveness that would turn most men into jello.

He simply stood his ground and looked at Maya up and down without any expression.

"A voyeur," she thought. She had to speed along the transaction so she coyly smiled to disarm him and said, "Let me make you comfortable by taking your jacket…"

But as she took a step forward, he took a step backward and put his hand up nervously, warding her off. She stopped, taken aback by his gesture, and she coyly eased back.

"Sorry," he uttered. But in that one word, a deep sense of shame could be felt. "I sorry to waste your time, you not her." He placed his hand into the right front jacket pocket, and Maya instinctively placed her right hand on her earpiece and was prepared to utter something. A brown wallet came out, and he gently began to open it.

She pursed her lips, the momentary sense of caution washed away as she realized he was only getting his money ready. With his short sentence, she started to profile him. Chinese, she thought, English as a second language and not fluent. She could feel that the transaction was about to be done, and this would close the deal on what would happen next.

"You're a man of few words, I see, but money can do the talking. What would you like, a massage?" she asked politely.

"Sorry, how much for your time?" he said quietly.

"How much time do you want? 30 minutes? 1 hour?" she answered.

"No, no time. You not her."

A wave of confusion came over Maya. He was rejecting her, she realized. What the hell, she thought. Was she not seductively attractive to him? And what did he mean when he said, "You not her?" But she was quick on her feet, and she solicited him again, "I can be anyone you want me to be. Who do you want me to be?"

He looked at her with his sorrowful eyes as he placed a twenty-dollar bill on the dresser and simply said, "You not my daughter."

Maya was stunned by his answer as he grabbed the doorknob. She froze for a moment until the voice in her earpiece stammered with urgency, "Is it a go?" Maya didn't answer as the doorknob clicked and again the voice pierced through the earpiece, "Did he show any money? Do we bust him?" The door opened as the hallway light silhouetted the Asian man's frame. She quickly placed her hand on her earpiece and said, "Stand down."

"Affirmative, standing down," replied the voice from the earpiece as the Asian man disappeared into the hallway.

Maya looked at the twenty-dollar bill on the dresser's edge, which was not in the closed circuit TV's view, and quickly stepped forward, clasped it, and tucked it quickly into the only pocket of her satin robe.

The overweight white man appeared at the door, his brass-colored police badge dangling from the metal beaded chain from around his neck. He looked at Maya, who came toward the door. "Couldn't close the deal, could you?"

Maya looked at the officer with a bit of contempt, but she hid it from her expression and simply replied, "No, he wasn't looking for anything, but someone."

"*Someone?* That's an odd sexual request, what do you think..." but before he could finish, Maya turned around and opened the closet in the room. She quickly threw on her mid-length raincoat and threw her cell phone, holstered sidearm, and her badge into the front pockets. She grabbed the right edge of her coat and pulled it close to her body and with her left hand, she wrapped the left side of her coat over her right arm.

She rushed in between the officer and the doorframe and into the hallway, to which he exclaimed, "Hey! Where are you going? We've still have work to do!"

"We haven't had one customer all night with this rain, I have to go!" she said curtly.

She rushed past another set of doors and into the lobby, which was set up as a front to lure customers who wanted sex instead of a massage. Her eyes met the eyes of another older Asian woman, also another officer who was playing the *mama-san* of the massage parlor. She couldn't utter a word as Maya rushed through the front door.

It was raining hard earlier, which was much needed for the drought-laden part of Los Angeles County. But it had let up, and it was only a drizzle whose drops could be seen under the few street lamps.

Maya saw him. He was not far from his car. An older model grayish Toyota Camry. Her high heels clicked on the wet asphalt with each quickened step.

"Wait!" she stammered, and it was on the second holler that her plea to wait caught his attention. He turned around bewildered and saw the Asian woman coming toward him.

With a few feet separating them and the cold chill beginning to work its way through her raincoat, she started, "Hi… hey… I know this is awkward. I'm not who you think I am," she said.

The Asian man still looked confused but listened intently.

"I'm a police officer," she said as she produced her LAPD police badge, which caught the glint of light from the street lamp.

A panicked look leapt to the Asian man's face and he put his hands together in a pleading manner, "No trouble please! Please, no ask you do anything wrong!"

"No, no… you are not in trouble. Please, you are safe. I didn't mean to frighten you," she said pleadingly and soothingly. She no longer saw him as the potential perp but as someone from her Chinese American community. "I want to help."

"I not in trouble?" he asked.

"No, you are not. But can we talk in that diner across the street? I'm really cold," she said.

He nodded approvingly as they began to walk to the diner.

* * *

The diner was ordinary with its worn-out black-and-white linoleum checkered floors and its green vinyl-covered booths, a few of which had tears. The grayish-and-white streaked laminate on the tables was waxy, after having served thousands of people in its lifetime.

They were almost alone in the diner, aside from the cook in the kitchen and the sole waitress, who was a slim woman with her hair up and too much make-up on. There was one lone customer at the bar with a blue LA Dodgers cap on. He stared at Maya, with her seductive dolled up make up, curvaceous legs wrapped in her sheer back hosiery, and black high heels.

But when Maya caught him looking, she flashed her badge and he quickly averted his gaze back to the half-eaten cheeseburger on his plate. What a strange couple the older Asian man and herself were, Maya thought to herself. She felt suddenly self-conscious as she pulled in her raincoat to cover the satin red robe underneath.

He held his coffee cup with his fingertips, feeling how hot the coffee was before drinking it. He stared down at the hollow, dark reflection that looked back at him. Maya stirred some cream and a packet of sugar into hers and waited for him to open up.

From his demeanor and reserve, she could only conclude that he had experienced something very painful in his life.

"I don't even know your name. Let me go first, I'm officer Maya Lim of the LAPD. I'm sorry that I frightened you earlier, but we thought you were going to solicit for sex…"

"I no such thing," he said curtly. "Sorry, I not mean to be rude," as he gently shook his head from side-to-side in shame, before he brought the coffee cup to his lips and took a sip.

A sudden sense of need to put things at ease between her and him arose. She relaxed her posture, to come across as non-authoritative. Then she said calmly, "No, I'm sorry. Please, just forget everything before. What is your name?"

"Ho, my last name, Ho," he said. "My first name… *Mo Meng*. You can call me Moe."

Maya nodded and said, "It's nice to meet you Mr. Ho, and if you don't mind, I'll call you Mr. Ho. I want to be respectful. My parents would expect me to do so as much. Are you Cantonese?"

Mr. Ho perked up a bit and said, "Yes, I Cantonese. From Hong Kong."

"My parents are from Hong Kong," responded Maya as she tried to make a connection to him.

Suddenly, Mr. Ho responded in Cantonese, *"Ah, we're kin. Were you also born there?"*

In her best Cantonese, Maya explained that her parents were from Hong Kong and arrived in LA in 1989, then had her in 1991. She was the oldest daughter of a family of five, two other brothers and sisters. She had been a police officer for the past three years.

A sudden sense of guilt intertwined with frustration washed over her, as she wasn't fluent in Cantonese and she felt she might miss parts of the story if she kept the conversation in Cantonese. But her Cantonese helped open the door, as some color seeped into Mr. Ho's face and he looked at her directly for the first time. He took another sip of coffee and nodded.

"Your parents must be proud of you, you police officer," said Mr. Ho.

Another wave of guilt stirred within Maya as she sighed under her breath. "Not really, they wanted me to be a doctor."

Mr. Ho let out a chuckle. "All Chinese parents dream."

"I guess so. But it wasn't for me. But after 3 years, I think they are OK with it now."

Mr. Ho looked at her with some sympathy and said calmly, "You good police officer. Not matter what you do, as long as you help people. Like you help me now."

Maya, took her cell phone out and started the voice memo app. She couldn't afford to lose anything in translation, between the Cantonese and the English. "I want to help if I can. You said earlier, that I was not your daughter. Are you looking for your daughter?" she asked.

"Yes," he said. "I look for my daughter," as his voice carried away for a moment. "She was kidnapped."

This took Maya by surprise, but she kept on listening as he began to tell his story.

"I come to this country, America. I come with my wife, much younger than me, but she agree to marry me. I feel so happy and lucky. I start work in restaurant. She also work in restaurant. It was very hard work for us, and we had our first child, a daughter, like you."

Maya felt a sudden fondness for Mr. Ho as he likened his daughter to herself. He continued.

"We so happy to have beautiful baby daughter. We name her, '*Hei Mon*.'"

"Hope," said Maya in a moment of realization. "You named her hope."

"Ah, you know word? Your Chinese is good," Mr. Ho chided approvingly of Maya.

Maya blushed as she received praise from Mr. Ho. He continued.

"So you say her last name and first, what it sound like to you?"

Maya paused and softly spoke the full name, "*Ho Hei Mon. Ho Hei Mon.* I get it. A lot of hope." She thought it was clever when she realized how the full name came together.

"Ah, you smart girl," praised Mr. Ho as he continued. "When we had her, we knew we had everything to live for, she our new hope as we work hard in America. We do OK. Restaurant business, always busy, so always customers. *Hei Mon* grew up happy child. We do as best to give her everything. When she seven, something happened. I win lottery. I come to America poor immigrant and suddenly, I'm multimillionaire. I don't know what to do. My wife and I think all our hopes are answered. But money turn out bad. Few days after I deposit check, I come home and no one home. No find my wife and daughter. I worry all night and I call police for help next morning. They come over, ask me questions and I get phone call. I answer and man on phone say he has my wife and daughter. I so scared, I give phone to police. Other man hang up when police officer speak. Many police come into my home, no take off shoes, make apartment dirty. But I trust them, they police, they supposed to help. They connect my phone to computer and tell me to keep man talking as long as I can. Man call next day and I answer. He tell me not to get the police and I tell him lie. I tell him that no police here. He tell me that he has my wife and daughter and he will give them back if I hand over my money from the lottery. I agree, of course. I ask to speak to my wife and they put her on. She is scared and tells me to do what they ask and I tell her I will. Then she cry and say so many things and then nothing. Man come back on phone and I hear my wife cry and yell in the background. They tell me get money. Then they call again to tell where to bring money. I agree. They hang up."

Mr. Ho paused and took a deep breath. His trembling hands created ripples along the coffee's surface.

"Could not trace call. Police say something about burning phone."

"Burner phone," Maya thought. The kidnappers used a burner phone and her police mind raced. Did they trace the number to the store where it was sold, and if so, was there a credit card associated with the purchase? They probably did, as it was it all standard procedure now. But there could always be sloppiness on the side of the kidnapper, especially if it was their first kidnapping or an overlooked step on the police side. She turned her attention to Mr. Ho.

"I tell police I go to bank to get money. I fight with police. They want more time. I tell them I no care. I happy to give all my money to get my wife and daughter back. They agree, but say they watch me. I OK with this, police supposed to help."

Despite the broken English, Maya was riveted by his story. Mr. Ho paused a little longer and continued as the traumatic memories coursed through his agitated expression.

"Next day, police help with bank and I get all money. So much money. Never see four million dollars. Was more, but government take a lot. That OK, gladly give all money to get my wife and daughter back. We wait and they call early evening. Very smart these bad men, they want me to give money at night. They tell me to meet them in underground parking. Police tell me no, but I agree and ask to talk to my wife again. Wife get on phone, she sound very bad. She scream 'Death! Death! Death! Death... tell me come get her and *Hei Mon*.' She scream so many words. I so scared, I tell her I will! Man come back on phone and tell me where to give money and get my wife and daughter."

"Police tell me they want to put something on me to hear. I say no! I worry kidnappers will find and I not see my wife and daughter again. I tell them, kidnappers want money, not wife and daughter. I tell them, I give money, and I get my wife and daughter back. Police say they watch me and follow the kidnapper back and arrest them."

A simmering anger crept into Mr. Ho's demeanor as his arms stiffened and fists clenched. He inhaled a couple of deep breaths and continued.

"I drive to underground parking garage and wait with money in big bag. I know police watch somewhere. I hear black van come really fast and stop. I feel hope that I will get wife and daughter back. Side door open. Man in black mask tell me to get in. I ask, 'Where my wife and daughter?' Man points gun at me and say if I want to see them again, I get into van now. I get into van and another man push me into corner. Another man drive van. Three men. First man open bag and sees money. Second man stare at me and point gun at me. I ask them, 'Where you taking me? Where my wife and daughter?' The man tells me to shut up. First man pull out something and wave it over bag. It make loud beeping noise. He yell, 'What is that?' I don't know what he talking about. He reach into bag. He take out small blinking wire. He yell really loud! 'You got cops! They place device with money?' I tell them I did not know. I tell them to believe me, I do not know. I beg so hard. Man is very angry. He drop thing on floor and step on it. The van go faster. He take out phone and he text. He look up at me and he put phone away. Van stop. They all get out and take money with them. I yell, 'Where my wife and daughter!' First man take out key from pocket. He throw at me. I catch it. It car key. I look up and other men go through door. The man said, find your wife, and he go through doorway. I hear car above me but I look at car key and press it. I hear beep. I look around and press key again and I see car light up. I run to the car, no one inside. I look at trunk. I press key again and trunk open. I open it."

Mr. Ho paused as his breathing labored and the words slowly tumbled out.

"I only see blanket. I pull back blanket. I see… I see my wife. Her eyes still open. I see hole… hole in her head… blood. They kill her…"

His clenched fists suddenly fall limp and flatten out on the table. His shoulders hunched over as his head also fell and he silently sobbed. All the anger that coursed through him was only enough to give him the strength to tell his story, but all that was left was heartache.

Maya's heart crumbled and emotions rushed into her, but all that she could do was reach out with her hands to his and held them as he quietly choked back on the anguished tears that flowed forth.

* * *

A steady cacophony of LAPDs finest went about their business; bookings, reading case files, interviewing verbose eyewitnesses or mime-like defendants, and even attending to dreaded paperwork. It was early the next morning, and Maya walked in with her slim-fitting blue jeans that covered black leather ankle boots, while a white blouse underneath her cropped black leather jacket established her LA fashion sense. The Beretta PX4 Storm compact, her personal sidearm, was holstered on the right, while her shiny LAPD brass badge was clipped right next to it.

As an undercover cop, she had most of her mornings and afternoons free while she worked the night shift. But on this day, she didn't sleep in like she normally would after a long night's undercover sting. The previous night was no normal night. After patiently waiting for Mr. Ho to get over his traumatic story, he composed himself and apologized profusely. His story flashed so many scenes through her mind as she tried to make sense of them.

Maya looked about her as she made her way to the precinct's cafeteria. The wisps of her black hair bounced with every step as she headed toward the coffee station. There she grabbed a medium-sized cup and fiddled the eco-friendly cup sleeve onto it. As the hot water dispensed into the cup and steam rose from it, she got distracted by Mr. Ho's story. How he was lured into the van and caught the police officers off guard. How he was threatened with a gun all the while, determined to find his wife and daughter. Then how they discovered the tracking device that the police did not tell Mr. Ho was in the bag.

"Ouch!" Maya let out as her string of fragmented thoughts were broken as hot water droplets splashed from the full cup onto her hand. Instinctively her hand shot up to her red lips to dissipate the pain. She reached into her inner jacket pocket for a packet of her favorite green tea. The mesh green tea packet sank slowly into the hot water and allowed it to seep. Once the plastic lid was fastened, she spun away from counter.

There were only a few officers in the cafeteria, but one stood out, and she smiled. She could always recognize Don from his buzz cut and wide-shoulder stocky frame. Her pace quickened toward him. He seemed to be filling out paperwork judging from the chorus of keyboard "tappity taps." There was an opened case file next to him, and judging by the half-drunk coffee, he'd probably been at it for a good half an hour.

She walked past him and yelled out his last name, "Cho!" as she spun around in a confident playful manner and pulled out the chair in front of him. He looked up and when he realized it was Maya, he stopped typing and smiled as he watched her slink into the white plastic seat. His eyes were unconsciously drawn to her slim legs when she crossed and dangled them off to her side.

"Well, if it isn't Maya. Aren't you up a bit early from your night shift stings?" he asked as Maya gently clasped the hot cup of tea with both hands.

"Well, if it isn't Cho, always here in the cafeteria doing paperwork instead of actually patrolling the mean streets of LA," Maya teased.

"Well hey, at least I get to wear a uniform. You just wear your Victoria Secret things to attract all the white men with yellow fever looking for their Asian fetish fantasy," said Cho as he let out a hearty laugh.

Maya scornfully beamed at him and abruptly turned away as her lush hair swung about providing a wall of black silence.

Cho stopped laughing immediately and his shoulders dropped. He reached out with his right hand but stopped. "Hey, I didn't mean it like that," he said, hoping to assuage her hurt feelings. But Maya's feelings weren't hurt. With a nonchalant look, she was simply listening, as she knew that guys didn't like the silent treatment from girls.

"Will you please turn around?" Of course she did not, prolonging the silent treatment. "Hey, I'm sorry, OK?" he said pleadingly.

A sly grin crept across her face as she heard the magic word. She turned around casually as if nothing had happened. Before Cho could collect his thoughts and utter anything else, she said, "Hey, as for last night. Something unexpected happened."

"Oh?" he said curiously as he was again unconsciously paying attention to her.

Maya recounted the details from the previous night, about the sting and how she met Mr. Ho, went out to talk to him because something about him was desperately asking for help. His story about winning the lottery, the kidnapping of his wife and daughter, the botched exchange, the murder of his wife and the unknown whereabouts of his daughter.

"I remember that case," said Cho as he typed away on the laptop with his pudgy hands. "Here," he said as he angled the laptop so that Maya could also see. As she leaned in, she could see that he had pulled up the case file. She began reading it along with Cho.

"So far, what he said to you seems to be all corroborated in here. It's a cold case; two years old. No one is assigned to it, it seems," said Cho. "The kidnappers outsmarted our very own that day. Instead of the intended exchange where our guys were prepared to identify the kidnappers and then stealthily use the tracking device to follow them, they lured Mr. Ho into the van, drove 5 floors below, and exited on foot through a service entrance that connected through to the other end of the mall. It's almost like they knew what was going to happen."

Maya pushed back from the table and leaned back into the chair as she looked perplexed. She thought for a moment and asked, "They seemed really organized, didn't they?" Cho nodded in agreement as Maya continued her line of questioning.

"They knew to alter the original plan for the exchange. They chose a parking garage with underground levels they could quickly escape to. They knew to look for the tracking device, and they had a pre-planned escape route that our guys were not prepared for."

"That sounds about right," replied Cho. "And since that day, there has been no trace of them. No follow-up ransom call because they got all the money. No forensic evidence from the dead wife or the car that she was in. It was stolen earlier that morning. The 9mm slug that was pulled matched nothing in our ballistics database."

"And how about his wife?" Maya asked.

Cho looked back into the case file, paused and fell silent. "It's bad," he said with resignation.

"Tell me," said Maya.

"She was raped. Multiple bruising on her inner thighs, possibly a gang…"

"Stop," said Maya as Cho's voice trailed away. She gathered a moment as her eyes looked to the ground before taking a deep breath and exhaling. "Did she fight back? Was there any DNA evidence from the assholes on her?" Maya demanded.

Again Cho looked down and then looked directly at Maya. "There were ligature marks around her wrists and ankles, it looks like she was tied down during the, well, you know."

Anger and hopelessness filled the void of silence that befell them.

"His daughter is still out there. I just can't bring myself to think what must be happening to her!" said Maya in a frustration-laced voice.

"The human trafficking here is horrible. How young Asian women are caught up in this mess pisses me off!" said Cho.

"We need to do something! I need to see if I can help Mr. Ho find his daughter," she declared as a fresh sense of determination came from her face.

"What do you expect us to do? I'm a beat cop and you're an undercover cop…"

Maya cut him short, "And do you want to be a beat cop all your life?"

There was a pause from Cho and he replied, "No, I'd like to be a detective one day."

"Then let's take this case. Like you said, no one is assigned to it."

Cho interrupted, "We can't just take it, we need to get the captain's approval first…"

Maya leaned in toward Cho and nudged his firm right shoulder with her left finger, turning him a bit to face her. He looked up and met her stern but mesmerizing eyes.

"There's a little girl out there that needs our help. We're her only hope…" as she paused and her eyes looked profoundly inward.

"What?" asked Cho.

"Hope, that's her name translated from Chinese, *Hei Mon.*" Maya looked back up with renewed determination and said to Cho, "If she's still out there, we're her only hope."

Either because of Maya's resonating determination or simply how beautiful she was, Cho's only response was, "OK, I'm in."

* * *

Later that afternoon, Maya briskly walked through the door of a trendy Korean coffee shop that Don frequented and had asked her to meet him at. The well-dressed Korean hostess, in her silky long- sleeved blouse tucked into a black skirt, stepped out from the hostess stand as her black high heels gave a couple of taps on the wooden floor. In a friendly gesture, she bowed slightly to Maya and said, "*Anh yan he seyo.*" Maya stopped and also bowed slightly with her head and replied in the same manner in her best Korean.

"Hi, I'm looking for Don…" Maya paused as she spotted Don easily sitting at a corner table with his back to the wall. "Never mind, I see him. Thank you," said Maya as the hostess smiled.

"Hey, you found me," said Don as Maya pulled back the chair and settled into it.

"It wasn't too hard, corner table, in an area not too crowded and good view of the entrance?"

Don chuckled. "Once a marine, always a marine. Basic situational awareness tactics."

"I like that," Maya added.

A slight pause filled the silence before Don asked, "Hey, would you like some coffee?"

Maya nodded and he pressed the little button on the table's edge to summon the waiter, a young Korean man with stylish wavy black hair. Don asked for coffee. The waiter promptly returned with a white porcelain cup and saucer with steaming coffee that was topped off with coffee art, in a tray with cream and a delightful assortment of sugars.

After taking a few sips, the fresh brewed coffee tantalized Maya's taste buds and the smell filled her nose as a warm feeling just fell over her senses. "That's good coffee," she said.

"It's why I come here. I don't know what my people do to the coffee, but it's pretty amazing here."

"I wouldn't have taken you for a coffee snob," chided Maya.

"I may be a beat cop, but I have higher aspirations when it comes to good coffee," sneered Don.

Maya smiled as she took her second taste of the coffee. "OK, what you'd got? I need to be back at the precinct in a couple of hours for my shift."

"So I poured over the report and nothing out of the ordinary. The kidnappers were good. There was very little forensic evidence. They were always in masks so nothing on the CCTV. The van they used was stolen, and the forensic team swept it and nothing was left behind. The car that held his wife was also stolen, and same story there. I also listened to the audio recordings, everything routine, well…" Don paused.

Maya looked up, "What?"

"Well, except for the audio. It's in Chinese and you know, I speak Korean…"

"But I speak Chinese, let me have a listen," she said as she pulled her ear buds from her pocket and plugged them into the headset jack on Don's laptop. He pulled up the audio. "Was there a translation?" she asked.

"The report only said that she was frantic and kept on saying 'Help' and 'Death' over and over."

"She must have been scared that they were going to kill her. OK, let me listen," she said as she cupped her ears with her hands and let her eyes drift downward as Don played the proof of life portion of the audio.

Mrs. Ho's voice was filled with frantic fear, and from the sound of his wife's voice, she must have been crying just before. In her distress, she muttered only Chinese words, "Help! Help us! Quickly. Death, death, death! Quickly, help! Death, death…death, death."

But it was the last word that didn't make any sense. Before the kidnappers pulled her away, she uttered one word: "hotel." In the background, her voice trailed off, and Maya couldn't make it out. She asks Don to replay the last portion and this time, with her eyes closed, she focused in on Mrs. Ho's voice as she visualized in her mind what was happening to Mrs. Ho.

She is pulled roughly by her arm as they place the phone to her ear. The kidnapper orders her to speak as her frightened eyes look up at him. Then she looks down and speaks into the phone, "Help! Help us! Quickly. Death, death, death! Quickly, help! Death, death…death, death…hotel." As they dragged her away, Maya is able to make out her trailing voice, "Death, death…hotel, death, death!"

Maya's eyes opened and she asked, "Is there a translation?" Don scrolled down the report and points at the translation. She didn't know why, but the word "hotel" was missing. She then uttered, "The translation, it's wrong."

Don looks curiously at her, "What do you mean?"

"Mrs. Ho was clever. She only spoke Chinese, knowing that her kidnappers probably didn't speak Chinese. She was trying to disguise her words. It sounded like she was saying "death" over and over again, when she was really saying the number four!"

Don then asked, "How do you mean?"

Maya went on to quickly explain, "She is saying help, and when she says 'Help us,' she's stating that she and Hope are alive. She does say 'quickly,' and she does say 'death,' the first time around but she doesn't say the actual word death all the other times. The Chinese word for 'death' and the number four sound really similar, but they are different. And she deliberately said 'four, four,' twice in four separate occasions. But what I don't get is why the translation doesn't mention the word 'hotel' that she was able to get in only once."

"OK, let's assume she says four and four, what does that mean?" asks Don.

Maya was silent. She didn't know.

"Are you sure she's saying the number four?" asks Don.

"Hey look! I went to Chinese school every single Sunday of my childhood and had a Tiger Mom. Every time I brought home anything below a 100 from school, she would say 'death' for the rest of the night! I know the difference between the number four and 'death'."

"OK, ok, I trust you," says Don reassuringly. "But it still doesn't tell us what she was trying to tell us."

"Yah, I know. So let's assume she snuck in the word 'hotel' in Chinese. Why wasn't it captured in the translation? Who did the translation?"

Don scanned the report once more and stated, "Says here, they took the translation directly from Mr. Ho at face value while he was emotionally distraught. Seems like he was quite emotional as he heard his wife's voice."

"So no third-party verification?" asked Maya, to which Don replied,

"None."

Maya took another sip of her now-lukewarm coffee.

"OK, let's put ourselves in her position. She's frightened, but she's got her wits about her. She feigns more distress, and maybe she knows something about the location they brought her to, and maybe that's the reference to the hotel," Don speculated.

"OK, I follow you, but now she needs to tell us where. She can't tell us the exact address, obviously, and she probably doesn't know, either. So what if she's telling us the approximate location of the hotel?"

"So what does four and four mean?" asks Don?

"Maybe it's not separate fours but forty-four?" speculated Maya.

"So like 88 Ranch but 44 hotel?" asked Don.

"Man, you're so Asian!" chided Maya. "But maybe there's a hotel with the number 44 in it?"

Don promptly turns the laptop toward him and with a furrowed brow that Maya couldn't help but notice, he Googled it. "*Nada*, no hotel with the number 44 in it."

"She can't give something exact, I would assume," said Maya as she thought aloud. "But something that she saw while being driven to the location."

"An exit!" exclaimed Don.

"An exit?" asked Maya.

"Yes, an exit number!" exclaimed Don as he pounced on the keyboard once more.

Maya became excited and jumped from her chair. She came around the table and leaned in close over Don's right shoulder to watch the laptop screen as he pulled up Google maps.

"Let's assume they're going west, what highway has an exit 44?" Don asked as he expanded the map and followed along the trail.

"Not the 105 or the 101," said Maya as the rest of the map filled in west of the 105 and the 101. "The 405!" they both said aloud.

"The 405 has an exit 44," says Maya. "What hotels are in the immediate vicinity?"

"Already on it," said Don as he pulled up the nearby hotels and red-pin-drops began to fall into place.

"Take away the chain hotels," said Maya as she placed her hand on Don's left shoulder and leaned further in from his right side.

Don eliminated the chain hotels, and the number of the red markers dropped to one.

"One, one privately run hotel off exit 44," says Maya.

"It can't be this easy," said Don suspiciously.

"I know, it feels too easy. But she couldn't make it too hard for Mr. Ho to figure it out either. I think she just assumed the kidnappers didn't speak Chinese. It's the only lead we've got," stated Maya.

"Better than nothing. I'm about to go off shift; let me do a little more digging while you get ready for your shift."

Maya let out a groan, "Another night of catching perverts. and just when we have a lead!"

"You better go! I got it from here, I'll call you when I find out more about this hotel," Don said.

"OK, you're the best!" said Maya as she quickly drew him in with her left hand and nudged her temple to the side of his head. She bounced upward and sauntered out of the coffee shop. But out of the corner of her eye, she couldn't help but notice Don watching her as she left. She didn't know why, but she smiled.

Back at the precinct, the captain was hunched over his desk reading reports. The short, combed-down white sides of his hair were all that was left of a once-full head of hair. His experience showed on his face with a 5 o'clock shadow of distinction, which gave him a good look for a policeman-turned-bureaucrat. He now headed a precinct with hundreds of officers and detectives under him, and the pressure never let up.

His focus was broken by a knock at the door. He glanced over at the time: 6:06 PM. "Come in," he mumbled.

The door opened, and Maya walked in as the door slowly closed behind her.

"Lim!" barked Captain Rourke. "Why are you still in your civvies and not getting ready for your assignment tonight?"

"Sorry, Captain, I just wanted to take a moment of your time. This won't take long."

The captain hesitated, looked at Maya seriously. He softened his expression and begrudgingly motioned her to the chair in front of him. She nodded and seated herself in the chair.

"Captain, do you recall that cold case where the kidnapping went horribly wrong with Mr. Ho? The one where his wife was killed and the daughter never turned up?"

He leaned back a little into his seat, looked up for a brief moment, came back level with her and nodded his head in the affirmative.

"Well I've been doing some checking on that case…"

"Why are you looking into that cold case? That's not your case," said the captain, cutting her off.

Maya composed herself and began to retell what happened the previous night, omitting any of Cho's involvement. Her intuition told her that she'd better protect Cho and gauge the captain's response first.

"So the father came looking for his little girl. I get it. But that doesn't mean you should go off and take this case on your own," lectured the captain.

Suddenly, a wreath of warmth encircled her neck all the while, a sense of urgency welled up in the pit of her stomach that just wanted to come forth.

"I'm sorry, Captain, I didn't mean to take on this case behind your back…"

"Let's get this straight, it's not your case," admonished the captain once more.

"Yes, I understand that but a little girl's life is in danger," argued Maya.

The captain let out a sigh, "We don't know that. I've been around the block a lot longer than you have, and these type of cases never end good. These immigrants get sucked into the Asian underground…"

"She's not an immigrant, she was born here and what makes you think the kidnappers were Asian?" interjected Maya.

"Come on, Lim! Who else could it be? These Asian gangbangers exploit your kind all the time!"

Shock came over Maya as her captain unloaded a torrent of unsubstantiated allegations. Suddenly, she felt everyone who looked like her were potential criminals or illegal immigrants in his eyes.

She needed to interject once again, "There's no evidence that the perpetrators were Asian! I'm not saying that they can't be, but the evidence isn't there!"

"Did you just raise your voice at me, Lim?" snapped the captain, glaring hard at her.

Maya froze. All of a sudden she felt 10 years old again, being scolded by one of her parents for doing something wrong and feeling guilty for it.

"I'm sorry, Captain, I didn't mean to…" responded Maya.

"You're suspended," said the captain curtly.

Another wave of shock crashed over her as she exclaimed, "But, the girl…"

"Bring me proof that she's alive, but for now, you're suspended for 3 days for insubordination."

"But how about the undercover sting for tonight?"

"We'll get Nagasaki, Nagamura, whatever her name is. She looks just like you. Now get out of here and come back with some respect for your commanding officer after 3 days."

A silent anger smoldered within Maya. She couldn't believe that she was suspended when all she was following up on was a cold case related to her job. But she finally understood that her captain only saw her as an Asian face on the payroll to fill a need to arrest more perps with an Asian fetish. She was not an officer who could do any real police work in his eyes.

"Yes, Captain," she responded as she got up, walked around the chair and out of the office as the captain went back to reading his dreary reports.

Her walk was brisk as each step on the floor was laced with seething frustration. Her eyes were focused on the floor, and she avoided eye contact with the other cops as shame descended upon her. But there was silent determination because her gut told her that a little girl was still out there, alive but scared. She reached the precinct's lobby when her cell phone distracted her swirling frustration.

She reached into her jacket for it. It was Don calling and a smile came across her face.

"Hey Don," she said but before she could get another word in, he said, "Maya, come to the hotel, I'll text you the address. I'm in my SUV parked across the street."

Each word from Don's voice was tinged with a serious undertone, and she responded laconically, "OK."

Don sat in his black Acura MDX and from behind the tinted windows, he watched the non-descript 10- story hotel from across the street. In his right hand, he held a DSLR outfitted with a telephoto lens that doubled as binoculars that rested on his right knee. His left hand tucked his Samsung Galaxy under his chin as he eyed the hotel.

The muffled sound of a car door closing and hurried footsteps caused him to look into the rearview mirror, and he recognized Maya's silhouette and flowing hair. He unlocked the car door and soon, Maya hopped into the passenger seat and closed the door. She quickly looked up at Don.

"Hey," said Don.

"Hey yourself. What do you have?"

"I'll make it quick as you have your night shift…"

"Oh about that, there's no night shift for me tonight. I got suspended," interjected Maya.

A moment of silence passed before Don stole himself away from what he was about to tell Maya. "What? What happened?"

"Ugh, it's a long story. Could we talk about what you found out?" asked Maya.

Don looked at Maya, who looked back at him with her inquisitive eyes. He collected his thoughts and began to tell her what he had gathered.

"So I came straight to the hotel and started casing it. I pulled the building history, and it's been around for quite a while. It started out as a bar and restaurant, which is still here. See over there, by the hotel entrance?" asked Don as he pointed to the restaurant on the ground floor.

Maya looked over and saw the sign for the bar and restaurant. She focused back on Don as he pulled out his tablet from the center console.

"So look here, the bar and restaurant was bought up about two decades ago from a local family. It was then expanded with the hotel built on top of the restaurant. Looks like the business did very well too, and then a decade later, it was sold to a private company. But when I dug deeper into the company. I saw that it was owned by a shell company that itself was also owned by another shell company. So right now, ownership isn't clear-cut, but it's a bit sketchy, if you ask me. I took a look at the Yelp reviews and it has 3 stars. It's pretty standard and nothing to hype up the business, which is odd, especially when you want to increase business. But given that, take a look at the hotel for a few minutes and tell me what you see."

Maya twisted her slim body toward Don and leaned forward onto the edge of the seat to get a better vantage point. Don leaned back in his seat and remarked, "Take your time, I've been here a couple of hours already."

"Hmmm… seems normal enough. There are valets, bellhops, a bit more security than I would expect. Odd, the windows in the restaurant are all covered up from the inside. And it looks like we're hitting the dinner rush hour, as more cars are pulling up."

"Odd for a restaurant that only has 3 stars, wouldn't you say? Something must be bringing them back because look at how the customers are greeted at the door by the security guy who seems to be in charge."

Maya peered over again. She noticed that almost every customer was personally greeted by the husky white man in a black suit, with a firm handshake and a smile. That was odd, she thought. Then she noticed another thing.

"All the customers, they're all men," she said in realization.

"Right. Now let me fill in the rest from what I've seen in the last couple of hours," said Don as Maya turned to him. "For a mediocre hotel on paper, they're doing a bang-up job in business. The parking lot is full of cars, and most of the customers have all been men, usually one but a couple of them here and there. But for a hotel, there is one thing noticeably absent: suitcases. Now that's odd. Another odd thing, so far, I've observed 20 men going into the hotel, and half of them have already left."

"They're running an illegal sex business inside the building disguised as a legit hotel," said Maya in disgust. Don nodded.

Anger seethed throughout Maya. It was something she was keenly aware of through her undercover work. The illegal sex trafficking of women, particularly of Asian women, was troubling. Some of them were children. She suddenly pictured Hope, who might be caught up in this mess. If Hope was an unwilling victim, what would she say to Mr. Ho? A sudden sense of hopelessness rose up from her, but that was intertwined with anger.

Her recent anger at how her captain dismissed her because she was Asian American and at the many times in her life she let others dictate her course of action. How she ended up being an undercover cop who played an Asian prostitute to cater to a group of men who had yellow fever and a disgusting fetish for Asian women. But today was different. There was a little Asian American girl who needed to be saved from the depraved hands of these disgusting men.

"We need to go in!" exclaimed Maya.

"Whoa, hold on…"

But before Don could continue, she exclaimed, "Hope can be in there, and she's just a kid! Who knows what disgusting things these men are doing to her! It must be a nightmare!" The anger made her voice tremble like a low rumbling thunder that was ready to explode into a roar.

Don put a reassuring hand on her shoulder, steadied her for a moment, and looked her in the eyes. "I know, I know. I'm with you, OK? I'm angry too. I have a little sister too who's only in elementary school. But as much as our observations are telling us that something is wrong with this hotel, it's all circumstantial. We need more intel on this place. So let's do our job."

He was right, thought Maya. They couldn't just barge in and shoot up the place and rescue a little girl who may not be there. But if Hope was in there, she suddenly felt like she wanted to go in there guns blazing. She turned to Don and asked, "How are we going to do this?"

Don smiled, "I have a plan."

Don drove into a lightly lit alley a block away. In the front seat, he explained that despite most of the customers being men, a few couples here and there had entered the hotel, so it would be best to follow them in to lessen suspicion. Despite the possible real motive of the place, there did seem to be a legitimate business to serve as a front. Since it was a bit after dinnertime, a couple going to a late dinner would be the best cover. They would first ask for a table that would give them best vantage point to observe the operation and go from there. Maya nodded, impressed with Don's operational planning, and said, "OK, let's go then."

"Hold on, we can't just go in there unprepared. Follow me," said Don as he exited the SUV.

Maya followed him to the back of his SUV. Don took a few furtive glances around and then opened the back of the SUV. On the floor of the cargo space, he had a perfectly sized hardened plastic case that snugly fit the width of the cargo space. He entered a few numbers into the centered combination lock and opened up the lid to reveal a neatly arranged arsenal. The ambient light from the SUV danced and gleaned off the black steel to show an assortment of guns, from Glocks, Berettas, and H&Ks, each neatly inserted into the black foam with its corresponding magazine beneath it. Embedded in the lid of the gun case were a shotgun and an AR-15 rifle.

"Wow," said Maya as she admired Don's arsenal. "You are prepared! It's like you were in the army or something."

"Marines, actually. Not career, though, but in the reserves. Unlike one of my buddies who is a colonel now in the Marines. He's career military, and no one deserves it more than him. What are you carrying?"

Maya sheepishly placed her hand on her one piece and said, "A PX4 Storm with 15 in the mag and one in the chamber."

"OK, but first, put this on underneath your blouse," said Don as he slipped her a slim bulletproof vest. "You can change in the back seat."

After she had donned the bulletproof vest, she came back around as Don had just finished buttoning up his shirt over his own bulletproof vest.

Without so much as looking at Maya, Don reached into the case and in tandem asked, "And how many spare mags with your fashion sense?"

Maya suddenly blushed, it was the first time Don ever remarked her on sense of fashion. "Just one other."

Don nodded and grabbed two additional PX4 Storm mags and placed them into a slim double belt magazine holder. "You can tuck this into your belt, I assume?"

Maya took the double mag holster and smiled, "I'll manage," she said. He cared about her, she thought to herself as she began to tuck the magazine holder into her belt next to her current one mag. Don handed her another two magazines, and she looked at him puzzled.

"You can place these two in that thing you call a pocket," said Don with a smirk. "You now have six mags and one in the chamber, for a total of 91. I think you're pretty well armed now," said Don.

"I guess I am," said Maya confidently.

"And for a backup?" asked Don to which Maya shrugged. Don looked back in his case and pulled a smaller handgun, "Glock G43 works?"

It was the way that Don asked her that caught her off guard. There was no doubt from him. He expected her to handle herself, and she saw a side of Don that she didn't catch before. "G43 works," she said confidently. He popped the mag to see that it was full, verified that there was one round in the chamber, then firmly popped the mag back in. He checked the sight quickly and then tucked it into an ankle holster of the nylon velcro type and handed it to her. As she began to outfit the backup piece she saw that Don began to outfit one himself.

"What are you arming yourself with?" asked Maya.

"Two Glock 19s, Gen 5 and 10 mags total. I know, it seems like overkill in civilian situations, but the firepower that the bad guys have nowadays, it's almost like we're in combat situations. One of the badass things that I was known for while in the Marines was my double gun action. I'm ambidextrous. A great skill to have, I tell you," explained Don as she watched him tuck away his firearms and mags along his body.

"And for a backup," teased Maya.

Don smiled and pulled out another Glock G43 and an additional mag for it. He looked and turned toward her and said, "You have my second spare, so I'll settle for the second G43 that I have." Then he winked at her. "OK, let me check you out."

Maya stood tall and allowed herself to be checked out by Don. He gave her a quick once over and suddenly said, "Are we forgetting something?" Maya suddenly felt some doubt and she remembered her badge and placed her hand over it. "And what else?" For a moment, Maya was lost and must have looked dumbfounded as Don interjected, "We need to swap out your holster for a concealable one. We're going in as civilians."

Maya felt a little flushed from her oversight. As a cop, she was always comfortable wearing her badge along with her sidearm in plain sight unless she was with friends on a night out. But as she worked the undercover night shift, she hasn't had one of those nights in a long time. She took the concealable holster from Don and swapped hers out. She was ready in no time.

Don then asked her to check him out, and though she was confident that he knew he wasn't printing, she didn't mind. His black blazer draped around his muscular, big-boned and broad-shouldered frame nicely. With his untucked dark grey collared dress shirt, he could more easily hide his firearms and ammo. She gave him a thumb up and smiled.

They got back into his SUV and drove to the hotel. Maya was feeling a bit nervous as she steadied herself. But Don was cool as a cucumber, having served in active combat and being a beat cop, his nerves were steeled for this kind of situation. They slowly drove up to the hotel and were unexpectedly stopped at the entrance. A man with slicked-back brown hair, a mustache, and medium build looked through the windshield, first at Maya and then Don. Don rolled down the window and the man came to the side.

"Evening, what brings you here tonight?"

"Just coming in for a late dinner with my girlfriend. We were in the area and Yelp popped this place up as the closest restaurant, so we'd thought we'd give it a try."

The man paused for a moment, continued to look at Don, then looked over at Maya, who peered over and gave a friendly smile. "OK, enjoy your dinner."

"Thank you," said Don as he rolled up the window and drove into the parking lot.

"Girlfriend?" asked Maya with a smile?

"Yah, we're acting right? Besides, you're too young-looking to be my mother," replied Don to which Maya let out a laugh.

After finally backing into a parking spot, Don and Maya stepped out of the SUV and joined up at the front. Don made an adjustment to his collar and then straightened up. Out of the corner of his eye, he caught sight of another couple headed to the restaurant in front of them. Don caught Maya looking at him and he then extended his arm. Maya looked caught off guard but gave a laugh, took his muscular arm and the two walked toward the hotel acting as a couple.

After following the couple in, they decided to head to the bar to get a vibe of the scene. The bar was adjacent to the restaurant and a part of the bar was open to the hotel lobby. Maya indicated to Don that they should set up at a vantage point that would give them clear line of sight of the restaurant and the hotel lobby. Don nodded and Maya surmised that he was thinking the same as he led her to a couple of empty seats that gave them that vantage point but was away from people.

Once at the bar, the bartender, a clean-shaven man with thick dark hair, parted on one side and swept backwards came over suspiciously. He greeted them and eyed Don. Don nonchalantly asked for two glasses of tonic water but specifically in lowball glasses and with ice. The bartender hesitated but nodded. He placed two lowball glasses with tonic water and ice along with a small bowl of assorted nuts on the counter. The bartender asked if there was anything more that he could get, and Don asked for two vodka tonics with lime in two lowball glasses as well.

Maya gave him a look. Though they were off duty, they shouldn't be drinking, but Don didn't seem to worry. Soon, the bartender placed two vodka tonics in front of them and went away to take care of other customers at the other end of the bar.

"Don," said Maya under her breath but it was as if he had anticipated her admonishment and he looked at her and simply said, "Do as I do." Maya hesitated but gave a nod.

He lifted the black straw stirrer from the vodka tonic and Maya did the same. He placed it into the tonic water with ice and she followed suit. He took the lime wedge and placed it also in the tonic water with ice and Maya mimicked the move. He then nonchalantly swapped the tonic water and ice with lime glass with the vodka and tonic glass, and by then Maya understood. "You are now drinking tonic water and ice while giving off the appearance of drinking alcohol. Cheers." Maya smiled at his cleverness and clinked glasses with him as they began their observation of the joint.

The restaurant didn't do a lot of business, but there were a few patrons in the dining area. In the bar area, there were a number of men, many of them keeping to themselves, nursing a drink or transfixed to the slow glow emanating from their mobile screens. Maya noticed also the lack of women, and every now and then, she received an uncomfortable lewd glance from the men. She responded by grabbing Don's arm and looking at him. Don played the part to make it look like they were a couple as they collected intel.

They observed that just about every man that went to the hotel front desk was greeted and directed to wait in the lounge area of the bar or the hotel waiting area. Ten to fifteen minutes would pass, and a pudgy man in a suit, with tussled brownish hair and a cropped beard, would come by and greet one of the waiting men and hand him a keycard. This was by far a very out-of-the-ordinary procedure for any hotel. He would direct the man to an elevator off to the side, where he was greeted by a security guard, who would let him through. After only an hour, sometimes only thirty minutes, would the same man reappear and leave the hotel. Maya noticed that the men's shirts were no longer neatly tucked in and some carried their jackets in their arms. The thought that these men were engaging in not just illicit prostitution but potentially raping under-aged children sickened her to her stomach. Hope continually came to her mind, and it disgusted Maya that she could be caught up this sordid affair. But everything that they saw was circumstantial until

Maya saw her.

A man in his late 50s with white-grayish hair that was parted on the side and neatly combed had just entered the lobby. He was wearing a navy suit, a crisp white shirt with the top two buttons undone, and leathery brown dress shoes. He was accompanied by two younger men, both with athletic builds and also in suits, presumably bodyguards of some sort. But it was the little Chinese girl in pigtails wearing a *cheongsam*, a traditional Chinese dress that caught Maya's attention. It was Hope.

The fact that Hope was being used like a pet in tow of this man further disgusted Maya. She saw that Hope was expressionless as she followed the man, and each time she would stop, the man would look back and make a whistling sound to get her attention, and she would continue on.

Maya tugged on Don's arm and brought his attention to Hope as she and the three men walked toward the secluded elevator. Don briefly touched Maya's hand, and she looked up as he said, "Stay right here, I'll be right back."

Don quickly stole himself away from the bar stool and took out his cell phone to pretend that he needed to take a call away from Maya. He crossed the lobby and took up a spot that was in better view of the elevator. The three men and Hope had just entered the elevator and after about a minute he came back to the barstool.

"Ten, they got off on the tenth floor," said Don. "Only one guard manning the elevator, and it looks like you need a keycard to get access to the elevator."

"We need to go now. Who knows what could be happening to Hope?" Maya stammered urgently.

Don nodded and pulled a couple of twenties and tossed them onto the bar counter. Don and Maya left the bar area, crossed the hotel lobby and then strolled to the secluded elevator. They smiled and pretended to be distracted by their fondness for each other.

The guard was not amused and stepped away from the host desk. With his hand out, he stated, "This is a private area."

"Oh, are these not the elevators to the hotel?" asked Don.

The guard was not amused and glared at Don and Maya. "No, the elevators you're looking for are behind you and to the left."

"Gotcha. By the way, may I have your key card?"

The guard looked confused, "My key card?"

In a blink of an eye, Don drew forth his gun in his left hand and pointed it at the guard and said, "Yes, the key card that's hanging from your belt. Hands up, now!" said Don firmly as Maya pulled out her gun and pointed it at the guard.

The guard's expression changed as he put up his hands, which exposed his key card clipped to his belt. Don kept his eyes and gun at the guard's head as he pulled off the key card and handed it to Maya. As she went to get the elevator, Don also withdrew the guard's gun, popped out the mag, which fell into a small wastebasket by the side of the host desk, and ejected the chambered bullet by catching the back sight along the top of his belt. Maya was impressed with Don's skill with gun mechanics.

The elevator door opened, and Don firmly told the guard to step in, and once the guard was in, Don commanded him to place his hands on the back of his head and interlace his fingers. Don firmly grabbed the guard's fingers and abruptly forced him onto his knees as the elevator door closed. He shoved the guard's forehead into the elevator wall, where he uttered a grunt. Don leaned in and asked, "How many guards on the tenth floor?"

There was silence from the guard, and Don shoved the muzzle of his gun into the base of his neck and asked again, "I ask one last time, how many guards on the tenth floor?" to which the guard responded, "More than you can handle, you chink!" Don swiftly pistol-whipped him as he fell unconscious.

"Well, we won't be getting much from him," Don said as he took out a few zip ties and quickly hogtied the guard. The sound of tape being ripped off caught Maya's attention. She saw that Don had several pieces of duct tape on the inside of his jacket, which he placed over the guard's mouth.

"You've done this before," said Maya, admiring his efficiency.

"Yah, while I was in stationed in Iraq. We had to quickly restrain insurgents, but let's talk about what we're going to do when we get to the tenth floor."

Maya nodded in agreement and knelt down as she held her gun pointed downward and away.

"We have no intel. We know that there are at least two guards along with the man in charge, so that's three. Seeing that this guy was armed, we need to assume they are all armed. We find Hope and we get out of there fast. Agreed?"

Maya nodded as she steadied her breath. She saw Don pull out his badge and clip it to his belt and she did the same.

"Maya, you may need to shoot someone today, are you ready for that?" asked Don.

Maya looked downward, let out a deep breath. Since joining the LAPD, she'd never had to draw her gun for any reason. But she was ready and believed in her heart that she was doing the right thing. She then looked up at Don and nodded.

"Trust your training. OK, let's put that key card in and let's go to the tenth floor," said Don.

The ding of the elevator caught the attention of the lone guard on the tenth floor. As the elevator doors opened, no one came out. That was odd, he thought, and as he looked left, he was suddenly staring down the muzzle of a gun. Maya slowly stepped out of the elevator and motioned for the guard to put his hands up, which he did. She disarmed him and then motioned for him to step into the elevator. As he did, Don, grabbed him by the back of the neck, pivoted him and pushed him onto his knees. With the muzzle of the gun firmly on the back of the guard's head, he instructed the guard to slip his hands into a looped zip tie and they were fastened firmly.

As Maya anxiously kept watch on the elevator, she took note of the ice machine and vending room on one end of the foyer and an exit stairwell on the other. Don leaned into the guard and asked, "How many guards are on this floor, and where is the little girl?"

The guard let out a contorted grunt and mumbled, "Six... corner room."

Don then pistol-whipped him as the second guard fell unconscious alongside the first guard.

"At least six, though I trust this guy as far as I can throw him. Looks like Hope is in the corner room," whispered Don to Maya. Maya nodded as the deafening quiet made her nervous. Only the whirring of the icemaker broke the silence. As Don finished securing the guard, Maya flipped up the hold switch, stepped out of the elevator, and saw a map of the floor on the wall.

"Oh no!" muttered Maya as Don stepped out with his gun and the second guard's key card.

"What's wrong?" asked Don.

Maya looked at him, "There are two corner rooms at the end of this hall."

"Damn it!" as Don looked up momentarily in frustration. "Let's hope we find Hope on the first try then. We gotta move, they will be wondering where the lobby guard is."

Maya nodded, and she and Don briskly but quietly made it to the first room on the left that had a key card reader. They lined up on either side as Maya used the key card to unlock it. Don flipped the door handle and went in, followed by Maya to cover his flank. The room was bare, aside from the mattress on the floor, towels, bed sheets strewn about, along with rope. There were also photography lights along with a video camera on a tripod fixed near the bed.

No one was in the room, and they quickly exited to repeat the same routine for the room across the way, and when they entered the third room, they found the same. Don looked downcast and then said quietly, "No one is in these rooms. I think we can assume they are all clear."

Maya wasn't certain. She felt that they needed to check all the rooms to ensure that no one would double back on them upon their escape. "How can you be so sure that there is no one…"

"I'm sure," said Don with a sense of irritation.

"But…"

"Damn it, Maya!" Don said in a slight raised tone, "Do I have to spell it out for you? These are rape rooms!"

Maya froze. The realization of what the rooms were sent chills down her spine, but they also sent up tendrils of anger.

In a hopeless tone, Don simply said, "These are the rooms where they break in new girls by filming their rapes, over and over again until they comply. If they were being raped now, we would hear the screams. Come on, we gotta go."

Maya let out a breath. They had stumbled onto something big, but she was beside herself with how long this nightmare may have been going on.

Don led the way. Maya followed and quietly closed the door behind them. Don quickly made his way down the end of the hall, and Maya took the left corner. They both peered down the ends of the hall, and there were no signs of guards.

"Damn it, where are the six other guards?" asked Don.

"He could have been lying," said Maya.

"Maybe," said Don resignedly. "OK, left or right?"

"Left," said Maya, praying that Hope was in that room.

Maya took the lead this time, and Don followed on her heels and took up position on either side of the door. Maya got near the door and could hear the low murmur of a TV and at least one voice. She indicated this with one finger to Don when suddenly two distinct laughs could be heard, and she signaled with a tight fist to hold. She then indicated two targets with two fingers.

Don got ready and placed his left hand on the door latch. Maya got into a crouch and placed the key card on the reader. There was a green light. Don forcefully pushed the door in and entered with his gun drawn. Maya swiftly came up behind and alongside him as the door closed.

Two young men were leaning and relaxing back on a couch with a beer or snack in hand. Don stood tall and aimed his gun at both of them as they froze, eyes widened. He tapped his LAPD badge and moved a couple steps closer. Their feet were propped up on the coffee table along with three holstered handguns.

As Maya stood up, she surveyed the room and noticed two other doors in the room across from the door they had just entered. Suddenly, a toilet flushed, and the bathroom door opened as an unsuspecting man came through laughing while twirling an empty cardboard toilet paper roll in his fingers.

"Hey guys, I think we're out of…" But he couldn't finish his sentence as Maya's gun was trained on his head. He kept his hands up, and she motioned for him to come forward. As she took a step back, he made a lunge for Maya and grabbed her hands. Don instinctively pivoted, quickly unholstered his left gun, and trained it on the third man, keeping the other gun trained on the two other guards, who froze, intimidated by Don and his two guns.

Despite the guard being bigger, her instincts kicked in, and she pushed her gun up over her head with all her might and kicked him in the groin as hard as she could. The man expelled a grunt and crumbled to his knees with his hands clutching his groin. Maya then hit him over the head with her gun, and he went unconscious to the ground.

Don smiled assuredly and trained both of his guns back on the other two guards before they could think to do anything else. Maya quickly came over to secure their hands and feet as Don nervously kept watch. Time was not their friend. Maya took the zip ties from Don and secured the unconscious guard while Don gagged the other two guards.

As Maya turned the unconscious guard onto his side to duct tape his mouth, a thud came from the unopened door. This caught her and Don's attention as they turned their attention to the door, which had a heavy deadbolt above the doorknob. Maya dropped the head of the unconscious guard and with Don following, made her way over to the door. There was no light coming from underneath the door. Don quickly produced two flashlights and handed one to Maya.

Don firmly grabbed the deadbolt and Maya quietly turned the doorknob. Don mouthed, "one… two… three," at which point he pulled the deadbolt and shoved the door in. Don went in on the right, and Maya followed on his left.

A chorus of screams came at them as the light from the flashlights danced about an untold number of scurrying bodies. Maya sensed fear in the room and brought her gun upward as her eyes tried to focus on the moving faces cowered in their own splayed hair. Don aimed his flashlight on the wall behind him, located a light switch, and flicked it upward.

Young Asian girls, barefoot, in nothing more than underwear and T-shirts, were all huddled in the back of the room. They covered their faces with their bound hands and wept in fear.

"Oh my God," uttered Maya who quickly holstered her gun and put her hands up in an unintimidating manner. "Shhhh… it's OK, I'm with LAPD, we're here to help."

Don angled his gun downward and took a position by the door.

There was no response from the girls apart from their indiscernible cries until Maya heard it, *"Mo-ah, mo-ah."* It was Cantonese and her heart ached. She instinctively responded in kind.

"Don't worry. I'm with the police. I'm here to help," said Maya in her best Cantonese.

Suddenly other voices spoke up, *"Please help us!" "Please stop them!"* but other voices spoke up that Maya couldn't understand when suddenly, Don uttered in Korean, *"Are any of you Korean?"*

Another chorus of anguished voices spoke up in Korean, and Don's sudden need to help kicked in. *"Please listen to my police partner. We're here to help, but right now we need you to be quiet."* The eyes of three Korean girls perked up when they heard Don speak Korean, and they nodded in acknowledgement under their muffled cries.

Other voices spoke up, but in a language that Maya and Don did not understand, when one of the girls who spoke Cantonese suddenly turned to the other girl and spoke to her in Vietnamese. That's when Maya saw the tattoo. As the girl turned her head, the tattoo at the nape of her neck was exposed. Soon, the Vietnamese girl nodded, her eyes flooded in tears.

Maya took a step forward, made eye contact with each of the ten girls, and calmed them. From what she could tell, five were Chinese, three were Korean, and two were Vietnamese, all victims of sex trafficking. Maya looked at Don with eyes that were filled with sadness, "We have to get them out of here."

Don, who was still by the door, looked down in resignation. The plan to only rescue Hope just got ten times more complicated. He looked at each of the young girls and saw a potential younger sister staring back at him. "I know, let's do this. You tell them what to do, I'll translate in Korean, tell the Chinese girl who spoke Vietnamese to translate to whoever speaks

Vietnamese. I'm calling for backup right now, but we gotta go now."

Maya gave out her instructions in Chinese, which Don translated into Korean, and one of the Chinese girls translated into Vietnamese, all while Maya cut the ropes tying their hands with a knife that Don had flipped over to her. Once the instructions were clear, Maya nodded to Don, who then led them out of the room. The unconscious guard and the two other guards were hogtied against the couch. The girls initially held back upon seeing the hogtied guards, but with Don's encouragement, they crouched along in single file along the wall as Maya came up to Don's position.

With their guns drawn, Don cracked the door and saw that the corridor was still eerily quiet, and he quickly raced over to the hallway leading to the elevator. He peered over and could see that the two hogtied guards in the elevator were no longer unconscious and were desperately struggling to free themselves from the cable ties. They needed to hurry, he thought. He motioned to Maya that the coast was clear.

Maya nodded in acknowledgement and quickly looked over at the frightened girls and told them to follow. Under muffled acknowledged cries, they quickly and quietly followed Maya as she raced past Don, who stood sentry at the corner. Maya made her way down the middle of the corridor with the ten girls in tow when suddenly a man in a black suit appeared from the left down the hall and yelled out, "Hey!" as he drew his gun.

Maya didn't hesitate to fire three rounds from her gun, but the man was able to duck out of the way. The girls suddenly screamed and turned around toward Don, who was waving them back toward him when the door to the other corner room opened up with another man holding a gun. Don fired and hit him square in the chest, knocking him backwards. A rambling of expletives came from the room and the door slammed shut.

Don looked down the hall and saw two men, one who managed to cross over to the other side of the hallway, taking aim at Maya, but the girls were precariously trapped in between him and Maya. Don looked back at the door to the corner room, and it opened a crack. He sent several shots into the door and it firmly shut again.

Maya fired the remaining rounds from the magazine as bullets raced by her. Adrenaline rushed through her as she heard the screams of the girls behind her. She popped out her mag, popped in a new one, and sent shots down the hallway, but she was entirely exposed and needed to protect the girls. She pushed herself up against the door and remembered the key card reader. She quickly grabbed the key card, placed it over the reader for the door behind her, grabbed the door latch for dear life as it fell open along with her. She shielded herself from behind the doorway and sent down several shots down the hall as she frantically signaled to the girls to quickly get into the room. They quickly did as she frantically fired the remaining rounds when finally, one of the guards was hit and slumped to the floor.

Don kept firing down the hall with his right hand to provide Maya cover fire, and once he saw that all the girls had scurried into the room, he strode over to the other corner and popped out both mags, placed his left gun atop his right, popped in fresh mags into both, tossed the top gun back into his left hand, and chambered both guns simultaneously by releasing the slide catch. He pointed one gun down at the corner room and shot out the peephole, then fired a few more shots at the lone gunman down at the other end of the hall. The gunman ducked out of the way.

Maya barreled across to the other door, badged in, and ducked inside the room. As the gunman appeared once more, Maya got him in the upper chest. Don quickly walked down the hallway to where the girls were when he heard the footsteps of a gunman behind him just as another gunman appeared in front of him. Don was in the middle as both gunmen took aim at him. Don stretched out his arms in a T and fired both guns just as the gunmen fired theirs.

The bullet from the direction of the elevator missed Don, but the bullet from the corner room sunk itself into Don's left shoulder, spinning him and sent the gun in his left hand onto the ground. However, both of his bullets had found their mark, and both gunmen went down.

"Don!" screamed Maya as she braced his fall by lunging into him. Don let out a grunt, but true to the soldier that he was, he kept his right gun up. He soon got onto his feet in a crouched position and he let out a gasp.

"Are you OK?" asked Maya and Don looked more disgusted with himself than anything else but simply said, "There's still one left."

"One," asked Maya.

"The head boss, he's got to be the only one left," said Don.

As their senses seeped back in, they could hear sirens from outside and knew that backup had arrived.

"We need to get the girls out," said Don.

"Yes, I'll tell them to follow you," said Maya.

"Follow me? What about you?"

"I need to find Hope," said Maya as she looked at Don with determination in her eyes. "Can you stand?"

"Yes, but…"

"No time," said Maya as she quickly crossed the hallway and shouted in Cantonese, "*Follow him!*"

The girls nodded and hurried to the door as Don rose up, his left arm held crooked as he trained his gun down the corridor toward the elevator. Maya looked at him and simply said, "Go!"

Don nodded, looked at the girls, and motioned with his head to follow as he raced down to the end of the hall to secure that position. Maya then quickly raced back up to end of the hall to the corner room and saw that it was clear. She looked down at the gunman, who took a shot in the upper chest. Her eyes went up to the now partially closed door as she popped out her mag, popped in a new one and chambered the first round. She crouched low, raced along the wall, and braced herself against the side of the door. Through the crack, she could see the body of a guard lying flat on his back. She took a deep breath and pushed aside the door to see a plush living room and office set up with a glass dining room table set up near the balcony. There was no sign of the man in the navy suit, though his suit jacket was on the back of an office chair. Her eyes came upon a closed door to her right in the corner. Moving into the room with her gun at the ready, she stepped passed the dead guard and approached the closed door quietly. She tested the doorknob. It was locked. Suddenly, splinters of wood blew past her along with the sound of three gunshots from behind the door.

Maya retrenched low against the side of the door, then sprung up and put three shots into the doorknob. She kicked in the door and lunged through in a crouch, training her gun ahead of her.

He had his left forearm around Hope's chest as he crouched behind her. She was small for a human shield, but that was the way of cowards. He held the muzzle of the gun against Hope's head as she winced. His eyes were calm and determined, and as he saw Maya barrel through the door in a crouch, he snickered.

"You got to be kidding me. They didn't just send a woman cop, but an Oriental?"

"LAPD!" shouted Maya as she placed her gun sights on the man's head.

"You come another step, and I'll put a bullet into her pretty head!"

Maya had to take command of the situation, but he shifted his weight too much to take any steady shot. In the firmest and loudest of voices, "I'm ordering you to…"

But the man interjected and yelled over Maya, "Order? Order me? You don't order me! I order you Oriental bitches to do what I say!"

He was trying to get into her head, demoralizing her using racial slurs to disparage who she was. She wasn't going to allow it so she changed tactics, "OK! Let's not do anything stupid, all I want is the girl."

"Oh, so do I! She's a bit young now, but in two years, she's going to be pretty, and I will sell her virginity to the man that wants to pay top dollar to pop this little China doll's cherry."

"You're disgusting!" screamed Maya as she steadied her gun on the man's head. But she couldn't help but look at Hope as well, whose frightened expression showed her helplessness.

"Don't pretend all you Oriental women don't want it in the end! You all end up with us sooner or later!"

Maya tried to stay calm and tried desperately not to let him get under her skin. "Look, let's talk…"

"I'm done talking to you! Drop your gun and then let me walk out with her! Be a good little Oriental bitch and listen to your master!"

Maya needed to end it and looked directly at Hope who was looking directly at her. She had to try. It was her only chance.

"She took her left hand off the gun and gently raised it, seemingly acquiescing to the man's demands and slightly took her finger off the trigger. The man smiled as Maya slowly angled the gun up. "Don't hurt her… *Hei*

Mon."

Hei Mon then looked up upon recognition of hearing her name.

"Tsk tsk, such a shame, such a pretty thing you are. My customers would have loved to break you in," as he began to point his gun at Maya.

Then in Cantonese, Maya screamed, *"Hei Mon, bite his arm!"*

Hei Mon didn't hesitate as she bit into the man's forearm. He flinched and released his hold as he dropped his gaze for a moment. The first bullet hit him square in the forehead, the second his neck, the third and the fourth into his upper chest. His gun flew out of his right hand as he was sent onto his back onto the wooden floor.

Maya stood up and crossed the distance between her and the man. She came around to his side, kicked away his gun, and looked at him. The red dot on his forehead indicated death as blood started to dribble from his neck, absorbed by his crisp white shirt. The whimpers caught Maya's attention, and she saw *Hei Mon* cowering up against the wall in utter fear.

Maya quickly holstered her gun and went to embrace *Hei Mon*, who crumbled into Maya's arms as her teary eyes looked away from the body.

In Cantonese, Maya whispered reassuringly, *"Don't cry, don't cry. Nothing to worry about,"* when suddenly Maya pulled her gun out once more and pointed it at the doorway as Don slammed himself up against the door jamb with his gun pointed at them.

"Don!" yelled out Maya as she lowered her gun.

"You got him? Is she safe?" asked Don who looked a bit frazzled as blood dripped from his left arm.

"Yes, and yes," Maya said reassuringly.

Two SWAT team members came in to assess the situation, which caused *Hei Mon* to bury her face in Maya's chest.

"It's OK *Hei Mon*, it's OK *Hei Mon*, I've got you now."

"Back-up came. The girls are safe. They're doing a floor-to-floor sweep right now. We should be good from here on out," said Don as he crouched down against the doorframe.

Maya smiled, holding *Hei Mon* and rubbing her back to comfort her. As Maya tried to straighten out *Hei Mon's* hair, she noticed a triangular tattoo on the back of her neck. The animals had already branded her.

* * *

Later, in the parking lot, as a light mist fell onto the active crime scene, Maya walked around the fleet of ambulances where the sex trafficking victims were being looked over by paramedics along with translators who could speak Cantonese, Mandarin, Korean, Vietnamese, Japanese, and other languages. The untold number of customers in different states of dress, were being led into the back of prisoner transport vehicles. Many were in quiet shame while others were more vocal in their denial of doing anything wrong. There was also the number of unscrupulous men, part of the illicit sex trafficking operation, being led into prisoner transport vehicles as well. She was disgusted by what they had put the Asian female victims through and couldn't imagine their nightmare and sexual abuse they must have endured.

As she walked toward one ambulance in particular, a voice hollered out and she looked over and saw one of the young Cantonese-speaking girls that she rescued. She uttered "Thank you," and the rest of the girls, uttered thank-you in mix of Cantonese, Korean, and Vietnamese.

A tear came to Maya's eye and she smiled and nodded toward them. She walked over to Don, who was strapped into a gurney as the paramedics were wrapping his arm.

"Hey," said Maya with a smile as she came up beside him. The paramedic was just finishing up applying a temporary dressing.

"Hey yourself," said Don as he looked a little frustrated.

"You were great back there. You had my back, and you really helped out these girls," said Maya admiringly.

"Yah, you did a pretty bang-up job. You got the head asshole and rescued Hope. I'd say, not bad for a day's work."

Maya smiled, "Yah, not too bad for a day's work."

"Ugh, damn bullet is still in the shoulder," uttered Don.

"Oh you big baby," Maya said and suddenly leaned and placed her lips on Don's unsuspecting lips. The paramedic just stood there frozen as Maya pulled back and looked at Don, who was still stunned.

"I'll drop by the hospital to see how you are doing," said Maya. "You can take him away now."

"Hey wait! My elbow is starting to hurt too now, can I get a kiss…" said Don just before he was pushed into the ambulance.

Maya smiled at him until they closed the ambulance doors and she turned around. She looked around the squad cars and found the one she wanted when a deep voice caught her attention.

"Lim!" said the captain as he walked up to her as she turned around to greet him. Maya stood her ground and simply looked him in the eye.

"You're supposed to be suspended," stammered the captain.

"I know," said Maya confidently.

"You know. And you still went after this cold case when I explicitly told you not to?" asked the captain?

"I went with my instinct," said Maya.

"Your instinct. So your instinct led you to this hotel that was a front for an illicit brothel specializing in Asian women," stated the captain.

"Yes," said Maya.

"And it was also part of a grander operation for sex trafficking young Asian girls, along with apprehending a number of criminals involved, in addition to killing the head of the operation, rounding up a number of the sick perps who were sexually abusing all these women and girls and rescuing them all too? Along with finding the little girl from that cold case?"

"Yes sir," said Maya confidently.

The captain suddenly liked the newfound confidence in his undercover officer and nodded. "Anyways, you may have stumbled onto something much bigger. This may just be a small piece, but what you did tonight was tremendous work."

"Yes, that's probably true," said Maya.

"So what's your angle here… what are you looking for, an accommodation?" asked the captain.

"No Sir," said Maya. "But a promotion to detective would be nice."

"Detective, huh? Is that all?" he asked incredulously.

"No, that's not all, Sir."

"Oh, there's more?"

"Cho too. I couldn't have done any of this without him," said Maya firmly.

"Huh, Cho too? He really was a big part?"

"You'll read it in my report, Sir," said Maya.

"Detective Lim and Detective Cho—that would be a pretty good public relations story, you know. I like the sound of that."

"We won't let you down, Sir," said Maya confidently.

"I guess not. Oh and Lim, I will read that report in the morning because I'm lifting your suspension immediately," quipped the captain as he put out his hand.

"Thank you cap," Maya said as she shook his hand.

"Good job tonight," said the captain, who then smiled and walked away, as he could hear the press with their yammering in the background.

Maya spun around and approached a squad car being watched over by a lone female officer. Maya smiled at her and uttered, "I'll take it from here."

Maya looked down into the misty rain-laden window and saw that *Hei Mon's* gaze was downcast, her hands neatly folded into her lap. She was in adorable pigtails on either side of her head and had cute bangs. They dressed her up like a doll to mold her into a product to serve an Asian fetish. Maya couldn't imagine what she must have been through. Suddenly being ripped away from her parents to serve as a pet to a criminal leader in Los Angeles. Maya put on a smile, opened the squad car's door, and crouched down. *Hei Mon* didn't move, but she slowly fidgeted with her fingers in her lap.

"*Hei Mon,*" said Maya in the sweetest of voices possible. *Hei Mon* looked toward Maya with a childish blank stare.

In her best Cantonese, Maya uttered, "*Do you understand me?*" to which *Hei Mon* nodded slightly. Maya smiled and slowly reached out to lay her right hand on top of *Hei Mon's* tiny hands. They were cool, but the warmth from Maya's hands slowly enveloped her little hands. "*You are OK now. I'm going to get you home,*" said Maya reassuringly, but *Hei Mon* didn't respond aside from a sniffle.

Maya caught out of the corner of her left eye another squad car stopping about fifty feet away, and a man stepping out of the back. It was Mr. Ho, who was directed by the driver in Maya's direction. Maya smiled and then looked at *Hei Mon* and told her gently, "*I need you to step out of the car now with me OK?*"

Hei Mon hesitated but soon she turned toward Maya and struggled like any child would getting out of the back seat. Soon her two tiny feet were planted on the ground, though she was still looking down and hadn't said a word. But she clutched onto Maya's warm hand.

The footsteps quickened, and soon enough Mr. Ho was crouched down next to Maya, facing the daughter who he feared was lost to him forever. There were tears in his eyes as he looked at this daughter. His expression was contorted, as there was probably so much he wanted to say, but all he could muster was a gentle and garbled, "*Hei Mon.*"

Hei Mon didn't look up and continued to look at her own hands in Maya's hands. As gently as she could, Maya steered *Hei Mon* to face her father. Then Maya whispered in Cantonese, "*Hei Mon, look who came to see you. Do you remember him?*"

Hei Mon looked up into her father's face, and she nervously held her gaze at the man, who was smiling and tearing up at the same time.

Mr. Ho then gently placed each of his hands on each of her shoulders and looked at his daughter and gently whispered in Cantonese, "*Hei Mon, it's Ba-ba.*" There was no response from *Hei Mon* as she continued to stare, and Mr. Ho said it a second time, "*It's Ba-ba.*"

"*Ba-ba,*" *Hei Mon* suddenly mumbled, and Mr. Ho excitedly nodded his head.

"*Ba-ba,*" said *Hei Mon* once again as Mr. Ho nodded his head vigorously as tears streamed down his face.

"*Ba-ba!*" said *Hei Mon* in a squeaky loud voice that only children can do as she let go of Maya's hands and reached for her father, who also embraced her warmly and affectionately. *Hei Mon* continued to repeat, "*Ba-ba!*" until suddenly she herself started crying into her father's shoulder while mumbling quietly, "*Ba-ba.*"

Maya couldn't help but feel her eyes well up with warm tears and her throat swell up in emotion. Mr. Ho then looked up from his teary eyes and whispered over to Maya, "Thank you."

Maya nodded and sniffled a few times as she slowly walked away from the emotional reunion between father and daughter. Once she was some distance away from Mr. Ho and *Hei Mon*, she fanned herself and wiped away her tears. She looked down at the wet asphalt and pulled out her phone. She wiped her nose, cleared her throat, and dialed a number. It rang a couple of times until a familiar voice picked up. Maya smiled and simply said, "*Ba-ba.*"

GREEN LIGHT

He stood there, statuesque, leaning slightly against the outside counter of the nurse's station. His single-pleated khaki dress pants draped lightly over his shiny black shoes. In the large left pocket of his white doctor's coat covering his pressed shirt and tie was his stethoscope. His elbow rested on the counter as his left hand held the patient's records. His eyes were intense, studying the patient's chart, hoping that it would miraculously say something different from earlier that morning. But the chart failed to deliver such a message. There was no change.

Dr. David Nguyen gently adjusted his black-framed glasses, which gave him the look of a professor of great intellect. As the hospital's chief neurosurgeon, he was not only the hospital's first Asian American chief of anything, he was also its youngest, a by-product of disciplined academic rigor instilled by a father who demanded it along with high career achievement.

David's father and his wife had come to the United States during one of the refugee waves after Saigon fell. They had nothing and left so much behind. After settling into Boston, Massachusetts, along with several other Vietnamese refugees, they worked as unskilled laborers and toiled away to try to make a living.

But despite their dire circumstances in a new land where they did not speak the language, they persevered like so many other Asian immigrants. David's father, Mr. Nguyen, was ambitious despite his challenges. In time, through interactions with Bostonians in the streets and in the restaurants that he worked in, he learned English. His wife, Mrs. Nguyen, was just as astute and picked up English as well. In the wee hours of the night, after their long shifts were over, they would practice with each other. There were no weekends for this husband and wife team, and vacations were far and few in the first few years. They simply worked and only had each other.

Everything changed however when their first son David, was born. Their already challenging life was now filled with an uncharted promise; the future of their family would be secure. This drove Mr. Nguyen to make a courageous decision: to take their entire hard-earned savings and open up a Vietnamese restaurant that would bring the culinary cuisine of his homeland to Boston.

The first two years were grueling. The Nguyens found themselves at the budding restaurant daily. They were in a city when the Chinese were dominant, and Szechuan-style cooking and General Gao's chicken were all the rage among the white populace. But the fledging Vietnamese restaurant took hold as it catered to a growing Vietnamese populace who missed the flavors of their homeland. Like the Nguyens, many of them worked long hours. They indulged in the convenience of ordering from a restaurant to get flavors of home.

More often than not, David was at the restaurant. Ever since he was an infant and for as long as David could remember, he had grown up in that restaurant and watched his parents working and sacrificing their youth to build a future for him. But soon, it just wasn't him, as Tracy entered into the world as the baby sister, and soon thereafter, baby Nicholas. It was widely rumored that baby Nicholas was a mistake, stoked from a night of passion to release the bottled-up happiness when the receipts for the restaurant that night were the most they had ever seen.

Regardless of the circumstances, the Nguyens were now a family of five, and the need to work even harder became a necessity. That work ethic was passed down into the children's studies, and the Nguyen children were expected to excel in their academics. The children were sequestered each and every day, and Mrs. Nguyen dispensed the academic routine to the children. The first priority was absolute mastery of the English language to spare them the ridicule their parents endured from unkind people who enjoyed mocking their accented and broken English when the parents first started to learn English.

The children excelled academically. The highest expectations were for their firstborn, David. He was going to be a doctor. Not that that was David's dream, but rather, it was his parents' dream. The parents couldn't have lived the lives they had wanted and could not fathom the opportunities that their children had. All the parents knew how to do was to sacrifice their sweat, muscles, joints, pain, and personal dreams for their children and to live vicariously through them. Their need for their children to have a better life and fulfill the American dream was the driving factor for Mr. Nguyen to demand nothing short of academic success for his children, especially David.

Being in the South Vietnamese army, the primary reason why he felt he had to flee to the U.S., he was a true disciplinarian. He would berate his children unrelentingly when their grades did not meet his expectations, and he did not tolerate any excuses. It was his children's obligation as Vietnamese sons and daughters to do well in school. And it worked. The Nguyens created three class valedictorians and got them into some of the best colleges.

Every now and then, Mr. Nguyen would break from his military style of rearing his children and remember that they were children. It was at that occasional family outing to a beach in Quincy where the children saw the doting father. But that side of their parents, the sympathetic and more compassionate side, was usually expressed by Mrs. Nguyen. Though she did not expect anything less of her children, she was the loving smile of the family and offered them comfort.

When David got into Harvard Medical School, his academic success became the pride and joy of the Nguyens. Though his younger siblings, Tracy and Nicholas, who preferred to simply go by as "Nick," were proud, they also resented their elder brother's success because it meant trying to surpass a bar of expectation that may be insurmountable.

However, David's upbringing and the extra discipline that he had to endure as the firstborn were ingrained into his competitive soul. In the end, he became an extension of his father and sought to achieve what his father couldn't. He aced his years in medical school; raced through his residency with a tenacity that brought admiration from seasoned doctors; and through a combination of keen medical insight, hard work, chance, and luck, he became the hospital's chief neurosurgeon. It was an achievement that his parents took much pride in, since their son's future was now secure.

As David stood there against the nurse's station, he flipped over another page. His consternation was still the same, intense and quiet. The patient had suffered swelling to his brain. It was ultimately relieved, but not before the patient went into a coma. All neurological scans were inconclusive. The inconclusive data could not determine a prognosis. The patient had simply fallen silent and was only alive due to the mechanical devices that tended to his life.

David was puzzled and paid close attention to this patient. He looked over and gazed into the patient's room and could see him lying in the bed. The white sheets were gently drawn midway up to his chest. He was wearing a white-and-blue-patched hospital gown. His arms lay by his side, waiting for orders from their host that might possibly never come again. His hands were worn, leathered by hard restaurant labor. The skin on his face clung loosely to his bones, clearly showing the shape of his skull. Gray hair had infiltrated his once-blackened eyebrows and his limp hair, which was neatly combed to one side. A breathing tube clung to his emaciated face, a sign of his weakened state. How ironic that David, the chief neurosurgeon, found that he could do nothing for this patient, his father.

"How is he today?" asked the nurse gently as she had maneuvered herself a couple of feet directly in front of David without him realizing it. She was in her nurse's scrubs of a light emerald color as she clutched a manila folder across her chest with both of her arms. Her black hair was pulled tightly back behind her. She looked up at David with her bright brown eyes that evoked a sense of concern.

David was caught off guard and fixated on Mabel with stern eyes. "He's the same," he said curtly. "You're his nurse, you know this already."

Mabel diverted her gaze immediately and looked wounded. "I'm sorry, I just saw you looking at your father and I…"

"There's no need to worry about me, just tend to my father," interjected David.

"Yes Doctor," replied Mabel.

After a pause, David ended simply with, "Thank you" before he walked off, leaving Mabel to pick up the patient records.

The glass door slowly swung back into place as David entered his office. He walked to the side of his desk and through the windows, saw that night had slowly fallen onto the city. He placed his hands at his sides and bowed his head forward, his shoulders slouching as he exhaled a sigh. His mind wandered as his thoughts hopelessly went back and forth as to why he couldn't figure out his father's mysterious condition.

It had been months, and though patients have miraculously awakened from comas after years, he hoped that this wouldn't be the case for his father. His arms shifted as one arm crossed his chest and the elbow of the other rested atop of it. He drew his clenched fist to his chin, to ponder the hopelessness of the situation. His eyes opened just a little and for moment, a tear nearly escaped, but it was held back as his eyes became focused on the pictures on the shelf behind his desk.

He walked toward the shelf and glanced across the photos that he had taken for granted. They were pictures of happier times. One of the pictures was of just his father as he beheld the diploma from Harvard Medical School. If one didn't know, one would have thought his father had been the medical school graduate. There was a casual picture of him and his parents eating at the hospital's cafeteria. But one picture caught his attention: The picture of his parents and him graduating from Harvard Medical School as his sister and brother stood off to the side. His sister, Tracy was beaming while his brother, Nick wasn't. It was more of a smirk. Though the picture hid the arduous family toil but for a moment, it revealed smiles.

Things at home had not been the same in the last year, and their father's coma had made them worse. David was the model son, Tracy was a quiet daughter, and Nick was the young rebel in the family. Lacking their father's discipline, their lives became unfocused. In their father's absence, David had become the patriarch of the family, a role he never wanted. It was also a role that his siblings could not accept, as he was their brother.

The troubles at home were not helping the situation, as if he didn't already have enough to deal with at work along with his father's unknown prognosis.

The ring tone of his cell sliced through his reverie. It was his mother. She was a strong woman, trying to be strong for the family. She was the dutiful mother to a fault and though she had much more success with Tracy, she could not reign in Nick, who had left home recently to live with friends. It worried her to no end as to how he was surviving on a day-to-day basis.

David answered his cell, "Hi Me. Yes, I'll be home for dinner. I'm just getting ready to leave. Yes, I'll check in on Ba before I leave. Yes, I'll drive carefully. See you soon."

David hastily made his way to his father's room as he meandered the white-walled hospital hallways. He had saw that that it was a bit after 6PM. He knew that the traffic getting back into Dorchester by way of 93 South was going to be nightmarish. He quietly stepped into his father's room. The silence was interrupted every now and then from the beeps that came from one of the many medical devices as the rhythmic hum of the respirator tempered the ambient noise from outside.

David walked up along his father's side and looked down at his frail body. The blanket that gently covered him outlined his slender frame. His forearms laid at his side, covered in deep streams of veins, betraying his weakened state as a zombie-like life force flowed through them still.

Satisfied for now, David nodded, turned away, and walked out of the hospital room for the night.

The thumping sound of the wiper was numbing as David sat at the red light. The stress dulled his senses as his mind ruminated for a prognosis. The ebbing waves of black umbrellas went unnoticed just as the wiper mechanically wiped away the rain. A frustrated honk woke him from his reverie. It was a green light. He eased his foot off the brake and drove on.

After luckily finding a parking spot only a couple of doors away from his parents' place, he made a dash to it. As he raced up the wooden steps, the front door opened and his sister, Tracy, appeared.

"Hey," she said as her eyes looked up to meet his somewhat rain-misted face.

"Hey yourself," he said with a faint smile as he passed into the doorway, where he quickly took off his shoes near the mob of paired shoes that seemed to worship a full shoe rack.

His mother called out from the kitchen in Vietnamese that dinner was ready. He nodded to himself, and Tracy reached out for his wet raincoat as he smiled and gently waved her away, "I got this. Go, go to the kitchen, I'll be there in a sec," he said to his always-helpful sister.

She nodded and then asked, "How's Ba?"

David gave a sigh and simply said, "The same. No change."

As they ate quietly at the dinner table, his mother took glances here at there to make sure that David and Tracy were eating. Cooking made her happy. Because she came from impoverished circumstances, being able to provide and cook for her family was all the humble satisfaction that she needed. But she couldn't help looking with sadness at the chair where her husband had sat in for decades and then at the empty chair where her youngest son would usually sit.

His mother's glance didn't go unnoticed as David blurted out, "I can't believe Nick isn't here for dinner. He's so disrespectful."

"Ai, shhhh," shushed his mother. "Don't give Nick so much stress."

"Please Me. What stress does he have? I'm the doctor in the family caring for Ba and he left the family," David said scornfully.

But all his mother could say was, "Eat," as she scooped another chopstick full of rice into her mouth.

David shook his head in frustration as he thought about his younger brother. He was bright, but he was rash. His selfish ways were a constant topic of David's chastisement, and Nick would usually just disrespectfully brush off his older brother's admonishment.

Nick had just graduated from college with a finance degree, but his heart wasn't into it. Instead, music was his calling. When he was not studying, he was playing his electric guitar and singing. In his room, he would create covers for his YouTube channel, and he was pretty good at it. But their father disapproved of it, thinking that it was a waste of time. There would be heated fights between Nick and his father, which usually ended up with Nick locking himself in his room as his father barked out one shaming comment after another.

Before their father fell into his lonely coma, Nick had moved out, no longer able to endure his father's constant bickering. As he rushed out of the house, the father yelled at his youngest son and accused him of being worthless, telling him he should never return home.

"Hey, fish?" asked Tracy as David was brought out his trance.

David fixed his eyes on his sister before extending his bowl of half-eaten rice to welcome the saucy fish that she dropped onto his rice. He quickly picked up the rice and devoured the delicious fish and as he chewed, he looked gently at his sister.

She was quietly eating and despite her calm look, he knew that she wasn't happy, albeit she played the role of the dutiful daughter of a traditionally minded Vietnamese parents. She had graduated with honors from Boston University and soon found an accounting job at a reputable company in Boston. She lived at home until she was to marry, per the custom of a traditional Vietnamese family. But that is where she went afoul of her family's wishes. She started dating a Korean American man, and her father strongly disapproved. It wasn't that the father disapproved of Korean Americans, but he expected all his children to marry Vietnamese. It caused great anguish in the family, and though Tracy said the relationship was off, David knew that they were still secretly seeing each other.

"Have more fish," said the mother to David as she held a chunky piece of fish out to him. David quickly placed his almost empty bowl underneath it as she dropped it in, to which he said, "Thanks."

"How is your father today?" asked the mother.

There was a pause as David swallowed the bite of fish. He gently placed his hands holding the bowl and chopsticks onto the table and looked up at his soulful mother. "It's the same. I don't know yet what is wrong," said a defeated David.

His mother looked up at her doctor son, the one who they had the most expectation for and could see the disappointment in his face. "Eat. One day a time. You'll figure it out. I'll visit tomorrow."

David nodded and plucked out another piece of fish before devouring it quickly.

The next day, as David was making his rounds, he slowed down on approach to his father's room. He could see his mother's back to him as she sat somberly in a chair pulled up beside her husband. The streaks of gray ran through her hair. His mother visited every single day, without fail. In the early days, she would spend hours at her husband's bedside, but as the days turned to weeks, weeks turned to months, her visits were more constrained. An hour per day, maybe two at the most.

She would speak softly to him in Vietnamese, recapping the previous day's events. Sometimes, she would recite a previous memory of them together and laugh. It was always her hope that somehow, he could hear everything so that when he woke up, he wouldn't have missed a day. She would reassure him that the children were all fine, but that wasn't the truth. Then there would be days where she wouldn't have much to say, and she only beseeched her husband to wake up soon.

David quietly stepped into the room and came upon his mother.

"Me," he said as she craned her head up toward her son as she offered a sobering look. Her silent gaze fell back onto her husband for a few moments, before she spoke in Vietnamese, *"David is here now. He knows what is best. I'll see you tomorrow."*

David's mother gently got up and turned toward her son. She didn't say much. All that could have been said, had been said. "I'm going to Chinatown to pick up some groceries now. I'll see you at dinner."

"Sure thing, Me," said David as he helped his mother gather the raincoat from the wall hook along with her umbrella.

"It's going to rain later, so drive slow," admonished his mother as she put on the raincoat.

"Sure thing, Me," said David. "I'll continue to work on Ba."

His mother fastened the last button on her raincoat and cast her eyes downward before looking up at her son. Her tired eyes told a story of weariness, yet resilience. Without looking at her bed-ridden husband, she turned and simply said, "Be home for dinner."

"Sure thing, Me," was all David said.

As the end of the day neared, David walked down the hall toward the nurse's station by his father's room. He stopped by the counter and could see that Mabel was updating another patient's profile. She hadn't noticed him at which point, he simply said, "Mabel."

She turned to him as apprehension appeared on her face. She turned away from him to reach for David's father file when David said, "Any day now."

Mabel dutifully got up and handed David his father's latest brain scans. He firmly took it from her as she took a step back and clasped her hands together in front of her. David reviewed the latest scan, and he didn't know why he would expect a change. The latest scan was the same as the one before, and the one before that and so on. He placed the file on the counter and without looking at Mabel, walked off.

The thumping sound of the wiper was numbing as David sat pensively at the red light. It was lightly raining again, and he was caught up in the evening rush hour. His mind jumped from one thought to another, but with his father's scan being the same again, he thought of his mother, his sister, and finally his brother. The sound of the wiper came once again followed soon by a sharp honk from behind. David shook off his thoughts and looked up at the bright green light in front of him, staring at it. Then the honk behind him became angry, and David suddenly knew, he had to move on.

His driving picked up as he confidently navigated between slower cars and pedestrians in the light rain. He called his mother to let her know that that night, he would not be coming home for dinner. When she asked why, he simply said he had to work late. He then texted his sister, and when she texted back, he nodded that she had texted him the information that he needed.

He arrived where he needed to be. After parking the car, he entered the Korean restaurant. He was greeted warmly in Korean by a young Korean hostess. David bashfully acknowledged that he was a party of one, but before he was led away to his table, he asked the hostess, "Is Sung Park working tonight?"

The hostess smiled back and responded, "Oh yes, he's here all the time. Do you want me to get him for you?"

"Yes, please, if you don't mind," said a gracious David.

As David folded up his umbrella, a tall Korean man in slacks and a pressed shirt appeared, and his eyes widened upon seeing David.

David turned to Sung and nodded and Sung offered a slight bow and stepped forward with his hand where David pressed his own hand into his.

"Dr. Nguyen," said Sung politely to which David grinned and quickly said, "Please, call me David."

Sung smiled and said, "Of course. Are you here for dinner?"

"Yes, it's just me," said David with some hesitancy.

Sung quickly dismissed the awkwardness and became the hospitable host to his restaurant and gently welcomed David with his right hand as he mouthed something in Korean to the hostess who nodded. He took the menu from her and led David to a grilling booth that would have seated four people.

"Oh, this is much too big for me..." said David.

"Please, it's the least I can do for Tracy's..." Sung suddenly paused, which David picked up on.

David reassuringly placed his hand on Sung's left shoulder and said, "It's

OK, I know that you and Tracy are still dating."

A cautious relief settled onto Sung's face as he let David settle himself into the booth before he passed him the menu. Before leaving, Sung recommended the Korean marinated ribeye, *deng shim*, as his choice of meat for grilling.

David noticed that Sung was very charming and gracious. He had only met Sung once when Tracy brought him to lunch one day, and it wasn't too long thereafter that she announced to the family over the dinner table that she was dating someone. Initially, her parents were elated until she mentioned that he was Korean. His father's tone suddenly changed, and he admonished her for choosing anyone other than a Vietnamese man. When Tracy was stunned into silence, their father continued into an angry tirade about how important it was to preserve their Vietnamese heritage while in America. It ended in an angry crescendo when he forbade her from dating Sung any further and his intimidating ultimatum held even David paralyzed.

It wasn't long thereafter that their father fell into a coma, and not wanting to add further tension to a difficult family matter, Tracy and Sung took to hiding their relationship. But David knew that they were still dating despite his sister trying to hide it. Over the last few months, a few clues popped up here and there which David took notice of, but unlike his father, he personally had no issue with Sung.

David looked up as he saw a jovial Sung leading a young Asian American couple to a booth not too far from him. Each booth was sectioned off with a contemporary light wood design and the tables were a dark stone, most likely granite. Each barbecue booth was outfitted with an in table grill and vent. It was evident that Sung spared no expense to create a memorable Korean barbecue experience. As Sung walked away, a smiling Korean woman approached his booth and quickly scattered about his table a delectable assortment of small Korean dishes, collectively known as *banchan*. There was everything from fresh kimchi, kimchi daikon, bean sprouts, spicy fried tofu and so many other dishes, that David's eyes and appetite widened in delight.

When asked, David requested a kimchi tofu *jjigae* and in his best attempt at Korean, he asked for the recommended *deng shim* for the barbecue. The waitressed nodded slightly and turned on the grill. As David sampled each of the *banchan* before him, his steaming and bubbling kimchi tofu *jjigea* arrived. It was one of his favorite stews, and he sampled each spoonful with appreciation. Soon enough, the *deng shim*, arrived and David had not realized that it was such a large cut of ribeye. The waitress smiled and assured him that it would be delicious as she placed it on the hot grill as the sizzling sound sung through the air.

As the meat sizzled, the delicious smell of grilling meat wafted through the air and the caramelization of the marinade tickled his nose. The waitress soon returned to flip the *deng shim* and scattered the grilling onion and mushrooms. Soon thereafter, she returned and expertly cut up the *deng shim* into bite sized pieces and gestured to David that they were ready to eat and pointed to the dipping sauce. David nodded with a smile and with the metal chopsticks, took a piece along with the sauce and brought it to his mouth.

His eyes closed as the sauce that coated the *deng shim* piece seemed to melt onto his tongue. Then came the char from the barbecue that seemed to revive some instinct of appreciating meat cooked upon an open flame. It was then followed by the tenderness and juiciness of the *deng shim* itself, and David quickly picked up another piece to devour.

To David's surprise, he had finished all the food, and he felt just right. If he weren't told so, he would have simply and happily ordered the barbecued *galbi*. The kind waitress cleared the table and David simply waited at the booth, while sipping on some hot tea.

Soon enough, Sung came by the table and David greeted him with a smile.

"How was the meal?" Sung asked.

"Sung, let me tell you, that was one of the best Korean meals I've ever had," said David appreciatively.

Sung smiled with a slight nod, asked, "Is there anything else that I can get you?"

There was a pause and David said, "Some of your time if you have it. I would like to talk to you."

Sung scooted over into the booth across from David and looked him in the eye.

"As I kind of let on earlier, I know that you and my sister are still dating. I also think you know that my father didn't like the idea of you dating my sister," said David firmly.

Sung looked away for a moment and then back at David, "Yes, I know."

David looked at Sung gravely and then said, "Well, what I'm about to ask of you will be hard," as Sung looked intently at David.

Just as David started talking, the sizzle of two meats from another table drowned out what David was saying to Sung.

After leaving the restaurant, David got into his car and let out a large sigh. He sat there in the driver's seat and started his car. The lights awoke and soon illuminated the dash in a smattering of lit icons. He looked at the time, and it was 9:00 PM. He took out his phone, found the text from his sister, and nodded.

A short drive away, he found himself in front of a wooden triple-decker home. After exiting the car, he walked up the rickety steps to the front porch. There were two side-by-side doors and in the dim light, he found the doorbell that he needed. He pressed it and could hear an agitated buzzer echoing from somewhere high and deep within. Sounds of descending footsteps were heard and soon the wooden door opened, and David's brother, Nick, was there.

In jeans, a T-shirt and socks, Nick looked up at his brother, who stood about an inch taller. His hair had gotten longer and was hanging off to the side of his face. He had also lost some weight since the last time he saw David. "How did you find me?" he asked.

"Tracy," David said. "She texted me your address. Can I come up?"

Nick looked at his brother dismissively and with a wave of his hand, gestured his brother to follow him. David walked through the door and up two flights of narrow stairs before entering the third-floor apartment. After following Nick through the apartment and passing two other young guys in the living room that reeked of college life, he found himself in Nick's modest room.

It was a small room, large enough for a twin-sized mattress on the floor in the corner, an old wooden desk with an opened laptop on top of it, a wooden chair and a soft-lit floor lamp that looked like it could have been bought at Ikea. There was a small refrigerator, a couple of amplifiers, one larger than the other, and a guitar case. It was open, but the electric guitar itself was lying on the bed.

Nick plopped himself down onto bed and propped himself against the corner. David just looked at him before he turned and quietly closed the door behind him. He glanced at the wooden chair, and Nick gestured toward it. David walked over to it, pulled it out, and sat down in it.

The silence was deafening until David said sarcastically, "I like what you've done with the place."

Nick looked up and retorted sarcastically, "Oh thanks, it's a dream home."

"Well at least it's neat," said David.

"Like how Ba always taught us," said Nick.

Another heavy silence fell on the two brothers.

"How is Ba?" ask Nick.

"He's still the same," said David as he was met by another pause from the brooding Nick. "Nick, come home."

Nick gently swayed his head from side-to-side.

"Come on, Nick. What are you doing here?" asked his brother.

"I'm living my life!" hollered Nick before he settled down.

"This is your life?" said David questioningly.

"Well at least it's my life."

"You can still have your life. Me and Tracy, we all miss you."

Nick looked up at his brother firmly as his eyes glistened. "Hey, do you remember Ba told me to never come back home if I was still going to do my music? Don't you?"

David softened his tone, "I do, but it's different now…"

"Sometimes, I just wish…"

"What? That Ba was dead?" David asked angrily.

Another blanket of silence floated down between the two brothers.

"No. Sometimes, I just wished Ba would have accepted me," said Nick as he sunk his head into his pulled knees.

"I didn't mean that, Nick," said David reassuringly. "Look, I want to help."

"I don't want your help," said Nick despondently.

David pulled out his wallet and produced a business card. He extended it to Nick, who stared at it before reluctantly taking it.

The business card had the logo for Berklee College of Music and a name.

"What's this?" asked Nick curiously.

"Grace Dunn, the professor on there, was a patient of mine. She had a brain tumor some years back, and I saved her life when I removed it. It's an amazing thing when you save people's lives, they say they are indebted to me. I never take it up, you know, it's just a saying. Well, I called her earlier today, and guess what? They need someone to teach guitar. I told them I have a person in mind. Interested?"

Nick looked at his brother dubiously, back at the card and then back at his brother. "Are you kidding me? This is Berklee College of Music? You just can't become a professor…"

"Don't get me wrong. It's not a free ride. You'd only be an adjunct professor. The rest you have to earn yourself," said David.

Nick hesitated and incredulously asked, "No strings attached?"

"Well, I didn't say that," said David.

"What does big brother want from me?" asked Nick as he let his hand holding the card droop across his knees.

"It's simple," said David as the piano music from Nick's roommate drowned out their conversation.

In the late afternoon the next day, David was anxious as he briskly walked toward his father's room. His mother had appeared as usual earlier that day and had gone home. As usual, she expected him home for dinner and asked if he wanted anything special, which he usually did not take her up on. But that day, he asked if she wouldn't mind preparing *thit bo voi bo*, one of the seven beef dishes of a traditional Vietnamese beef meal called *bo bay mon*. She was surprised by his request but obliged, as she hadn't prepared it in awhile.

As David approached the nurse's station, Mabel had just gathered up the latest scans for his father. He stopped in front of her without as much as a glance and took the file. He reviewed the scans, and as usual, they told the same story. He closed the file as his hand holding it fell to his side. He walked over to his father's room, but instead of stepping through the doorway, he leaned up against it and simply stared at his father.

There his father lay, motionless, a shell of the man that he once was. The low and steady beeps broke the silence that enshrouded the room. The life-supporting devices displaying green lights were a misnomer, as they didn't really display life—only that his body was biochemically functioning with the help of machines and nothing more.

David turned and walked back to the nurse's station to see Mabel waiting for him. She was a slender young Asian American woman in blue scrubs. Her black hair was tied back that day. Despite his curtness, her temperament was always steady. He stopped at the counter and for a moment took her in and slowly handed the file to her.

As she took the file, he said, "Mabel."

Mabel looked up surprised as he rarely addressed her by name let alone spoke to her. "Yes?" she responded.

"You've been the nurse here from day one since my father fell ill. You've watched over him and you always showed me kindness. But I don't think I have always been that nice to you, and for that, I'm sorry," said an ashamed David.

Mabel's eyes lit up in surprise and attempted to brush it off by saying, "Please, Dr. Nguyen, you don't have to apologize. You're under a lot of stress, I understand."

"No, please, it's no excuse. I've only been concerned for my father's status and I never paid attention to the others who have also watched over him. For that, I'm thankful," offered David.

Mabel nodded and with a grin she simply said, "Thank you and you're welcome. I know how you feel."

Her sympathy piqued David's curiosity. "How so?" he inquired.

There was a pause until Mabel answered. "I lost my father, to cancer. When I was younger, I remember visiting him in the hospital each day. It was really tough on my mom and my younger brother and sister. I was the oldest, and I felt the need to be the strongest. But on the day my father passed, despite all my prayers and hopes, I felt so hopeless and that I must have let him down. I couldn't stand being in that room, and I ran out. I didn't know where I ran to, but it was a nurse who chased after me. The same nurse who cared for my dad each day. In my hopelessness and lots of crying, all she did was hold me and tell me that I was so strong throughout the whole thing, and that I must have inherited my strength from my dad. She told me that life is sometimes unfair, but parents give to their kids strength to get them through the tough times so that they can move forward. That's when I knew I wanted to be a nurse. So that I can give others the strength to move on."

David was in awe of Mabel's story. It just reemphasized to him that for the last few months, he knew nothing of Mabel. He put his hands into his pocket and looked at Mabel, "I never knew. You've been this silent pillar of strength that I didn't know was there this whole entire time... thank you."

Mabel felt a warmth rush up to her cheeks at David's genuineness that she wasn't sure how to receive it from the stoic doctor that she knew him to be. "Please, don't think anything of it," said Mabel.

David for once looked at Mabel for more than being a nurse, the caretaker of his father, and the steward of his charts and offered, "Let's do lunch this week."

"Excuse me?" asked Mabel with a bit of a bewildered look on her face.

"Lunch, to say thank you. You eat don't you?" asked David.

Mabel grinned and said, "Yes, I do eat, and I'd like that."

* * *

Later that evening, Tracy heard the familiar footsteps of her brother and approached the front door. She opened it to a beaming David who just stood there blocking the doorframe.

"Are you coming in?" she asked.

"It smells good," said David as he still leaned up against the doorjamb.

"Me has been cooking since she got home. Why aren't you coming in?" she asked.

David smiled and moved to his left as Sung appeared from the side, with a sneaky smile.

Tracy's face lit up in surprise as she saw Sung, who was carrying two bags of what seemed like groceries. Tracy looked quizzically at David, who only said, "I know you two have been dating."

David entered and Sung followed. Tracy busied herself asking Sung why he was there as he took off his shoes. David let them talk as he went into the kitchen.

"Me!" he said excitedly. "It smells great!"

"I hope so. I've been cooking…" she then paused as she saw her daughter and Sung appear in the doorway to the kitchen.

David, stepped out of the way and gestured to Sung. "Mom, I want you to meet Sung."

Sung bowed slightly and then stepped forward with his hand. Mrs. Nguyen quickly wiped her right hand with the towel that she had and cautiously shook his hand.

Tracy quickly interjected, "Me, this is…"

"Yes, your boyfriend," said Mrs. Nguyen quickly.

Tracy looked baffled as her mother replied, "I pick up on a few things, I know," she said smugly. Tracy turned away bashfully, realizing she wasn't as secretive as she thought.

"I hope I cooked enough food…" said Mrs. Nguyen apologetically.

Sung then quickly chimed in, "Oh that's not a problem. David asked me bring some food from my restaurant. If you can just tell me where to set up…"

"I'll help," offered an excited Tracy, who only wanted to extricate herself from the embarrassing situation as she led Sung toward the dining room.

"What are you doing?" Mrs. Nguyen asked her scheming son.

David looked at her and said, "I'm moving this family forward."

His mother didn't offer a response; the lock turning on the front door distracted her. Nick stepped through wearing jeans with black low-cut boots, a loose T-shirt, along with a black leather jacket topped off with a baseball cap. His electric guitar in its black nylon carrying case was strapped to his back.

"Nick!" exclaimed his mother as she rushed past David and over to her youngest son.

She stopped a couple of feet in front of him with a smile that betrayed her worry about him. He turned to her with a smile that hid his sense of remorse.

"Me, I'm sorry. I didn't mean to leave home," said Nick as he looked down at his mother with downcast eyes.

She grabbed the hands of her youngest son and simply said, "Come eat, and you can meet Tracy's boyfriend."

"Oh, Sung is here too?" asked Nick.

After the introductions and Sung assuring Mrs. Nguyen that the portable grill that he brought over would not set off the smoke alarm, everyone sat down together to enjoy a Vietnamese and Korean barbecue dinner of sorts. With the addition of Sung, David found that he took the seat that his father would have normally occupied. He insisted that Sung introduce his mother to his new favorite Korean barbecue meat, *deng shim*. Sung also made sure that he had brought Tracy's favorite *banchans*, particularly the dried anchovies. The number of *banchans* that covered her table amused Mrs. Nguyen, but she thoroughly enjoyed them, especially the fried tofu.

David's mother then proudly explained the beef with butter dish, *thit bo voi bo* and how it was part of an elaborate seven course beef dish. This intrigued Sung as he watched how she prepared the meat as he took in the delicious smell.

During dinner, Nick announced that he had gotten a job at Berklee College of Music. Though he was excited for the opportunity, he humbly said it was a starting gig and that he would need to work hard to make it a permanent position. He also let everyone know that it was David who put him in contact with a professor there. Mrs. Nguyen couldn't help but give her older son another suspicious look.

After dinner, David insisted that everyone retire to the living room as he helped his mother clear the table. As he helped his mother wash the dishes, him shaking off the excess water and placing the dishes in the dishwasher rack, his mother remarked, "He seems nice."

"Sung? He's seems like a really good guy," said David.

"He owns and runs his own restaurant?" asked his mother.

"He does, and it's pretty busy," said David.

"And Nick? You helped your brother get a job?"

"I just put him in contact with a friend. Nick really didn't like finance. But maybe he can be a musician."

"He'll never make any money," said Mrs. Nguyen disdainfully.

"Musicians can make decent money. Maybe he'll be on TV someday," said David jokingly.

"Don't be funny," admonished his mother.

That's when they heard the electric guitar playing and David beckoned his mother to the living room as they dried their hands.

During their living room conversation, Tracy had mentioned that Sung was a pretty good singer and Nick was trying to coax him to sing. Sung was reluctant but was relieved when Mrs. Nguyen and David entered the living room.

Sung politely got up and with an appreciative smile, "Dinner was delicious, Mrs. Nguyen. I couldn't have done better myself at my restaurant."

"You will take me to your restaurant," said a witty Mrs. Nguyen.

"Yes! Of course, it would be an honor to have you and everyone at my restaurant," said an excited Sung.

"Eric Nam!" said Nick as he started to play a few chords from the popular Korean K-Pop musical artist.

Sung gave Nick an annoyed look and asked disapprovingly, "You think that just because I'm Korean I listen to K-Pop?"

Nick didn't look fazed as he continued to slowly pluck out a few chords from one of Eric Nam's popular songs.

Sung shook his head, looked at Tracy and then to Nick, "You're right. I do, and I know this song too."

"Then sing it!" said Nick gleefully and got into the natural rhythm of the song. Soon, Sung began to sing, to the delight of everyone there. Tracy seemed the most moved by the song, and she listened to Sung singing melodiously as Nick brought the song to life with his electric guitar.

Though Mrs. Nguyen couldn't understand the song, she could appreciate the melody and was simply delighted to see her family together in her living room. David noticed this as well, and it made him smile.

A little later as David prepared to leave, he left Nick, Tracy and Sung in the living room. His mother followed him to the door, curious to see where he was going at such a late hour.

"Where are you going? It's dark out and dangerous," said his mother cautiously.

"I'll be fine, Me. I just need to take care of something at the hospital," said David.

"Your Ba?"

"No. He's still the same, Me," said David under his breath.

"Will he ever wake up?" she asked as she looked up at her son.

There was a pause and David simply said, "I don't know."

His mother nodded her head a couple of times and said, "OK. Get home soon."

"I will Me," said David.

* * *

Later that night, with the lights of the hospital hallways dimmed somewhat for the night shift, David made his way over to his father's room. The night shift nurse manning the nurse's station only gave him a cursory glance. He entered his father's room and closed the door behind him. He looked at his father's frail body as the blue blanket neatly draped over his body. His skinny arms were at his sides as veins could be seen coursing along them.

He pulled a chair alongside his father and faced him. He gently clasped his father's unmoving right hand, whose skin felt clammy and disconnected from his hand. But he held his father's hand firmly and looked toward his father's motionless face.

"Ba. You've been through so much in your life. You sacrificed your whole life for us. You've been the strength of the family. I wanted to let you know Me is strong. She's been dedicated to you each and every day. Ba, I know you're not happy with Tracy and Nick, but you need to let that go. I met Sung, and he reminds me of you when you started your restaurant. I think if you gave him a chance, you'd like him. I know you felt Nick was wasting his life with his music, but it's OK, I got him a job. He's not going to starve. He's going to need to find his own way, and I'll be there to help him. Don't worry."

David rubbed his thumb along the web of his father's hand, trying to comfort his father or to draw strength.

"But Ba, you need to believe you gave us the strength to move on. I'm the doctor you wanted me to be, but there is still so much for me to do. I see you here, lying here, wasting away. I have to believe that I can help you to move on too. I need to have the strength to let you move on."

David then glanced through the half-drawn blinds and saw the night shift nurse was engrossed with her phone. With his other hand and only with a slight pause, he carefully and quickly unclipped the pulse monitor from his father's index finger and transferred it to his own without skipping a beat. He looked at the EKG and everything looked normal, and he carefully took another look at the nurse's station. Nothing was amiss.

Keeping his profile low, he leaned up toward his father's face and placed his forehead to his father's forehead for a moment. He closed his eyes for a few seconds and then lifted away from his father's expressionless face. Then with care that only a son can give to a parent, he carefully pulled out the breathing tube and set it to the side of the bed.

He sat back in his chair and clasped his father's right hand with both of his hands and looked at his dad as he took in his last breaths.

A tear slowly streamed down from his left eye as emotion started to ripple through his face. He rubbed his father's cold hand. "I know why I'm a doctor now," said David in grief as his father exhaled his last breath.

FLOWER GIRL

Definitely too fast, or was I too slow? I'm not even sure now. It was so long ago. But I do remember thinking how fun it would be until the moment came. Butterflies in my stomach began to swarm. Yes. That's how it was. Those pesky butterflies. I thought I was so pretty in my little dress; it was peach in color and very shiny. My aunt dressed me all up for the day in white stockings, which were itchy as can be. And those little peach-colored shoes, which were more like slippers, were simply adorable. I liked them a lot as I would poke my feet out from under my dress to either look at them myself or point them out to others. It was a simple job that I had for my aunt's wedding: I was to walk down the aisle, step by step, and drop a few petals from my basket every now and then. So when the time came for me to march down the aisle, I saw all those people, and the altar seemed like miles away. I got so nervous, I just stood there and froze, my stomach went queasy. Everyone whispered, "go," and when someone finally gently nudged me forward, I reluctantly started to move, one step at a time. Everyone was looking at me, then I heard people whisper "flowers," and in forgetful horror, I grabbed a handful and threw them in front of me, causing a few people to laugh. But when I was halfway through, I got better as people were whispering, "Isn't she adorable?" and I started to smile. I saw my dad as he smiled at me. He was sitting near the front. And when I reached the end, it was all over and I still had half a basket full of flowers. I was all but five years old then.

I never met my mom. She died when she was giving birth to me due to unforeseen complications. It was one of the most traumatic days in my father's life. He was in the waiting room when he saw several hospital attendants rushing into the delivery room. His gut instinct told him that something was wrong with the delivery. He tried to rush in to see what was happening, but he wasn't allowed in. It took three men to hold him back as he screamed my mother's name from the swinging doors. He could hear her screams, the kind of screams that instinctively sends a chill down a person's spine; a horrific slicing scream that indicated that something was terribly wrong. When the screams abruptly stopped, my father's frantic attempts to reach my mother ceased, his posture froze, one arm outstretched and the other pressed up against the hospital attendants. His body gave up hope and he was wrestled to the ground as tears rushed to his eyes. But after a brief silence, he heard my cries as I breathed in my first breaths of air. My father told me that when he heard me utter my first cries, some sense of hope rushed into him, replacing his grief.

I don't remember all the memories, but my father has told me his. When I was very young, my father would bring me to my mother's grave. I was too young to understand, and I innocently asked, "When is Mommy coming home?" and to that my father replied, "Mommy's sleeping now, let her rest." My father made many trips to see my mother, they were young when they married and it was only in the first year of their marriage when I was born. He never wanted my mother to think she was alone, and I would accompany him, probably once a month on a Sunday. But I grew to understand more. I once asked my father, "When is Mommy going to wake up?" and he replied, "Not for a long time." Then I knew that my Mommy was never going to wake up.

When I realized what death was and that people never woke up from it, it made me very sad. I went through a time thinking that it was my fault for my mother's death. My father in his soft tones assured me that that was not the case. He made it a priority for me to know my mother. He would tell me stories about her and showed me what pictures he had of her. My parents met in college, graduated, lived with each other for a year over their parents' objections; even though it was a forgone conclusion that they were most likely going to get married. They were married a year later. He had so many plans until my mother passed away. Whenever he talked about my mother, he would describe how intelligent, warm, compassionate, graceful and beautiful she was. It would always bring a smile to my face to hear my father talk about her in that way and he would usually say, "And someday, you're going to grow up to be just like Mommy."

From the pictures, my mother was indeed a beautiful woman. Her warm smile was always evident, and my father looked so happy whenever he was near her. There were pictures when they were at parties, at formals, on the beach, at the park, barbecues, and with their friends. There was one favorite picture where my mother was leaning against a window during the fall season where a tree grew directly outside. She was wearing a white buttoned-down shirt tucked into her jeans. Her arms were crossed as she looked out of the window. Her hair was held up that day, and she looked so elegant. I always wondered what she was thinking at that moment, in that seemingly private moment of hers. This was the one picture that I kept for myself. She was about twenty years old then.

He was always there for me, dropping me off at school. He was a nervous wreck on my first day of kindergarten. My aunt would usually pick me up afterwards and bring us all to Chinese school, since her son and daughter, my cousins, all went to the same school. My cousins and I jokingly called our parents evil tyrants for subjecting us to more schooling. Though studying was a required regimen, I remember a few times when my cousins and I were just the most mischievous students. My father always made sure that I studied and was always there to help me out whenever I didn't understand something. He was a very patient man, wanting to always spend every possible minute with me. His excuse was that he didn't want to miss any part of my childhood. In some ways, he seemed more involved with my childhood than I was. I just wanted to sit down in front of the TV to watch Sesame Street with my cheddar-flavored Cheetos. As I got into my teens, Cheddar-flavored Cheetos were still the snack of the day, but the Disney Channel had replaced Sesame Street.

My teen years were quite troublesome, just as in any other teen-parent relationship. I didn't want to go to Chinese school anymore, and after much arguing, my father relented. I was already fluent enough in Chinese that I didn't need to read those awful English subtitles in Chinese movies. It was tough growing up without a mother, without someone whom I could ask questions. Even though my father always told me that I could talk to him about anything, sometimes it wasn't comfortable. There was always my aunt and my girlfriends, but still, it just wasn't the same. It would have been different having a mother around.

Case in point: When I first got my period, I rushed to the bathroom. My father came to the door as well and asked frantically if I was okay. I told him that I was having my period, and he panicked. I heard him bustling about the door until I heard him snap up his car keys from the hallway table, rush out the door, slamming it behind him, and the sound of the car speeding away. By the time I cleaned myself up, pondered this new change in my life while trying to gauge if I felt any different, my father came rushing back through the front door. He came in with a brown paper bag tucked underneath one arm, the cell phone held up to his ear, and an opened tampon in the other hand all the while asking my aunt how to use a tampon. You can imagine my embarrassment as well as my disbelief as he ushered me into the kitchen despite my protests. In frustration he handed the phone to me and said, "I didn't know what to buy so I bought everything." With that he emptied the bag, and out came packages of Kotex maxi pads, Stayfree with wings of course, Lightdays panty liners, Tampax deodorant and non-deodorant tampons, Gyne Lotrimin and Vagisil. I picked up the Vagasil and asked,

"What do I need this for?" My father walked away in frustration and said, "I have no idea, but it sounded like you may need it." He quickly left the kitchen clearly embarrassed, but not more so than I. I told my aunt everything, and we began laughing as hard as can be. "Your father, my brother can be one crazy guy," she said, and I replied, "Now I know all guys are weird," and we laughed some more.

There was one night in particular when I hurt my father terribly. I was 17, a senior in high school, feeling invincible and on top of the world, and my friend wanted to drag me to this college party. She said that she heard around town that there were going to be a lot of cute guys there. Of course I wanted to go and see what a college party was like. But I stupidly told my father where it was going to be, and he forbade me from going. In my typical adolescence arrogance, I told him that I was old enough to go, make my own decisions, that he was being stupid and paranoid. I went up to my room, not wanting dinner that night despite my father's futile cajoling from behind the locked door, which I responded curtly with, "Go away!"

My father turned in early that night, probably from being upset with me. But I was determined to go to that party. I quietly got dressed into my party clothes, an outfit that made me look older than I was. I sneaked my way out of my house and exited through the back door. My girlfriends that I called earlier were waiting for me at the end of the street, and I hopped in the car as we giggled in excitement. The party was loud. There were people outside and inside. People were smoking, drinking, and yelling to each other. The entire scene was very intimidating, but my friends were plainly excited and dragged me along. A lot of the guys, in their drunken state, welcomed us in. There were a few references made especially to me as some guys snickered, "Hey, look at the Asian chick." The music was deafening, and people were bumping into each other. My friends and I stood about in a large room as we watched the mingling of bodies against the music. My friends picked themselves up a cup of beer, which I refused.

Eventually these three obvious college guys came up to us. They yelled over the deafening music. It seemed that they were more interested in my friends. Finally, they were able to motion to us to the dance floor. Two of the guys led my friends away. The third guy came out of the shadows and took my hand. I reluctantly went. He was able to introduce himself, "I'm Paul" and I responded, "Karen." As we danced he brought me in closer but I tried not to get too close. A friend of his passed him a cup of beer, which he took a few sips from before offering me some. I refused of course, but he was so insistent that finally I took a sip, which turned into another, then a gulp. I had to admit that the beer was loosening me up. I saw my other friends who were dancing very close now with the other guys, so I did the same and pressed my body into Paul's. He continued to offer me beer, and there didn't seem to be an end to the amount of beer in that cup of his. What I didn't notice were his friends who were passing him the beer. After a couple cups of beer, I noticed that the taste wasn't that bad anymore. As we danced, I began to feel his warm kisses along my neck, and soon I found myself kissing this guy that I didn't even know. He wasn't even that cute if I recall. Slowly and deliberately he moved me over to the couch. In my state, I wasn't sure what I was doing and found it rather amusing. He laid himself on top of me and began kissing me. I could sense that something was wrong. I tried to push him off but he was too heavy. I tried to tell him to stop, but he didn't hear me either because he did not want to or he didn't care to. Suddenly I felt his disgusting hand trying to go up my skirt and I could feel the tears coming to my eyes as my mind cried out "Daddy, help me!"

At that moment, his mouth came over mine as he shoved his tongue into my mouth. I bit hard and boy, did I bite hard! He lurched his head back and looked at me with such angry eyes. In that moment, I took the palm of my hand and shoved it at his chin sending him reeling backwards and off of me. With the adrenaline racing throughout my body, I quickly got off the grotesque sofa, and the other partygoers just looked on. The jerk was on his bottom as I quickly pulled down my skirt back and looked about for my friends. I saw one and ran to her and tried to get her to go with me. But she looked at me angrily as she waved me off. I couldn't find my other friend when a rough hand whipped me around and I was face to face with the jerk. Instinctively, like my father had always taught me, I kicked him hard and fast between the legs. Paul fell to the floor in a fetal position clutching at his pathetic excuse for manhood. Everyone else looked on. No one cared what was happening. Everyone thought that it was a joke. I was alone as I made my way past the drunken partygoers, and as I left I heard, "There goes that Asian chick."

After having tried to run in my high heels, which made a lot of noise, I finally took them off and held them as I walked the route back to my home. I was all alone. No one in the world cared at that moment. Even though I was in danger, no one at the party would have lent a hand. With the adrenaline dwindling, the effects of the alcohol began to resume its wobbly control of me. I sat myself down on the curb, exhausted, wondering to myself, what am I going to say to my father? How am I going to face my friends on Monday? A patrol car came by and an officer came out and asked if I was okay. All I said was, "I want to go home." I gave him my address, and I was seated in the rear of the car. By the time we pulled in front of my house, the lights were on, and I knew my father had figured out that I was gone. By the time the officer escorted me to the front door, my father had met us. I couldn't look him in the eyes, I didn't want to see the anger that may or may not have been there. As my father thanked the officer for bringing me home that late night, it was 1:30AM. All I wanted to do was go to my room and lock myself away from the shame that I had felt. How could I have been so stupid? I asked myself. I put myself into a compromising situation where I could have been raped, and no one would have stopped the jerk.

My father closed the door and looked at me. The silence was unbearable. I still couldn't look at him, staring at the floor the whole entire time. In a disappointed tone he finally said, "If your mother was alive now, she would be upset with you." With so many thoughts swirling through my head, mixed emotions entangled with hatred and heartache, I unleashed them at the closest person to me.

"Mom's dead! She died a long time ago! Just accept it, Dad!" the anger in me flowed forth like raging water breaking through a levy and it didn't stop there. I wanted to hurt someone, I wanted someone to feel the pain that I was feeling. My father was having a hard time at work lately, and I used it against him. "And you're such a wimp, Dad! You let people walk all over you at work. You let them promote the people that you yourself trained. That's pathetic! You're pathetic, and you're a rotten father!" I spun away from him and quickly went to my room, locked myself in and cried myself to sleep.

I woke up the next morning, with the biggest headache that I could remember. Had my first hangover at the age of 17. Not exactly something to feel proud of. As I rubbed my hand against my face, the night's events slowly seeped in, one awful image at a time. The images came back to me, and no matter how I tried to replay them, the scene with my father was heartbreaking. How could I have said that to him? I went to the bathroom to rid myself of last night's mess, threw on my bathrobe and went to my door. My hand held the doorknob and froze. I could feel my chest tightening and a huge lump forming in my throat. I eventually opened the door and let myself through. My bare feet sunk into the plush carpet. It was mid-morning, and my father was not in his room. When I heard him in the kitchen, I made my way down there. I stood in the doorway. His back was to me, drying a few dishes. He hadn't noticed me. I stepped onto the kitchen ceramic floor, which made the unmistakable noise of skin on ceramic. For a brief instant, my father's hands stopped drying the dishes and then continued. "Dad?" I whimpered. My father stopped drying the dishes, but he had not turned around. He just stood there, looking down at the dish in his hand. The tears in my eyes welled up, and I whimpered, "I'm sorry" as the tears came down my face.

My father took me into his arms immediately. I hadn't even noticed how quickly he put down the dish and covered the eight feet of distance between us. I cried into his shirt like a little girl as he stroked my hair, his chin on top of my head, comforting me as I choked back the words against my tears, "I'm so sorry. I didn't... I didn't mean that about Mom. And... and... and I didn't mean what I said about you."

My father held me there for who knows how long, but he was there for me, listening to me as my guilty conscience told him of last night's events. When I told him that I kicked the jerk in the groin, there was a moment of silence, then he asked, "Did you kick him real hard?" With a sobbing chuckle, I replied by saying, "Yes, very hard," and all he had to say to that was, "Good, that's my girl."

After I finished soaking my father's shirt with my tears, he sat me down at the kitchen table. I knew then that I wasn't going to get off that easy. Crying can only so far. In his stern yet comforting voice, he lectured me for being disobedient, but he explained to me it was for my own good, that he was just trying to watch out for me. It's an old cliché that every kid hears and ignores, but when it matters, the words just hit home and make a lot more sense. I was just fortunate that nothing more happened. As teens, we think nothing can hurt us. We think we're not given the credit that we are due and arrogantly think we know more than our parents, in my case my father. I kept my head down the entire time listening to his words until he finally told me to look at him. "You're the only thing that I have left of your mother, can you understand why I'm so protective of you?" and with that I replied, "Yes, I know. You really loved Mom, didn't you?" which was an out of place question, as I already knew the answer. He looked at me and said lovingly, "Yes, I loved her very much, and I continue to love her by loving you," which made me smile.

"How's the head?" inquired my father.

"Still a little dizzy," which I shamefully admitted, but in an amusing embarrassed manner.

"Serves you right," said my father, which was a totally different answer than the comforting answer that I was expecting.

"Daddy!" I exclaimed with a laugh. "You're not going to let me forget this moment are you?"

And my father's answer was an emphatic, "No."

He led me to the stairway, his arm around my shoulder, telling me to sleep it off, and I asked where he was going. He said that he was going to do some shopping. Though my father could see the gleam in my eyes at the mere mention of the word "shopping," and as much as my heart wanted to go, my mind said sleep. I slept in most of the day, but was awakened when I heard my father come home later that day. I sleepily walked down the steps when I saw boxes and bags from Staples. Then I saw my father come in once more with more boxes. I asked what was going on, as my curiosity was definitely piqued.

He apologized for waking me, and he told me, "I'm taking your advice. I'm going to quit my job and go it alone."

At first I was shocked. My father was going to quit his job? What of his 401K? But what about my college fund to some perfectly landscaped college campus in suburbia? He was going to go it alone? He was 42 which was old, another distorted perspective of being a teenager. But then it hit me, what advice? My father looked at me once more and in a confident nonchalance, told me of his plans.

"When your mother passed away, the responsibility of raising you was tremendous. I had never envisioned being a single parent, nor had I ever thought of raising a daughter alone. The financial obstacles were going to be huge. As you know, I haven't been happy with the way I've been treated at the company for several years now. There were days where I didn't want to work, but every time I thought about you, the reason to put up with going to work was obvious. I went to work for you. I saved as much as I could, and I planned out your college money from the very beginning. There was no life insurance money simply because your mother and I thought we were going to live long and watch our kids grow up together. But life didn't turn out the way I had planned. There was just you and me. Yesterday, there was something odd and uncanny about the way you yelled at me. The advice you gave me would have been the same advice your mother would have given me. So I'm going to listen to it. Effective Monday, I'm unemployed but self-employed. I need an office manager. Would you like the job?"

From the makeshift basement home office, my father started his data science consulting business. Things went better than planned. The companies that he worked with at his old job called him. It seemed my father developed a loyalty that rewarded itself in the end. Next thing my father knew, his clientele started to attract some really cool social media companies. I came home every day from school to happily help my father out and gain some very valuable work experience. For one of the first few times in my life, I saw my father being truly happy. There's no telling what life would have been like if my mother had lived.

As I'm older now, I can understand the sacrifices my father made to ensure that I would be able to go to college. I also understand the effort he put in to understand me as a daughter. I will never know exactly what the impact of my mother's death had on my father. However, throughout my life, he has been there for me, as I'm sure he would have done for my mother had she lived. My mother's death probably made him more sensitive, as many of my girlfriends have told me how lucky I was to have such a great father. Many of them wished that they could feel the same kind of love and understanding that my father had so unconditionally given me.

College was liberating. I returned home every summer to help my father's growing business, which outgrew the modest basement. He had a new office with a staff of 17 people, 18 during the summer when I worked there. As promised, my father saved and invested for my education years before, making the four years of college a breeze. Though my father's business was successful for a small company, he still led a modest life. Well, he did buy that cool Lexus LS sedan for himself, and I had to plead for the Lexus NX, in black, of course.

So it is on this day that it is even more special to have my father. Ironically I'm standing on the same place where I stood 20 years ago. Those pesky butterflies, they're back. However this time, a reassuring arm came to mine. I looked over to see my father, all decked out in his tuxedo. He looked very handsome for an older Chinese gentleman. No wonder my Mom fell in love with him. I could see the happiness in his eyes. His daughter was getting married, and though he was giving me away, I will always be Daddy's little girl to him. As the church doors opened, I could see the altar, which still seemed miles away from me. But I knew I'd get there. I turned to my father and whispered, "I wish Mom could be here," to which he replied, "She is, she's inside you." In many ways my mom married the best father a daughter could ever have.

PERFECT MATCH

It dazzled. The fleeting glances of angled blues, reds, and yellows radiated each time it passed under a highway light. Michelle couldn't but look at it with spellbound awe, and her smile was unyielding. Happiness enveloped her, as she knew whom she would be spending the rest of her life with: Michael. She peeked up at him as he drove, admiring his clear jaw line and how his black hair gently swooped over his right ear. His hands were steady on the steering wheel, as she nestled into the leather seat. He was gently humming, exuding the same sense of happiness he showed when she said "yes." She smiled again and looked down at the diamond ring, when the entire windshield became engulfed in a white light. She felt the car swerve. Michael's arm came across her chest as she let out a scream, before everything went black.

Beep. This was followed by another faint beep.

A blurry pinhole of light pierced the darkness that muffled any sound, but only for a moment. Then a sliver of light crept in, and faint, audible voices clumsily tumbled through the dark void, and the beep echoed within. There was something beyond the sliver of light. "Michelle," she thought she heard. She needed to see. There was something to see, and she tried harder. Beyond the blurriness, she saw the movement of ghostly silhouettes. A few struggled blinks were enough to begin to ward off the blurriness, but the light hurt her eyes. Slowly, she could make out the images of her parents on her right and a couple of other people on her left. She wanted to say something, but found that she couldn't. She blinked a few more times and could hear her parents calling out her name. She turned to their familiar voices. She blinked a few more times until finally, her eyes adjusted to the light. She felt tightness across her chest as she struggled to take a deeper breath. "What's going on?" she thought.

Someone clasped her right hand.

"Mom? Dad?" she finally mumbled.

"Yes, yes! Michelle, we're here," said her mother soothingly.

She tried to pull herself up but the soreness across her chest held her at bay and she relented as her body fell back into the bed. "Where... am... I?" she asked as her mind was still in a fog.

"You're in the hospital, Michelle. Doctor, how is she?" she heard her father say.

An unfamiliar man's voice came from her left, and she strained toward that direction while she gently felt her bed being inclined.

She pursed her lips and tried to clear her parched throat.

"Hello Michelle. I'm Doctor Murphy. I'm sure you must have a lot of questions..."

"Michael?" asked Michelle suddenly as she felt a panic in her heart.

There was silence as Dr. Murphy looked at her parents' grimacing faces. He then looked back at Michelle, and all she felt was a sudden void that filled the room.

"Where's Michael?" asked Michelle as her chest began to tighten. She took in a deeper breath as she could feel something amiss.

"Michelle. You and Michael were involved in head-on collision from a driver who crossed the median," said the doctor. "Michael suffered a head injury. Despite everything we tried, he unfortunately did not make it."

The void collapsed in on itself and burst open in heavy sorrow, followed by pooling tears around her lower eyelids. "What?" she asked incredulously as her heart raced trying to comprehend what she just heard. "What do you mean?"

She felt her father's hand clasp on top of hers and her mother's. Her left hand found the strength to cover her grief-stricken face. Tears fell forth from her glistening eyes as they began to stream down her face.

"Michael did not survive the accident. I'm sorry," the doctor said remorsefully.

"No!" she uttered as her parents suddenly tried to console her distressed mind.

"Michelle," said the doctor. "I also need to inform you that you suffered an injury as well." Michelle suddenly turned to the doctor: What was she about to hear next?

"Your chest was pierced by a metal object from the oncoming car. Your heart was damaged beyond repair. You were minutes away from dying yourself, but we had one chance to save you," said the doctor gravely before he paused.

Michelle's frozen expression of disbelief fell over her as she continued listening.

"In order to save your life," began the doctor. "We had to perform a life-saving transplant of Michael's heart into you. He was the perfect match for you."

The tears seemed frozen on her cheeks. She looked at the doctor's grim expression, and the nurse behind him looked stupefied. She broke the clasp of her parents' hands, and pulled down the flimsy hospital nightgown to see the clear medical tape and white gauze running down her chest. Suddenly, she felt her hands pulled away from her as she sank back into the bed and started to shake in grief.

"No! Michael!" she yelled out as her vision became watery as heartache so deep within her chest welled up. "No! No!" was all she remembered saying as Michael's heart pounded furiously within her chest.

* * *

The shades of blades seeped through the blinds even on that cloudy day. The shadows splayed themselves evenly along the grayish rug like bars on a prison. They moved ever so slightly as the sun slowly arced over the sky. For three months, this was all Michelle could do during her leave of absence from work, as she lay on her side on the white sofa in a loose fetal position. She was alone, her one love taken away from her and unimaginably put inside of her.

She heard the footsteps at the door, the fumbling of keys, the turning of the lock and finally the creaking of the door as her parents came in. They had been calm and patient all the while concerned for their daughter's health. Her mother came over, gently bent down, and tapped her daughter's shoulder.

"Hi Mom," said Michelle with a reticent smile as she continued her gaze at the shadowy bars on the living room rug.

"Hi, Michelle. Your father and I brought you good food to eat. Come eat when you're ready." Michelle nodded.

Her mother quietly left Michelle and went back toward the kitchen, where her father was busily taking out homemade food in plastic containers salvaged from previous take-outs. This had been their routine after the life-saving surgery: They would come over to check up on their daughter, bringing over food and cleaning up where they could. Then, every other week, Michael's parents would do the same.

When the smell of the reheating food wafted through the air, Michelle pushed herself off of the sofa of desolation. She pressed down her T-shirt and sweatpants. "Hi Dad," she said as he carefully brought over the hot dishes to the glass dining room table. He always smiled at her in a loving way, as any father would for their little princess. He encouraged her to eat.

They would eat in silence, dabbing at the simple foods with their chopsticks, which she also enjoyed. She didn't have much of an appetite during those days, and Michelle found herself nibbling at her food. If it wasn't for her and Michael's parents, she was certain she would have died of starvation.

After dinner, when her parents packed up and organized the food in her refrigerator, she stood at the opened door, as her parents would look at her with worried faces. She would put on a strong face for them and thank them for the week's worth of food. There was an exchange of awkward hugs, and her parents would then gingerly walk away down the hall as she closed the door. She felt guilty for having to put them through this extraordinary effort for her, but the will to live had left her long ago.

As she stepped out of the shower that night, she stood naked in front of the steamed-over mirror. She rubbed the top portion of the mirror to reveal her young pretty face with her hair in a bun. She stood straight up and placed her right hand against the mirror and with each swipe came a squeal.

The young scar that looked like a fault line that ran down between her breasts stared back at her. She gently ran her fingers down the scar from the top, pushing down droplets of water until she reached his heart. She flattened her palm along her chest and closed her eyes. She could feel the beating of Michael's heart from within. She listened for him, as every beat was his way of telling her that he was still there. "I miss you," she whispered with her eyes closed holding back a few tears.

That following Saturday, Michael's sister, Julie, dropped by in the late morning. She was a few years younger than Michelle, but the two bonded when Michelle dated Michael. After eating a few of the pastries she brought over almost every Saturday, they sat on the sofa talking, though it was mainly Julie. Julie would talk about work, her on-and-off dating life, the latest K-Pop news as she was a hardcore fan, but overall, she was trying to cheer Michelle up. She was supposed to be her sister-in-law. Michelle liked having Julie around as she reminded her of Michael.

As Julie finished talking about the fashion sense of one of her K-Pop idols, Michelle looked up at Julie fondly. Her bright brown eyes were set back on her glistening skin, with just enough makeup to accentuate her youthful beauty and her thick black hair was pulled over to one side and rested on her shoulder.

"Thank you," said Michelle humbly.

Julie looked up at Michelle, who was no longer the vibrant woman she had been months earlier. Sadness masked her face, her eyes were a slight puffy red, and her hair was simply tied back in a ponytail that day. Julie reached out for Michelle's hands, which she allowed, and the warmth of their hands comforted each other. Though Michael was gone, Julie's fondness for Michelle never left as she uttered, "You will always be my *unni*."

Michelle looked up at the cute pair of eyes looking back her, and she laughed, something she hadn't done in a while, and Julie pulled her in for a sisterly embrace.

* * *

Michelle knew the day would come, but she couldn't bear it. But slowly and surely, she started to pack Michael's things. On some days, she would simply pick up one of his items and stare at it fondly as a memory would steal her mind. Items that sparked such memories, she would keep, but many other items simply piled up as reluctance stole away her will to pack them away. But the closet was the hardest. She would often lean up against the side of the closet, where she could still smell Michael. Seeing each shirt and pair of pants had more meaning since she could see him in them and remember what he looked like. She would even sometimes hold onto one of his shirts and inhale his scent, and she was certain that she felt his heart beat a bit harder each time. But as the days went by, she neatly folded his pants and shirts. She left on the closet rod only the ones that had the fondest memories or scent on them. Michael was very fond of shoes and would even stock up on them. One night, she decided to tackle a few boxes of new shoes in the back of the closet.

She was amused by the opening of each new box of shoes, which gave her a momentary respite from the sadness. She couldn't complain about his modest excess, as her own penchant for fashionable shoes was so large that the guest closet was devoted entirely to her shoe collection. She came across two boxes of sneakers, which baffled her. She opened up the first box, and it was a pair of gray women's sneakers with blazing purple striping, her favorite color. A Post-It note was right on top of them that simply had one word written on it: "Michelle." She put the box down and held up the Post-It note. It was indeed Michael's handwriting. But she was dumbfounded as to the purpose of the note. She put it down and picked up the second box and opened it. In it was a similar pair of gray sneakers with purple striping, but the men's version, and it too had a Post-It note. She peeled off the Post-It note from the sneakers, and it read "Bucket list, Boston Marathon!" Her heart skipped a beat.

Michael was indeed a casual runner, having run a few 5Ks here and there. She on the other hand, definitely was not. She was entirely fine with her yoga and barre classes. But she stared at the note, and then down at the two matching pairs of men's and women's sneakers. He had mentioned running a marathon only in passing but never seriously, and definitely never about them running one together. She knew she would have balked at the idea. But with Michael gone and yet still close by, she stared down at the sneakers and especially the Post-It note. This was his bucket list item, she said to herself. She carefully put the opened sneaker boxes aside, placed the Post-It note back on top of his sneakers, and turned in for the night.

The birds chirped the next morning as the bright spring sun shone through the bedroom windows. After her morning shower, Michelle sat quietly in front of the sneaker boxes. It was as if the boxes beckoned for her attention, but the note from Michael had her transfixed. She held the note with each thumb on each bottom corner as she looked at it. The fact that he had bought her a pair of sneakers didn't go unnoticed, and she smiled when she imagined in her mind how Michael would even try to convince her to run the marathon with him. She chuckled at all the excuses she would have given him to avoid running 26.2 miles as she tried to imagine all the ways he would have tried to convince her.

She brought the Post-It note to her lips and gave it a gentle kiss as his heart fluttered from within. "I'll run this marathon for you, Michael," she said as a smile crept across her face.

With that, she did a quick change and did her best to mentally prepare for a light run. She hadn't run in ages, but she was generally fit and toned and drew confidence from that. She grabbed her keys and cell phone and put on her weekend sneakers, which she never ran with. She briskly walked down the flight of stairs from her second-floor condo, pulled opened the front door, and stepped through onto the top of the stairs. She hadn't been outside in weeks, and for the first time in a long time, she took in a deep breath of air and could feel her lungs fill.

She looked about and saw a few people here and there walking along the sidewalks. She let out a few breaths and took a deep breath. She bounded down the steps. Her strides were even and in her mind, she was going to run one mile that day. But about midway to the end of the long street, she found herself bent over and steadying herself over a neighbor's fence. She was panting hard from being out of breath as Michael's heart pounded furiously within.

As Michelle caught her breath, she turned back to where she came from and could make out the steps to her condo. She felt totally embarrassed and defeated. But at the same time, she felt Michael, with each pounding beat of his heart and she smiled. In between each breath, she muttered, "Twenty-six... miles... this... is... your... bucket... list... item? You're... crazy... crazier... to... think... I'd... run... along. Oh... my... god." She straightened up and with her breath steadied, she decided to at least walk briskly around the block for day one, and even that was a struggle.

That night, she researched online what it would take to run the Boston Marathon. She studied the course and how to enter and looked at training schedules. The sneaker box containing her sneakers sat to the left of her iMac, and on top, she had placed Michael's sneakers. In the left sneaker was the Post-It note with her name and in the other was the other Post-It note, "Bucket list, Boston Marathon!" She looked at them and smiled with a hint of annoyance, almost wishing his bucket list item wasn't so ambitious. But at the same time, she felt a sense of purpose.

The next morning, her eyes widened, not because of the sun that crept into the bedroom but from the aching pain in both of her thighs. Her legs felt like two beached whales, and each time she struggled against the stiffness, pain would shoot down each muscle tendril of her thighs. She was able to turn herself over and suddenly felt like a turtle on its back. She found herself panting a bit, but she could feel Michael's heart, as if he was with her every step of the way. She laughed at her situation. After a few minutes of realizing that she wouldn't be running that day because she wasn't even sure if she could get out of her own bed, she reached for her iPhone.

She looked at the home screen, which was a picture of her and Michael sitting on the grass in Boston's Public Garden. He was holding her from behind as she took that selfie of them together. She then scrolled through some of their last text messages. The last one from that fateful day telling her he was on his way and the last text from him being, "Love U!" A smile came across her face as her eyes glistened. There weren't too many voicemails, but he did leave a few, and they went back years. She hesitated and clicked on his last voicemail, wondering why she'd never done so before. It was the first time she'd heard his voice since the day of his death.

"Hey beautiful! For dinner tonight, why don't you wear that dress that I love seeing you in? You know the one. The one that bares your shoulders that makes me want to nibble on them. OK, about to head into a marathon of meetings today, so I'll be glad to see you tonight! Love you!"

Grief, happiness, and regret raced through her mind. She wiped away the tears that gathered between her eyelids and she did something unexpected: She called Michael.

"Hey, you've reached Michael. Leave a message. Thanks!"

After the beep, Michelle froze but soon she mustered her words, "Michael… Michael. I missed you so much. I haven't stopped missing you. I wish you were here and in some strange way, you are, with every beat of your heart. Thank you for keeping me alive. Your parents have been great. They have been bringing me food every other week. Julie is great," Michelle paused.

"I found your sneakers for your bucket list item, along with the ones for me. I don't know how you would ever have convinced me to run with you. I can't even imagine. But I liked the purple on them," Michelle lets out a soft laugh.

"But as long as you are still beating within me, I'll run the marathon for you. At least you can't quit on me," laughs Michelle. "I promise. I love you," said Michelle before she ended the call. She turned up toward the ceiling and could still feel the throbbing pain in her thighs that reaffirmed that she would not be running that day.

Shopping for the latest fashions and trying on new shoes made her quite happy. But since Michael's passing, that no longer seemed important anymore. However, she decided that if she was going to run, she should have proper, if not fashionable, outfits for the training. She bought a new pair of sneakers to train in and had decided that if the far-off possibility of running a marathon was going to be a reality, then she'd wear the sneakers that Michael had bought her. But on that day, doubts about running a marathon held firm, and perhaps she'd just end up running a bit more.

After dumping out the new leggings, shorts, tops, and light windbreakers onto the bed, she selected her outfit for her second running attempt. She stretched out her somewhat-sore legs a bit in the living room before exiting into the cool air that waited outside for her. Her eyes panned the quaint tree-lined street, and she took a smooth breath through her nostrils. She started running down the sidewalk with confidence, but soon, she had to stop. Her legs could no longer power her forward and she was out of breath. She was almost at the same place where her body gave out the first time around but she wasn't unhappy. Through every labored breath, she could feel every single beat of Michael's heart pounding away. She could feel him more than ever.

She stood up with a solemn face as her breath caught up and she smiled, "OK, take me home Michael." She jogged back toward the brownstone, and every single beat of his heart brought a smile to her face. The run back to the condo wasn't that bad, and feeling Michael, she knew that she would be running again.

By that Friday, as she rounded the block toward her brownstone, her strides were no longer graceful and her arms were flailing a bit. But upon seeing the stone stairs to her brownstone, she felt a happiness that had left her so seemingly long ago. Michael's heart was feeling stronger with each thump inside her chest. She believed that his heart was happier too, to finally be doing something instead of moping around.

That night, as she was nestled into her bed, she called Michael once more, "Hey honey, you'll be so proud of me! I jogged around the entire block without stopping! But I think you already knew that," she smiled. "I can feel you now, you're finally a part of my life again. I love you."

That Saturday morning, she had run comfortably around the modest block and she felt a sense of accomplishment. Her breathing was steadier, and the rhythm between her breaths, her strides, and the beat of Michael's heart were coming together. She felt she was making progress, one stride at a time. She bounded up the steps with a newfound sense of energy, which suddenly abandoned her as she saw her parents in her condo.

Michelle sat in the middle of the couch, withdrawn into her own cocoon. Her hands were clasped in between her knees and her head cowering as each scathing scold from her mother stabbed at her. It was the condo of flying daggers except that each dagger was laced with poisonous guilt, propelled in a mixture of Chinese and English. It was in a sense, a verbal death by a thousand cuts. But these cuts were emotional, and each was designed to attack from each side. Some were more pleading, while others would reach a crescendo that made her shudder as her mother circled her like a vulture taunting its prey. Her father stood silently by, leaning up against the wall listening.

The guilt was overbearing, and she could feel the weight of her mother's admonishment. But it was her mother's last admonishment that seemingly pierced not her heart, but Michael's, that hurt the most. "Michael died for you so that you can live, how can you be so ungrateful! His family already lost him, and now you want to kill yourself too? If you died with his heart, how do you think Michael's parents would feel?"

Toward the end, her mother beseeched her to stop running, and Michelle reluctantly agreed by nodding her head. Her reluctant assent to her mother's wishes elicited a calming voice from her mother who placated her earlier admonishment by assuring her that she was making the right decision. She sat down next to Michelle and looked caringly at her disappointed daughter.

"Your father and I only want what is best for you. Michael would want that for you too. Don't be foolish. Be good and get on with you with life," lectured her mother before she left along with her father later that morning.

The next morning, despite all the motherly admonishment, she was flushed with rebellious determination. Normally she would give in to her mother's wishes, but maybe Michael's heart fueled a surge of will, and she welcomed it. She put on her outfit, laced up her sneakers and opened the door when Michael's parents appeared before her with his father in mid-knock. She felt Michael's heart sink.

Her parents must have told Michael's parents. Her mother was good, wielding an Art of War strategy to wage a war on two fronts to stretch an army's resources.

But Michael's parents were calmer despite her being outfitted in running gear. Michael's father had a rounder face but distinct features, and his hair was slightly graying. His rounder stature was befitting an Asian man in his later years. His mother, on the hand was always well put-together and her shoulder-length hair danced about her face, which was accentuated with makeup.

Michelle insisted on making tea, but Michael's mother usurped that, not in a rude manner but in a caring one.

"Why are you running?" Mr. Kim asked in his usual firm voice.

Michelle explained to Michael's parents about finding the sneakers and how it seemed to be a bucket list item. Though she had to explain what a "bucket list" was to them.

"Michelle, you don't need to do this. Michael would just want you to live. Please don't endanger his heart," pleaded Mrs. Kim.

What could she say to Michael's mother? The one that gave birth to him and the one that had to bury him at too early an age? Michelle fell silent.

"Listen to your mother and listen to us, you don't need to do this. Michael would be fine with what you just did, but he wouldn't want you to put your life in danger. He gave his heart to you to live, not to run," said Mr. Kim in a pragmatic tone.

Mrs. Kim stifled a couple of whimpers at the sound of how her son donated his heart.

Michelle felt like she was in a dramatic Korean drama scene where suddenly, the camera fell onto her. As Michael's father beamed at her and his mother looked up with teary eyes, she acquiesced to not running. She could feel purpose being hollowed out of her chest as Michael's heart stood on a wobbly column of hope, ready to fall into the abyss, but it did not.

When Michael's parents left her grayish condo, she was all alone. Dreariness settled in, and she found herself on the couch once more. She was ready to defy her parents, and that in itself took all her will power. But her clever mother masterfully played her last hand by sending Michael's parents. It was more heartache than she could bear, and she felt her face crumble in tears borne of guilt and shame. Was she being foolish? she asked herself. The parental guilt worked its manipulative ways. Was she being selfish? she asked.

As each tearful emotion showed on her face, no one could hear her lonely sorrow, except for each beat of Michael's heart racing to keep up with her emotions. But with every single thump of his heartbeat, she could feel him. She placed her hands on her heaving chest as a small smile crept across her lips, and she nodded her head.

The next morning, her guilt from the night before washed away along with a flood of tears. His heart told her, and she knew in Michael's heart what he wanted to do. They were going to run, in defiance of their parents' wishes.

Her eyes were all puffy from the previous night, but she ignored them. Her hair was in its usual ponytail, and she donned her usual running outfit. She was ready, and as Michael's heart fluttered with each step she took down the stairwell, all her motivation was extinguished. A man was waiting outside, at the bottom of the steps on the sidewalk. It was Mr. Kim.

He looked at her with his stern eyes and with his hand, motioned for her to come outside. She turned the old brass doorknob with trepidation, exited the brownstone and slowly walked down the stone steps with a sense of shame. She ended up in front of Mr. Kim, suddenly feeling tiny. He beamed at her, in his loose jeans, a windbreaker and worn out sneakers. His hands gently landed on her shoulders. Michelle was prepared for the worse, but in a low tone, Mr. Kim said, "If you run for Michael, then I run for you."

Her mouth opened slightly as she looked up incredulously at Mr. Kim's sympathetic eyes. Mr. Kim wasn't prone to emotions, but in that silent moment, Michelle felt his emotional support for her and a grateful smile came across her face.

"Really?" she asked sheepishly.

"Yes. Where are we running this morning?" he asked?

"Just around the neighborhood. I'm only up to a mile now. I'm still training, Mr. Kim," replied Michelle, which led her to ask, "Are you OK to run?"

"Don't be foolish, I used to run in high school, I'll be fine," said Mr. Kim confidently.

"Oh, ok, just follow me then. I have a regular route that I mapped out on my iPhone," said Michelle.

In about two blocks, Mr. Kim was barreled over gasping for air. Michelle tended to him with her hand gently on the back of his shoulder. When Mr. Kim caught enough of his breath, he waved off her hand and said, "Go... you run... I'll meet you... back at your place."

He offered Michelle a weak smile and after feeling reassured that he was getting his breath back, she continued the run, but she couldn't help being amused at the happy thoughts dancing in her head. A horrible weekend of not one set of Asian parents scolding her, but two sets, had turned into a thoughtful moment.

As she turned down the block toward her condo, she could see Mr. Kim waiting for her as he sat on the steps. He smiled and waved to her. She finished her mile run and she could feel Michael's heart was steady. She sat down to the left of Mr. Kim, and he asked, "How was the run?"

Michelle smiled, "It was good, I can feel myself getting stronger."

Mr. Kim nodded in approval and paused before he said, "I guess I need to get into better shape."

They both laughed gently.

"Micheal's heart... strong?" asked Mr. Kim as he looked at Michelle, who would have been his lovely daughter-in-law.

Michelle looked at him and without saying a word, she took Mr. Kim's right hand in her hands and pulled it toward her. Mr. Kim hesitated but she looked at him reassuringly and he relaxed.

She took his warm hand and placed it on her chest, and soon, he could feel it: the beating of his son's heart, thumping away without skipping a beat. His eyes closed as tears seeped through the seams of his eyelids. As he tried to hold back his emotions, he nodded his head several times. He opened his teary eyes, looked at Michelle, and muttered, "My son, he is strong and... you are a strong girl."

Michelle smiled and leaned into his shoulder. He placed his left arm around her, like a father would with his own daughter. They stole a moment together against the slight ruffling of morning leaves, finding purpose in a man whose beating heart was all they had left.

That Wednesday, after another morning run with Mr. Kim, who made it around the block while still huffing and puffing, Michelle found herself in her kitchen making tea. The unexpected buzzer to her condo startled her and when she answered it, she realized it was Julie. Julie sounded chirpy as usual, and when she arrived at the door, she came with a big hug and Korean pastries. The two chatted on the couch about nonsensical musings, while they nibbled on pastries and sipped on tea.

But after a while, the talk went quiet, and Michelle couldn't help but notice that Julie was distracted. Michelle looked at her and in a cajoling manner asked, "Is everything OK?"

Julie looked up and cautiously started, "My dad told me that you started running."

"I did," replied Michelle.

"And that you're running for my brother."

Michelle paused, "I am."

"*Unni*, are you sure that is the best idea?"

Michelle smiled, "His heart is very strong, I can feel it and I can feel that this is what he wants."

Julie eked a smile, "And you know so, because you can feel him?"

Michelle's eyes glistened for a moment and with a sniffle, she said, "I can feel him each and every day."

Julie looked at Michelle and asked cautiously, "My dad said you let him feel Michael's heartbeat. Can I feel it too?"

Michelle was taken back by the tender request and never thought how carrying a part of Michael within her could provide to his family a way to connect. She outstretched her arms and welcomed Julie to come close to her. She motioned to Julie to rest her ear on her chest. Julie was reluctant, but she deftly swept her hair back behind her ear and gently placed her ear on Michelle's chest.

Sure enough, the beating of her brother's heart resonated through Julie's ear and through a mix of glistening eyes and a smile, she uttered under her breath, "*Oppa*."

The previous weekend had begun on a note of admonishment and defiance. The week began with an unexpected alliance. The middle of the week was a sentimental one, but the next weekend, it was resurrection of her mother's will to stop her from running when she discovered that Michelle had defied her.

Michelle's parents had arrived early Saturday morning and started to berate her, pleading with her not to run. Her mother exacted all her Wushu moves of guilt and shame, but Michelle was stronger this time around. She held steadfast, but her will could only last so long until Michael's parents arrived. Her mother thought that by bringing Michael's parents for a two pronged assault, would it finally send some sense into her daughter. But to her mother's surprise, she was betrayed by Mr. Kim, who went to Michelle's defense.

Mr. Kim was very respectful and played to Mrs. Wong's sensibilities, but she would not hear of it. At times she feigned death, acting as if her own heart was going to give out from the pressure that Michelle was putting on her. But no one paid much attention to her Oscar-worthy act. That's when she realized that Mrs. Kim was silent, and she asked, "How about you? How do you feel about all of this?"

Silence suddenly fell into the room, and all eyes shifted to Mrs. Kim. She looked up and glanced furtively at her husband and said, "I don't think Michelle should run."

"Finally! Someone with common sense!" exclaimed Mrs. Wong, but Mr. Kim quickly interceded in an effort to turn the tides of alliances. In an excited exchange of Korean, Mrs. Kim turns to Michelle and asks, "This is what my son wanted?"

Michelle turned to her and respectfully nodded, to which Mrs. Kim asked, "How can you be so sure?"

Michelle stood there, stupefied for a moment until she knew what she had to do. She asked for a moment and dashed into the bedroom and came back with the box of sneakers. She stood in front of Mrs. Kim and held the box in one hand. Mrs. Kim looked down at the box and then up, dumbfounded. Michelle pulled up the lid and placed it underneath the box. She gently pulled away the tissue paper and pulled out the Post-It note as Michelle's parents came closer.

"When I was going through Michael's things, I found this new pair of sneakers. He wrote this," said Michelle as she handed the Post It note to Mrs. Kim.

Mrs. Kim, nervously took the note and immediately recognized her son's handwriting. She read the simple note, "Bucket list, Boston Marathon!" Mrs. Kim looked up at Michelle, "This is what my son wanted?"

Without hesitation, Michelle says, "In my heart..." but Michelle paused as she placed her hands over her chest, "In his heart, I can feel that this is what he wanted."

Mrs. Kim's lips trembled as she looked up at her husband. Then she looked back at Michelle, and she simply said, "Then run for my son."

Michelle quickly smiled as she was able to get Mrs. Kim onto her side but the celebration was short lived as her mother intercepted in Chinese, *"Oh the dizziness, my head, it's spinning."* She knew she had lost, but she wasn't going to lose without some compensation, so she looked sternly at Michelle's father. In a militant tone, she barked at him, "If our daughter is running, then you run with her too!"

Mr. Wong almost buckled over at hearing what his wife wanted him to do, and he stammered, "You want me to do what?"

"You will run with our only daughter to make sure she is OK," commanded Mrs. Wong.

"But he's running with her," he protested as he looked over to Mr. Kim.

"I don't care, if our daughter is running, then you're running with her!"

"But what happens if I have a heart attack?" asked Mr. Wong?

"Who cares if you die? It's our daughter's life that we have to protect!" she responded to her shocked husband.

However Mr. Kim found an opening, "Don't worry, if you have a heart attack, I'll give you mouth-to-mouth."

That's when the whole room erupted into laughter, except for Mrs. Wong, whose frustration could be seen on her face. She turned to her daughter, "If you're going to run, then your father is running with you!"

"But Mom," protested Michelle, but it was to no avail as her mother silenced her with a hand slicing gesture, "Your father and Mr. Kim will run with you, and that's final!"

With those last words, war was averted, diplomacy executed at its highest levels, concessions doled out, and a treaty was brokered. Michelle would continue to run, but her progress would be monitored.

The next morning, Mr. Kim was waiting for her. He was gently stretching in newly-bought running gear, and he looked more energetic. Michelle felt relieved that her marathon goal was out in the open. Despite strong opposition from her mother, she was cleared to run. She and Mr. Kim jogged alongside each other. She wanted to push herself to run two miles that day by simply running around the Back Bay neighborhood a few times. Mr. Kim soon called it quits after about a mile and waved her on, indicating that he would wait for her at her condo.

Michelle's pace was good as she felt her body developing a rhythm and she could feel Michael's heart ever more. It pleased her that she could hear that he was there for her, pumping warm oxygenated blood throughout her body. The soreness started to spider web itself around her thighs, but soon she rounded the corner and her condo was in sight. As expected, Mr. Kim was there, anxiously waiting for her, and this brought a smile to her face.

The following Monday morning, she found Mr. Kim and her father talking outside, and she couldn't help but giggle. Her father looked up, donned in running gear that must have been in storage for decades. It was as if the 1990's had come back to life. Her father had always supported her goals in life, and this was he going above and beyond, though she was sure her mother's strong encouragement was at play. She asked her father if he was OK to run, and he dismissed her concern with a smile. She and Mr. Kim knew better.

With two miles comfortably under her belt, she lengthened her course to three miles and decided to run along the Charles River. About a block in, her father was panting and grasping at his left side as exasperated gasps escaped him. But like a concerned daughter, she helped her father to a set of stone stairs while Mr. Kim jogged lightly in place with a slight smirk.

"You... go... on," uttered her father. "I'll walk back to your place and wait for you there."

"I'll run with her," said Mr. Kim reassuringly.

Mr. Wong nodded his head as he winced in exhaustion and merrily waved them on. "I'll be right back, Dad," said Michelle as she then ran with Mr. Kim. The Charles River was quiet at that time in the morning. Mr. Kim kept up a steady pace alongside her. There were a few other runners too, and she wondered how many of them were also training for the Boston Marathon. She looked down at her smart watch, saw that she had crossed the two-mile mark, and with determination, was on to mile three. She crossed over a footbridge, one of several along the Charles River, and ran along to the other side. Mr. Kim started to slow down, and she slowed down for him. But he waved her along and told her not to wait up for him. She nodded and she surprised herself by how steady her pace was. But more importantly, she could feel Michael's heart beating each step of the way.

She crossed over another bridge and saw that she was close to the three-mile mark and jogged in place to wait for Mr. Kim who sauntered over the bridge. He caught up with her, and together they jogged back to her waiting father at the steps of her condo.

Later that night, as she prepared for bed, she looked at her phone's wallpaper of herself and Michael. She called his number and heard his voice, to which she smiled. "Hi Michael, you won't believe what I did today! I ran three miles! And both of our fathers ran with me, well, to keep watch over me. But I'm happy they are running with me. Your dad is keeping up, but you should have seen my dad. He was wearing workout clothes from so long ago. I think I need to take him shopping. He didn't do so well on the first day, but I think he'll be fine if he keeps it up. I miss you so much, and I hope you are cheering for me from above. I love you."

Over the next few days, each time the early morning alarm went off, she wasn't always looking forward to the run, but she eventually pulled herself out of bed. As always, her father along with Mr. Kim was outside waiting for her. Their promptness annoyed her at times, and she wondered whatever happened to Asian time. Her dad had gotten into a soft jog while Mr. Kim was doing a good job of keeping up with her.

She was able to identify a closed-looped course along the Charles River that gave her just about a mile each time, and she simply started repeating it. She could feel her body feeling leaner and more toned, and her legs were definitely firmer. She was confident to break five miles that day.

Her father called it quits after three miles and decided to rest on a nearby bench as she and Mr. Kim carried on. At the four-mile mark, Mr. Kim decided to join his new running companion on the bench as well, leaving Michelle to finish mile five. It was just her from there on, every single pump of her arms, her steady breathing and each footfall on the path. She crossed over the first bridge and ran along the other side of the Charles. She was feeling some stiffening in her thighs, but her breathing was steady. She crossed onto the bridge to see how much further before breaking the five-mile mark, and she had about a quarter of a mile. The anticipated milestone brought new energy to her run. By the time she crossed over the bridge and made it back to the bench, she passed the five-mile mark, and she gave herself a congratulatory fist pump. Never in her entire life did she ever think she would run five miles.

Later that night, she could feel soreness in her joints. The repeated impact to her joints was causing them to stiffen up, and she found she needed to massage them. She rolled playfully onto her stomach, which caused her black hair to swing to one side. With her phone in hand, she called Michael again, "Hi honey! I did it! I ran five miles today! It felt great, but I'm starting to feel the pain, so I hope this will be all worth it when I run that marathon! I can't believe I just said that. I'm going to run a marathon! I can't believe I'm really doing this. I hope you are proud. I'm doing this for you! I love you!"

The mild summer lent itself to comfortable running, and as the week wore on, the sixth mile came down, along with the seventh, the eighth, then the ninth mile. It was getting harder with each mile, and she found that running the same loop around the Charles and over the bridges was getting kind of boring. But she was always happy to see her father and Mr. Kim, who had both made great progress. Both had lost weight and looked better for men of their age. But they both agreed that stopping at the five mile mark was more than enough for them as they waited for her at the bench. Each time she passed them, they would cheer her on and that made her smile. Mile ten was in reach as she crossed over the bridge. Another big milestone was going to be broken that day.

She crossed over the footbridge, her smart watch alerted her that she had just hit mile ten. The smile that spread across her face widened. She quickened her pace in excitement toward her the two fathers, who had become cheerful chums over the past few months. She saw them playfully thrusting their hands up into the air as they also knew that she hit mile ten. As quickly as she smiled at the scene, the smile fell from her face. The air in her lungs suddenly vanished. A sharp vise-lock of pain clenched at her chest, and soon, she could only see darkness.

***

Beep. Seconds later, another faint beep wobbled through the cocoon of darkness. The fleeting light was brief as it soon faded away, followed only by another beep. She heard herself exhale slightly and could hear smothered voices close by. The slit of light opened wider and the view was out of focus as shadows moved about her. Something unintelligible could be heard through the cloudy vision, as the light grew stronger. Something gently held her hand. It was warm, reassuring and familiar. The grogginess soon lifted, and she could see her parents along with Michael's near her.

Where was she? she thought. What happened?

"Michelle," cooed her worried mother as she held her hand.

She turned to her mother in confusion and struggled to utter, "Mom. What happened?"

Her mother placed her second hand on Michelle's and rubbed them. She cast her eyes downward and didn't say a word as her father stepped in somberly behind her mother.

Michelle turned to Michael's parents at the end of the bed to see their worried faces.

She was in a hospital, she soon realized. A state of confusion entered her mind as she drew her hand over her chest. Just then, the doctor stepped into the room and he smiled as he saw that she was awake.

"Michelle, I wasn't expecting to see you again," said Dr. Murphy.

Michelle looked confused but asked, "What happened?"

"Well Michelle, let me just be up front and tell you. You had heart a mild heart attack."

Michelle was in disbelief as she clenched the nightgown about her chest. She felt she had to ask, "Will I be OK?"

"Oh yes, you'll be fine. I heard you were running for the marathon! Usually most people take it easy after a heart transplant, but others, like yourself, decide to do something challenging. You'll be back up and running in no time…"

"She will not be running anymore!" stammered her mother as she beamed at the doctor's incredulous suggestion.

"I assure you and Michelle, this was just a mild heart attack, with some rest, she can get back on her feet and… "

"She will not!" exclaimed the mother. "She will no longer do something so foolish!"

Michelle could feel all the worries and anguish course through her mother's hand into hers.

"But Mom…" pleaded Michelle as she could feel Michael's heartbeat quickening.

"You will run no more!" stated her mother firmly as the room fell silent and Michelle felt completely alone.

***

The shadowy bars splayed across the rug once more, slowly moving along the rug as Michelle simply stared at them. She had lain on her couch, without purpose, for the better part of the past month since the heart attack. Bereft of her only means to connect with Michael's heart in a meaningful way, her sense of purpose was replaced with loneliness.

Haunting thoughts and questions held steadfast in her mind. Did she not wait long enough after the transplant to pursue running the marathon? Did she train too hard, even though she could feel Michael's heart yearning for the blood pumping through his heart? Was Michael's heart not strong enough? But what bothered her and she continued asking herself, was she letting down Michael by not running? Was his heart weighed down by the disappointment that she immeasurably felt? What if she died and his gift to her would have been in vain?

Michael's family had invited her and her family over for Thanksgiving dinner. It would be the Kims' first Thanksgiving dinner without their son, and having Michelle over would symbolically bring Michael into their home. Michelle was grateful for being around family that supported her recovery and short-lived marathon stint.

The mood was warm and cheerful. The two families had been through so much together and had become closer by it. Michelle along with her family had gathered at the dining room table, which was filled with a traditional Thanksgiving meal, from fresh cranberry sauce, smooth and creamy mashed potatoes, moist stuffing, juicy corn on a cob, and the centerpiece, a perfectly roasted turkey and instead of ham, was a stack of deliciously fresh off the grill *galbi*, a typical Korean barbecued beef short rib.

Michelle sat next to Julie on one side of the table, while her parents sat across from her. Mr. Kim took the end seat near Michelle while Mrs. Kim took the other end seat. Despite her mood and the heaviness in her heart, she couldn't deny her stomach all the mouth-watering food set before her. Her nose was drawn to the *galbi* as the smell of the caramelized marinade on the barbecued short rib wafted through her nose and tempted her stomach.

Before she could dig in, Mr. Kim acknowledged everyone and her parents graciously thanked him for the hospitality. Mr. Kim took up his glass of white wine and everyone else followed suit.

"Before we feast on this meal, that my lovely wife started to prep for the previous night, I just wanted to say that I barbecued the *galbi*!" said Mr. Kim to laughter.

"Hey, I worked on the mashed potatoes!" Julie interjected playfully.

Mr. Kim nodded in his daughter's direction, smiled and continued. "This year has been a difficult year for both of our families. Michael is no longer with us," Mr. Kim said, pausing before he recollected himself. "But he is at peace now. And if his last act was to propose to you, Michelle, to tell you that he loved you, then I want to think he was the happiest man alive at the moment."

Tension wove through Michelle's chest along with a slight quivering of emotion around her eyelids. But she stayed focused and listened intently.

"Michelle, I know that Michael is no longer with us, but if he was, I know that you would have been a lovely daughter-in-law. I want you to know, along with my family, we will always consider you to be a part our family as you hold Michael's heart."

"You'll always be my *unni*," said Julie as she gently placed her hand on top of Michelle's to which she smiled and reciprocated the gesture.

"Michael lives on, in you, and I want to think he would want you to live to life's fullest."

Michelle could feel Michael's heart beat faster as a flurry of emotions flooded her mind, but she managed a smile as Julie's warm hand on hers offered her support. Then Mr. Kim continued.

"So Michelle, live on for Michael and also live for yourself. OK?" asked Mr. Kim.

Michelle composed herself and she was heartened to hear others at the table sniffling from the heartfelt words. Despite all the gloom, one thought that entered her mind was Michael's elated expression when she said yes. This made her smile, and she looked back at Mr. Kim and said, "I will."

Mr. Kim looked approvingly. "Well then, everyone, cheers," said a somber Mr. Kim as everyone brought their glasses up to the sound of that familiar clink. Everyone then dug into their favorite dish while Mr. Kim began carving the turkey with hungry anticipation.

Black Friday was chilly, and all Michelle wanted to do was to stay in the cocooned warmth of her bed. She could still feel the heft of the Thanksgiving meal in the deepest pit of her stomach while the *galbi* glaze seemed to have coated itself around her own ribs. But soon enough, she begrudgingly walked into the bathroom to begin her morning routine. After her hot shower, she stepped in front of the steamed mirror. With a couple of broad swipes from the washcloth, she looked at herself in the mirror. Her pale complexion stared back at her along with her brown eyes and damp wavy black hair. Emptiness stared back at her.

She unwrapped the towel from her chest and let it simply drop around her feet. The scar ran down the middle of chest, an ugly reminder of that fateful night but a hopeful reminder of what lay beneath, the beating heart of the man she loved. She ran her fingers along the scar, feeling each ripple of scar tissue until she flattened her palm against her chest. Her eyes closed and she smiled as she felt each heartbeat, it was steady and smooth. Michael was still with her.

With her eyes closed, she listened intently, letting the heartbeat reverberate through her hand, up through her arm, and finally to her ears. She nodded gently a few times in silence and then opened her eyes. She pursed her lips and nodded to herself in the mirror and finished her morning routine.

She came out of the bedroom dressed in running gear as she tied up her hair into a bun. With determined briskness, she knelt down by the shoe rack and put on her running shoes. As she tightened up the laces, she paused and she could hear herself breathing, and she could feel Michael's heart beating faster. She didn't know if it was her nervousness or his yearning in anticipation of the run. Her hands came together upon her knees and she rested her head on them.

"Don't give up on me, Michael, and I won't give up on you," she muttered underneath her breath. Then in a swift motion, she donned a windbreaker, grabbed her keys along with her phone, and was through the door.

The chilled, crisp November air filled her nostrils with every breath and she could feel it being warmed in her chest. She soon found that she needed to take in bigger breaths through her mouth. But she was determined not to stop a meager block away from her doorstep like in her inaugural run. She slowed down, pursed her lips, and was determined to at least make it around the block despite the pangs of fatigue eating at her sides. But what kept her going was finally feeling Michael's heart beating inside of her, pumping blood filled with air to her muscles. She didn't want to doubt his heart despite the mild heart attack. She wanted his heart to prove to her that it would be there for her, to love her back in a way that she could only remember.

Soon enough, she was back on the steps of her condo. It was a struggle, but the run to redemption was laid as she gulped in big breaths, feeding each heartbeat. She stood up, arched her back, and relaxed. She looked up and down the street and knew she was starting all over again. With the marathon only five months away, she knew that it would be an uphill battle.

That night, she slowly slipped under her covers as the lethargy in her thighs started to take hold. She rolled onto her side as the ruffles of the blanket gently hugged her back. For a moment, she took in the warmth that enveloped her and then opened her eyes as they focused on her phone. She reached out for it, swiped to Michael's contact. It had been a while since she called his number to listen to his greeting, but that day, she needed to hear him.

Soon after hearing his familiar voice and the beep asking her to leave a message, she said, "Hi Michael. I'm running again. I hope you are not mad. Your heart seems to be fine," then she paused as a tear seeped out of her eye. "I know your heart is strong, and I know you loved me, so if you want to prove that you still love me, then don't fail me. I'll do this marathon for you so you'll have no regrets about this life. I miss you. I still love you."

The next morning, the dulling pain in her thighs foretold a painful run. After spending more time stretching and warming up in her living room, she left her condo in measured steps. Her heart skipped a beat as she was halfway down the stairs. Through the front door, she could see Mr. Kim's somber eyes staring back up her.

She hesitated but when he gently gestured to her with his hand, she cautiously went through the front door, down the stone steps and stood in front of him. Her hands were clasped in front of her while her eyes were slightly cast downward.

Mr. Kim beamed down at Michelle and in a low tone, he simply said, "You run for Michael, I run for you."

Michelle looked up at him as his words shed any shackles of guilt or shame that may have lingered. Her doubtful expression rippled away as a sense of gratefulness started to tremble along her skin and she instinctively moved toward Mr. Kim for assurance. At that moment, Mr. Kim saw how lonely Michelle was, who would have been his daughter-in-law and his fatherly senses arose as he opened up his arms to her. She leaned into him as he gave a couple of soothing pats across her shoulders. Michelle closed her eyes, and for a moment, she didn't feel alone.

As they parted, she asked, "How did you know?"

Mr. Kim paused, "Your eyes told me during Thanksgiving dinner. And Michael would not quit, so I knew you would not quit."

Michelle smiled and retorted, "Michael would not have quit. But I have to tell you, we have to go slow today, I'm a bit sore."

"Oh, thank goodness! I haven't run since a few months back, so slow is good for me!" stammered Mr. Kim as they both laughed.

They ran in measured steps for one block that Sunday afternoon.

A week had barely passed, and on that fateful Saturday morning, Michelle sat in the middle of her couch. The Kims along with Julie were standing off to the side, their faces resigned. Her father stood behind her from behind the kitchen counter. But her mother furiously paced back and forth behind her while uttering mumbled scoldings. But every now and then, she'd sharply turned to Michelle and launch a sharp verbal stab at her. Michelle had her defenses up, but she still cringed as each of her mother's zingers bounced off her mental force shield. The verbal guilt laden torment was going on for an hour without a cease-fire in sight. Her mother could definitely yell for a marathon's length, and even the Kims were a bit taken aback.

"How could you be so foolish?"

"Do you want another heart attack?"

"Do you want your father and me to watch you die? Go ahead then!"

"How can you break my heart?"

"Why would you do this?"

"Answer me!" stammered her mother as she looked in Michelle's direction.

Michelle clasped her cold hands tighter and with her head reticent, she uttered, "I'm sorry."

"I'm sorry? I'm sorry! That's not enough!" screamed her mother because for Michelle's sorry to have any depth of remorse, she would need to repeat it many times over.

"Are you going to run again?" asked her mother sternly. There was no answer so she asked again, "Answer me! Are you going to…"

Julie screamed out before Michelle's mother could finish, "Stop it! Please!"

Julie's face was pained in anguish. She rushed to Michelle's side and shoved her warm hands onto Michelle's hands, which made her look up in bewilderment. They locked eyes and in a heat of the moment, she uttered, "If Michael's heart fails, Michelle can have mine!"

"No," said Mrs. Kim, "Don't say that, Julie!"

"Yes, I miss Michael too, and if Michelle wants to do this for Michael and his heart fails, then she can have mine," said Julie.

Michelle's composure was mixed with humbled thankfulness. But she knew Julie's largess was more symbolic and heavy in selflessness. But that selfless act was what it took to give pause to Michelle's mother's scolding.

Michelle's mother looked resigned, and finally exhaustion claimed her as she crumbled to her knees before her daughter.

"Mom!" screamed Michelle as she instinctively broke from the couch and rushed to her Mom. Julie wasn't far behind as the Kims leaned in while Michelle's father made his way around from the kitchen counter.

Michelle's mother put her hand up to ward them off. The circle of people around her moved aside from Michelle, who dropped down to her knees in front of her mother. Michelle's mother slowly put her hand down and placed it on her knee along with the other. Her head was downcast and the once vociferous warrior that she was, looked defeated.

"I can't lose you," she said.

"Mom, you won't," responded Michelle soothingly.

"My heart will break if I lost you," said her mother.

Michelle reached out for her mother's hands whose fingers reached outward to interlace awkwardly with her daughter's.

"I always wanted another child but after I had you..." Michelle's mother paused as her husband suddenly knelt by her side, uttering "Shhh," under his breath.

"No, Michelle should know," said Michelle's mother as she slowly raised her head and looked into the bewildered look of her daughter.

"After I had you, I had an infection. I was in the hospital for days, but after I recovered, the doctor told me that I could no longer have children. My heart broke forever. But holding you gave my life hope. Do you understand?"

Michelle looked shocked as she gripped her mother's hand even tighter. She kept her gaze on her mother, who looked fatigued. In that moment, unfathomable emotions intertwined that helped connect mother and daughter.

"Are you still going to run?" asked Michelle's mother.

Michelle looked into her mother's face and moved in close. She slowly raised her mother's right hand and flattened out the palm. Michelle's mother hesitated, but Michelle reassured her and with a tug, placed her mother's hand over her chest to feel the beat of Michael's heart.

Michelle's mother looked out of place, but surely, she could feel each beat of Michael's heart, and she looked up at her daughter.

"You gave me my first heart to live. Michael gave me his heart to live on," said Michelle. "Yes, I'm going to run."

Michelle's mother nodded her head gently then looked at Michael's parents, "Was your son as stubborn as my daughter?"

Mrs. Kim smiled and looked up at her husband, who smiled fondly at her, and she said, "They were a perfect match."

"I'll be running with her too," said Mr. Kim reassuringly to which Michelle's mother looked at her husband and said, "You're running too."

"*Aiyah...* OK," said Michelle's father reluctantly.

* * *

It wasn't long before she got her running rhythm back, and she hit the one-mile mark. Each morning, her father and Mr. Kim were there for her. The first few days, her father fell behind as he built up his endurance, but he urged her and Mr. Kim to go on.

The next weekend, Julie greeted her at the bottom of the steps and said that she would run with her while giving their fathers a break. Michelle welcomed that, but what she didn't expect was to see their mothers at the green wooden bench that would usually mark the beginning of her run around the Charles. While Mrs. Kim smiled, Michelle could see the worry in her mother's eyes. However, it was the red plastic container with the white outline of a heart that caught Michelle's attention.

"Mom, what is that?" asked Michelle.

"It's a debil..." her mother took a moment to say it right. "It's a defibil... ugh, it's to shock your heart!" she stammered with frustration.

"A defibrillator?" asked Michelle in surprise.

"Yes, that's it."

Michelle was surprised, "Where did you get that?"

"Amazon! You can buy anything on Amazon," said her mother confidently as she patted the plastic box lightly.

"Oh Mom, I'll be fine. I feel great right now," said Michelle with a grin, though she was touched. Her mother rarely showed her emotions directly, but it was through Asian parents' actions that show how much they cared.

"I hope so," said her mother, but her tone betrayed the fact that she still disapproved of her daughter running.

"There, there... let her run, don't make her worry. She needs to run with good thoughts, and Julie will be with her," added Mrs. Kim.

"I got her. Don't worry, Mom and Mrs. Wong. I'll be with Michelle all the way!" said Julie excitedly as she gently tugged Michelle, who followed her onto the asphalt path as a worried mother watched on.

* * *

Michelle slid beneath the covers of her bed, albeit a little more gingerly. Her black hair was gently swept back behind her ears as she turned over onto her side toward the end table. Her eyes transfixed on her cell phone for a moment before she reached out for it. She called Michael and as her eyes closed briefly, she listened to his greeting.

"Hi Michael. I hope you can see the progress that I'm making. Your parents have been great, and your sister has been awesome! My Mom stands there, worried you know, holding onto that silly defibrillator. It's getting really cold out there now and you know how I feel about the cold. I miss your warmth when you used to pull me in tight against your chest during the winters. I really do miss you, but each time I feel your heart beating when I'm running, I know you're with me. I still have a long way to go so, be strong for me. I miss you."

The daily runs continued, and soon her breathing was smooth, and Michael's heart was beating in sync by mile three. Her father and Mr. Kim were able to finally keep up with her, but by mile five, they decided to settle onto the bench where their wives, dressed in down-filled coats, had warm tea and coffee ready for them. Michelle was warmed by the closeness of the two sets of parents. In some tragic way, losing Michael and then having his heart transplanted inside of her gave their parents a reason to become closer. Though the Kims would never be her parents-in-law, the heart within her was drawn to them.

By mile eight, her endurance never felt stronger. Having to wear layers became a necessity during the mild winter, though it made her feel bulky and sluggish. Even the Apple Watch, a Christmas present from her mother, who insisted on her wearing it to allow her to track her daughter, seemed heavier. Though the snow was light, the cold was not always merciless, and the only thing that kept Michelle running was the beating warmth of Michael's heart.

One particular Monday in late January, it was a mild winter day, the sun was creeping up, and Michelle was still running. The fathers had retired earlier to the bench with hot beverages from their doting wives. When Michelle was out of sight, her mother would glance down at her phone to track her daughter's progress. But on this day, the milestone Michelle was approaching was different. It was the ten-mile mark.

The anticipation of it haunted her. She tried to put it out of her mind but found that that worry was close on her heels. As each sole of her sneakers touched down onto the asphalt with a thud, demonic thoughts started to spring up: tragedy, dread, loneliness, and even death. They started to run alongside her as well, and although Michelle quickened her pace, she couldn't outrun these ethereal demons, and the only one who wasn't running alongside her was Michael.

Why did he have to die so that she could live? Why couldn't she have died with him? Why couldn't they be together? The thoughts started to gnaw at her and exacerbate her survivor's guilt. She was fighting through a cloudy glistening vision of tears that she had held back for months and choking back on them soon interfered with her breathing, but she pushed on, trying to outrun the demonic runners of tragedy, dread, loneliness and death.

"Why did you have to leave me, Michael?" she found asking herself.

The feeling of the four demonic runners about to close in on her, to strip away her will, caused her to mumble angrily, "Everything I have done is for you, so you better not fail me now!"

The sharp vibration on her wrist along with the loud beeping suddenly distracted her and she looked at the watch, "10.0 mi" it read. Suddenly, the four demonic runners were shredded away by hope. Michelle had reached the tenth mile, and she was still running. Elation suddenly replaced her dread. She stopped for a moment, placed her hands over her chest and could feel Michael within her, and he was beating strong. She enthusiastically nodded her head and looked down the asphalt path and said under her breath, "You keep on beating for me, and I'll keep on running for you!"

She then ran, accelerating her speed, and she felt Michael's heart keeping up with her. The thankful elation erupted on her face as she also took a few moments to spin into the air until finally she was in sight of the parents. She wiped away her tears of joy as she ran full throttle at them, which caused them to stand up in concern.

She slowed down her pace and jogged into their concerned arms. She calmed them down and found that they were still asking if she was all right, until between breaths, she just said, "He's still with me!"

Silence fell over the parents as they looked at each other to see no one else around at such an ungodly hour in the waning winter, running no less. Michelle chuckled and said, "Ten miles. I just passed ten miles and…" said Michelle as she paused to look at Michael's parents, "And Michael is still with me, inside me, beating strongly."

Mr. Kim pursed his lips and reached for his wife's hand. She looked up soulfully as she leaned into him, "Michael is still here," he said simply with a smile.

"I'm going to run another mile, maybe two!" said Michelle excitedly.

"Just one more!" stammered Mrs. Wong as everyone abruptly looked at her. Noticing that she had drawn attention to herself, she whispered, "It's cold, and I'll treat everyone to *dim sum*," she said sheepishly as everyone laughed.

"I'll be back, I…" Michelle paused, "We feel great!" as she turned and happily ran away.

Later that night, she called Michael's number and felt that the natural runner's high of that day had never left her. "Michael! Michael! I did it! Not only did I run ten miles, but I ran two more. Twelve miles total! I'm like almost halfway there!" Michelle paused before her excitement softened. "I'm not even sure why I'm calling you. It's just such a stupid thing to do, but it feels like the right thing to do at the same time. Ugh, I'm so confused because when I hear your voice, I just feel you are listening to all my messages. How many, I can't even begin to tell you. But I want to think you're listening to them, to me. You didn't fail me today, and I could feel you even more today. I'm going to finish this Michael, because... I still love you."

* * *

After mile fifteen and later that night, Michelle let out a groan, a groan interlaced with fatigue and relaxation. Her damp hair dangled freely as she leaned back as much she could in the chair with her robe loosely fitted around her. Her eyes were closed as her breaths were deliberately long. She gripped the ends of the armrests and pulled forward leaning over her legs as she stared down at her two tired feet, soaking and being pampered by the Epsom salt bath.

The soreness in her legs was starting to take a weekly toll. She looked down at her smooth legs and could tell that they were the most toned they had ever been. Her calves were shapely, and she wondered if she'd be able to maintain them after the marathon.

She reached into her robe's pocket to reveal her cell phone. She looked down at the wallpaper of her and Michael and smiled. "Call Michael," she said using the newly enabled voice command feature. "Calling Michael," the phone responded.

After the familiar greeting, she gently swept her damp hair behind her ear and grinned.

"Hi Michael. It's me. You won't believe what I'm doing. I'm soaking my feet in Epsom salt. I thought only old people do this," she said with a chuckle. "I hit mile fifteen today. Yeah! The running has been good, but it's really wearing down my body. But you'd be impressed by how fit I am, and my legs look great! I know how much you always loved my legs," she said with mischievous grin. "Your parents have been great, and they're taking turns with my parents. As my miles are getting up there, I'm spending more time running. A bit over three hours now, and that's a lot of time for our parents to watch over me. My mom taught everybody how to use the defibrillator. Isn't she so cute? Oh! Spring is coming. It wasn't a bad winter, thankfully. And your sister runs with me each weekend and tries to keep up. We all miss you. But I think when your parents and Julie are with me, they feel they are still with you. The marathon is only a few weeks away now, and I think I'm making good progress. I think once I hit mile 20, I'll feel a lot better. I can feel your heart beating stronger now and I know you won't let me down. So I won't let you down. I love you."

* * *

"Heartbreak Hill!" exclaimed Julie as she came bursting through the door that Saturday morning, two weeks before the marathon. Michelle grabbed onto the door to prevent herself from losing her balance.

After the abrupt entry, Michelle quickly closed the door and responded, "Um, what are you talking about?"

Julie pulled out her laptop and set it out on the breakfast kitchen counter. Her morning demeanor was unusually serious, and she pointed to the Web site that she was looking at before. "*Unni*, listen. I was looking at the Boston Marathon route, and did you know there are some crazy elevation changes?"

"Sort of but…" but before Michelle could finish, Julie interrupted, "*Unni*, look at this!"

Michelle looked at the Web site that listed the elevation changes starting in the town of Hopkington through every single mile before finishing in front of the Boston Public Library in Copley Square.

"It's downhill most of the way, but at mile 21, it goes from 143 feet to 228 feet," stated a concerned Julie. "By mile 21, you're going to be really tired, but you need to make it over this hill. Can you believe it's called Heartbreak Hill!"

Michelle absorbed what Julie was saying along with what was on the Web site and admitted that she hadn't reviewed the marathon route in detail. "Heartbreak Hill is at mile 21?" she asked herself. "How tired would she be?" It would be awful to run 21 miles only to find heartache at Heartbreak Hill.

"*Unni*," pleaded Julie as Michelle looked back at her. "We need to run a hill before this marathon and get Michael's heart ready for it."

Michelle's felt Michael's heart skip a beat, and she found herself disarmed by Julie's sincere compassion for her as a smile crept across her lips.

"I have a plan!" exclaimed Julie.

"You have a plan too? Tell me," asked a smiling Michelle.

"Seeing as your Mom won't let you out of her sight, we'll run about 5 miles around the Charles, and then we'll run toward Beacon Hill. Once we get to the top of the State House, we'll run back down through the Common and run up the hill again from Arlington and Beacon St. Sounds good?" asked Julie,

Michelle eyes widened at the idea and asked, "And how many times should we run up Beacon Hill?"

"Ten!" responded Julie,

"Three," said Michelle with more practicality.

"Five!" said Julie as she turned to Michelle with a smile. It was smile that was full of youth, which matched her pretty face and positive energy.

Michelle smiled and acquiesced, "OK, five."

"Yeah!" said Julie as she lunged in for a hug that Michelle accepted wholeheartedly. She held onto Julie for a moment longer, to appreciate everything she had done for her.

As they parted, Julie looked down at Michelle's chest and said fondly, "*Oppa*, be strong for Michelle." Then she nodded quickly and looked back up at Michelle with a smile.

"You're the best *moy moy* an *unni* could ever have," said Michelle lovingly as she placed her hands on her chest to feel Michael's heartbeat inside of her.

"I know," said a confident Julie.

Later that morning, after mile five, Julie lagged behind Michelle as they trekked up the sidewalk toward the State House for the third time. Michelle's jog was steady, but she struggled, since most of her training was on flat ground. But Julie was panting and tugged at her cramping sides. When she got to the State House to an awaiting Michelle, she was panting, to which Michelle said, "And you wanted to do ten?" to which Julie said, "Three would have been better," and they both laughed and ran back down to finish the last two.

* * *

On the same day that she hit mile twenty-three, Michelle eagerly picked up her official marathon bib and she felt grateful for the charity that sponsored her. She was so excited to bring it home. Julie was hanging out with her that day and was equally excited. She encouraged Michelle to pose with it while she took pictures. Michelle looked down at the white bib with the number 8118 and couldn't help but notice that the numbers coincidentally represented Michael's and her birthday, August 1st and January 8th. She was instantly in love with the number and thought it was fortuitous. Julie's jaw dropped upon realizing the number's significance. She quickly Instagrammed the bib number for her friends to see.

Tickled by the bib's providence, Julie suggested that they go shopping for new clothes for marathon day. Michelle laughed, but jumped at the opportunity. She hadn't been shopping for much lately.

Later that early evening, both Michelle and Julie hung out in the bedroom. Michelle laid out the assortment of running gear that she planned on wearing on marathon day. The weather forecast called for a mild day with temperatures rising after noon. So she bought options that she could layer. If temperatures were going to rise beyond her comfort level, her sports bra, a tank top and running shorts were all that she needed, along with her Boston Red Sox cap. If it stayed cooler than expected, she would wear an outer zipped fleece that she could take off at any time if it got warmer.

"What do you think of these together, Julie?"

"Try it on and let me see!" Julie responded with excitement as she tossed herself onto the bed. Michelle smiled and gathered the cool-day choices, hinting she'll be right back as she made her way to the bathroom.

When Michelle came back out, she was in her dark-gray running shorts and a purple tank top. She sported her Red Sox cap and pulled her hair through in the back. Her ensemble accentuated her fitness and slender physique.

"*Unn!* You look so pro! Let me Instagram it!" exclaimed Julie.

"One sec!" said Michelle as she went into the closet. When she came out, she had donned the sneakers with the purple stripes that Michael had bought for her and held Michael's sneakers in the other hand.

The gesture did not go unnoticed by Julie. She put her camera down. She felt a tear or two form at the corner of her eyes, but soon, a smile replaced her emotions as she asked Michelle to wait another second. She jumped off the bed and went into the dining area where she came back with the bib. She carefully pinned the bib to Michelle's tank top. She stood back from Michelle and said, "Now you're Instagram ready!"

Michelle laughed and she posed as gracefully as any runner would all the while, displaying Michael's empty running shoes. In between each giggled shot, she could feel Michael's heart flutter.

"Let me see," asked Michelle, and Julie excitedly showed her the pictures she took of her. It was one shot though where her right arm folded beneath the bib with her left arm folded toward the camera holding onto Michael's shoes while she turned her torso to the camera that caught her attention the most. It projected graceful confidence, and with the bib mostly in sight along with the sneakers, the reason for her running the marathon became crystal clear.

"*Unni*, you look like a K-Pop idol here! I love it!" exclaimed Julie as Michelle blushed at her compliment.

"Send it to me, too!" asked Michelle. Then she added, "Send them all to me."

Julie looked up with a smile and replied, "Of course!"

Later that night, after Julie had left an evening of sisterly bonding, Michelle slipped beneath the covers and as usual, had her phone in hand. She swiped through the impromptu fashion shots and came back to her favorite one. A warm smile came over her face as she texted the photo to Michael with the message, "For you, Michael, love you."

The night before the marathon, she had returned from a carbohydrate rich meal of Korean noodles with her parents and Michael's family. They were all so supportive and even her mom tossed away her nervousness and expressed how proud she was.

She had laid out her running gear on her dresser and the sneakers that Michael had bought for her were by the door. Her damp hair clung to her as she sat in the middle of the plushy carpet of her bedroom. Her white cottony robe draped about her, with her legs somewhat exposed. She fiddled with her phone, and a quick nod indicated that she finalized her playlist for marathon day.

She then she called Michael, and though she had heard his greeting a thousand times, his voice always brought a smile to her face.

"Michael. It's the night before the marathon. It's finally here, and I still can't believe it! I just wanted to let you know how much you meant to me during this time, through all the training, my mother's yelling, your family's support, the cold weather, the days when I ran through the rain and the really lonely days when you weren't with me but in some way, you were always inside of me."

Michelle turned her left hand over and a glistening light came into view as her engagement wedding ring appeared. A tear seeped out slowly as she managed a smile.

"We'll never get married in this life, Michael but we'll always be together. I put together a playlist of the songs that I think we would have played at our wedding. Okay, they're probably more my songs, but you would have liked them too. Wish me the best of luck, and you'll be with me at the finish line. I love you."

The next morning, a cool crisp day with temperatures hovering in the mid 50s greeted Boston Marathon day, a celebrated day in the city's history. Michelle found herself in the throngs of thousands of like-minded runners. Michelle hung back and was in her own world. She wasn't thinking about the other runners. She wasn't out to break any new records. She was only concerned with running over the finish line with the heart of the love of her life and completing something for him in return for his gift that saved her life.

As she jogged lightly in place, in her running gear, covered in a zippered running top that still managed to show her fit slim figure while donning her Red Sox cap with her hair pulled through the back, she listened to her marathon playlist. But soon she was distracted by a shadow passing in front of her and she looked up.

A man with brownish hair and a reasonably fit physique smiled as he got Michelle's attention. Michelle pulled away her right ear bud.

"*Ni hao*!" he said.

Michelle suddenly cringed inwardly but responded politely, "Hi there."

"Oh, you speak English? That's great. Is this your first marathon?" he asked.

"Yes it is."

"It's like my fifth, I'm a pro at this," he said confidently.

"That's great to hear, I'm just little worried about Heartbreak Hill," Michelle said politely.

The man came a step closer to continue the conversation. "You should be, it's a tough hill. I'll tell you what, why don't we run together. I'll slow down my pace for you as this is your first marathon, and I'll give you encouragement when we get to Heartbreak Hill," he asked as he flashed a veneer smile.

Michelle started to get a sinking feeling in her stomach as she said, "Um, that's okay, I'll be fine running by myself."

"Well, suit yourself. Hey, my name is Jeremy. Maybe I can get your number and we can meet up after the marathon, you know, to support one another after such a tough run?" he asked once more as he started to flex his upper body

That's when Michelle flashed her wedding ring and the dazzling light came in between the interloper and Michelle.

"Oh, I see you have someone waiting for you at the finish line. Too bad he couldn't run it with you," he said disdainfully as he trotted away.

"What a creep," thought Michelle. She suddenly felt Michael's heart beat harder before it settled down. She wasn't sure if Michael's heart felt anger toward the obnoxious runner. Regardless, Michelle chuckled at the warming feeling of Michael's beating heart as she placed her ear bud back in place.

The marathon was about to start and the start pistol would soon signal the first wave to begin. She was so far back that it would take almost 20 minutes just to jog to the starting line. Michelle felt Michael's heart beat nervously as she waited in the second wave along with a tingling sensation in the pit of her stomach. She took a few deep breaths to calm her jittery nerves until the start pistol went off.

It was slow going at first as she jostled between other runners on approach to the starting line. The pace picked up until she was at a slight jaunt, then a jog, and when her sneakers crossed the starting line, she started the timer on her smart watch and muttered until her breath, "Here we go, Michael."

As expected, the first few miles were mainly downhill and steady as she ran through the towns of Hopkinton, Ashland, Natick, and Framingham. Her heartbeats were steady, along with her breathing. Her eyes suddenly caught sight of something ahead of her, to her right. It was a struggling runner, whose arms were having a hard time keeping up with the smooth pumping motion of runners in better shape. His panting was heavy as he leaned slightly forward. As she came up alongside him, she smiled. It was Jeremy.

Her heart quickened pace as she passed him, saying, "*Sayonara!*"

She blew past him and didn't let up for at least half a mile, enjoying the vindication for herself and Michael.

Her ears perked up as she heard a chorus of screaming women, and she knew, that she was approaching the infamous Scream Tunnel, made famous by the women of Wellesley College. The energy was amazing as she looked at the many enthusiastic college students with signs reading everything from "Kiss Me, I'm A Journalist!" or "Kiss Me, I'm A Foodie!" She along with many other runners took in the excited energy, but when she approached a bunch of young Asian American women, she saw their eyes light up as they started to point at her yelling, "Asian woman represent!" and soon they all cheered her on. Though she felt sheepish about the attention, Michelle flashed them a big smile along with a thankful wave. The energy gave her a tailwind, and she felt lighter on her feet as she looked ahead for the second half of the race.

The next two to three miles were pretty steady running through a taste of suburban life until she felt like she was running downhill again. She looked up, and to her right, she saw the iconic store sign, "Lower Fall Wines." From what she remembered when Julie showed her on the route, the next few miles was going to be hilly before the approach to Heartbreak Hill. Michelle relaxed her pace, not wanting to push herself unnecessarily.

The dulling pain in her lower right side was festering, and she grabbed it often. Her breaths became labored over the hilly route. It was not something she trained for from the comfort of the flat asphalt around the Charles River near her home. She felt Michael's heart pounding to send much-needed oxygen to the parts of her body that yearned for it. Her steps were becoming irregular, but Michelle tightened her fists and pushed onward to Heartbreak Hill as the dulling pain started to weigh on her.

The base of mile twenty marked her last obstacle, the storied Heartbreak

Hill. Everything Julie warned her about was looming directly ahead, and despite the cheers from the onlookers, her legs started to feel strained. She was pretty much on autopilot, her body simply throwing one leg in front of the other, and the dull pain was now a full-blown cactus needling her every step of the way. Droplets of sweat ran down her anguished, furrowed eyebrows.

She was exhausted, but she knew she couldn't give up with only about 6 miles to the finish line. She grabbed her side and massaged it while opening up her chest to take in more air, and Michael's heart responded by thumping harder and faster. She looked dead ahead, shortened her strides and barreled forward.

Each step was a struggle, with the tip of her sneakers scraping along the asphalt when she didn't have the strength to pick up her knees any higher. Her forearms felt like rods of iron, and the fists that she maintained throughout most of the race started to unravel. With every breath, the pain in her side pierced deeper, causing her to wince. She was faltering, and Heartbreak Hill seemed to have no end in sight. The sun was starting to bear down on her head.

The music from her playlist was no longer providing the motivation she needed, so she turned it off. The sounds of cheering onlookers were replaced by the deadening thuds of her sneakers on asphalt and her labored breathing. But the loudest sound was Michael's heart as it furiously pounded within her chest. He wasn't ready to give up, and she nodded to herself, neither would she.

"Hey Boston Red Sox!" yelled a man to her left who was looking down at Michelle with a smile.

Michelle looked up and saw a tall Asian man with an impressive athletic build. He was wearing a red T-shirt emblazoned with a yellow lightning bolt for the superhero known as the Flash. He tilted his head toward her with his blue lens sports sunglasses as the navy New York Yankees logo on his baseball cap came into full view. "You're not going to let this proud New York Yankees fan beat you in your own city, are you?" he asked teasingly.

Michelle smiled and for a moment, the dulling pain abated and she let out a grin. "Definitely not!" she exclaimed with a smile.

"Good! You can do it! You're in the home stretch! Think good thoughts, and you'll cross that finish line!" he said with a wave before he said, "Catch me if you can!" and he pulled away from her.

Michelle took the competitive teasing well and kept her eyes focused on his red shirt as she tried to keep pace with him. But soon, he faded away over the hill. That's when she realized she was close to the top of Heartbreak Hill!

She pushed through the seemingly hardest steps of her life when suddenly she too crested over Heartbreak Hill. She could see the downhill route ahead of her. She let out a sudden gasp of exhilaration and smiled gratefully. She shook off the weight from her forearms, re-clenched her fists, and enjoyed the downhill run.

But her exhilaration was short-lived. The reverberations of each pounding downhill step shot up her legs, stealing energy and stiffening them. The thorny pain at her side was still there, clinging like a stubborn cactus-like parasite. Her legs felt as if they were pushing through waist-deep water. Each push was exhausting, but Michael's heart continued to pound within her chest, giving all that it could. Anguished tears started to seep out from the corner of her eyes, hidden away from view by the brim of her baseball cap. Each breath was choked back by emotional surrender. She couldn't see feel how she could finish the next six or so miles.

She could feel her legs slowing down. She wanted to stop and put her hands to her knees and just rest, but she knew if she did, she could lose her momentum and not finish the marathon.

That's when a cool breeze grazed her from the right, and she looked toward it. There it was, the Chestnut Hill Reservoir, and she smiled. Michael had taken her on many strolls around the serene reservoir, and she had enjoyed them so very much. The way he held her hand warmly and glanced down at her with that charming smile of his. Everything good in that memory started to fill her with a new sense of energy. She smiled, wiped away her tears, and took in heavier measured breaths. She could feel Michael's heart enriching itself with reservoir air. She looked ahead and pushed her legs forward, freeing itself of the sensation of waist-high water they had been in.

She crossed the tracks of Cleveland Circle and could see lines of cheering Brookline residents along Beacon St. She saw the Dunkin Donuts and laughed out loud at a memory of Michael bringing out a strawberry Coolata for her when she had a sudden craving. They were already late meeting up with friends for Sunday brunch, but he had made a U-turn nonetheless to get her what she wanted because she was being bratty that morning. However, it made that morning so much happier for her, and he loved doting on her. She smiled at the memory, which invigorated her as a newfound energy started to spring up in her legs.

She ran down Beacon St. looking around and saw Athan's bakery after crossing Washington Square. A romantic night with Michael one evening when she was frustrated with work seeped out from her memories. There he indulged her in her favorite dessert, tiramisu. All the while, he patiently listened to her and by the time she took her first bite of the tiramisu, she had forgotten her frustrating day at work. Instead, she had enjoyed a pleasant night out with Michael, who just smiled at her from across the small marble table. She was flabbergasted when he scooped up the last Tiramisu bite, but after a devilish grin, he fed her the last bite and she savored the chocolaty, creamy mascarpone filling and the taste of amaretto. The memory from that night fueled her even more, and she ran past with firmer strides.

The exuberant crowd at Coolidge Corner was infectious, and she could feel Michael's heart feeding off of it, pumping ever more smoothly for Michelle's last few miles. The grin across her face only got bigger when she saw her favorite Japanese restaurant to the left, Fugakyu. There she and Michael had enjoyed many date nights enjoying delicious sushi. The Sake Aburi being one of her favorite appetizers featuring torched salmon on top of a seafood salad. But it was the in-house green tea crepe cake that was the highlight of the night. Michelle had a weakness for all things sweet, and Michael would watch her endearingly with every sweet bite she took.

She found a new spring in her steps. She was past mile 24 and she had come so far, she knew that the finish was in sight for both Michael and herself. As she approached Kenmore station, a haunting but profound memory came rushing in. She and Michael were just leaving from a Red Sox win at Fenway station when they were taunted by three drunk white men. They made suggestive sexual remarks toward her and racist remarks at Michael. Anger welled up from within her, but at the same time, she was afraid, since there were three of them and only just the two of them. Michael shielded her from the three harassers and told her to ignore them as they made their way to the train station. But one of the men brazenly came up to Michael from behind and wouldn't be ignored, and Michael quickly swung around and pushed the man back. That man then tried to take a swing at Michael, who ducked out of the way and punched the man in the face, knocking him flat on the back, unconscious. The two other men hesitated, but Michael stood his ground and they backed off. He then shepherded a stunned Michelle down the steps into the train station. Michelle would always remember how Michael always protected her.

She found her fists clenched in anger, and she knew that Michael's heart was fueling it. But she relaxed her clenched fists and took the new energy in stride, continuing onward toward the finish line. The sidelines along the marathon route were overwhelmed with onlookers, but she became more focused upon seeing the "One More Mile" sign. She choked up in happiness.

She started to veer to the left, and she could see the Massachusetts Avenue underpass. That was it: Once she emerged from the underpass, she would take that right turn, then a left to emerge onto Boylston St. That emergent scene from TV news coverage of previous marathons was famous. There was no one else in front or back of her for about one hundred feet.

Soon she descended into the underpass, and for a moment, all the deafening noise of the onlookers and the ambient city sounds seem to disappear. She could hear each footstep hitting the pavement as her tired calves reverberated to absorb the impact. Her breathing was loud, but it was Michael's heart that seemed the loudest, amplified by the concrete along the short, open-ended chamber. Time slowed down as finally, it was just her and Michael, speaking together through heartbeats. She smiled and muttered under her breath, "Thank you, Michael."

The noise of the marathon soon rushed in as she emerged from the underpass. The last of the pain holding her right side had finally worn off, no longer able to feed off the despair and pain that she had felt many miles back. She was finally free to finish the marathon unencumbered, and she took the right turn with determination onto Hereford St.

She made quick work of Hereford St. and took the left onto Boylston St. The end was in sight, and she started passing many other places where she and Michael had enjoyed sweets, but at that moment, she only wanted to savor the sweetness of crossing the finish line for Michael. She passed the Prudential Mall on the right and finally, her sneakers crossed over the iconic blue-and-yellow finish line.

Her arms pumped upward as she savored the finish, and the seconds thereafter passed quickly. As she slowed down, volunteers threw a silvery foil blanket over her and handed her a bottle of water as she slowed down and took in more breaths. Without looking, she stopped the timer on her smart watch and was led to the medical area.

She was exhausted, but she found herself to be well enough to walk. Michael's heart pounded away, and she was thankful for it. She went to the tent to pick up her Boston marathon medal, and when she held out her tired arms and hands to receive it, she was overjoyed with happiness. It shone and dazzled in the ambient light and its meaning was just immeasurable. That's when she was distracted by a volunteer.

"Excuse me, but I think your phone is ringing," said the young blonde girl, who looked college aged.

"Oh, my arms feel like jelly, I couldn't feel the vibration," said Michelle.

"And you're Michelle Wong, right?" she asked as she looked down Michelle's bib.

"Yes, I am," replied Michelle.

"I just want to be sure, and congratulations again!" the young woman said.

Michelle nodded with a smile and turned away. She looked at her phone and saw that there were several missed calls and texts from Julie. Michelle had forgotten that she had taken off her headset and quickly plugged it back in.

"Julie!" exclaimed Michelle.

"You finished!" screamed an excited Julie from the other end.

Michelle was all smiles and nodded when Julie told her that they were by Trinity Church waiting for her. Michelle hung up and gingerly made her way to the meeting point, which wasn't far.

As she walked there, it wasn't long before she could pick out her parents and Michael's family, who began to walk briskly over to her. Before long, Michelle was overwhelmed with hugs and congratulations. The expected, "How are you feeling?" was asked several times, and Michelle responded that she was tired, but she felt so gratefully happy.

Michelle then produced the Boston Marathon medal as it twirled ever so lightly in the air. Everyone simply admired it.

"Instagram time!" exclaimed Julie. "Put it around your neck!"

As Michelle did, her mother came over looking flustered, quickly produced napkins, and started to blot the sweat from Michelle's brow. Michelle laughed and let her mother dote over her. When she was ready, she beamed as Julie took a few shots, then said, "Selfie time!"

Michelle's parents along with Julie's parents awkwardly posed around Michelle as Julie got in front of her parents and asked everyone to look into the camera.

"Excuse me," said an older man, who had on a Boston Marathon cap and matching windbreaker. He approached them from behind with a clipboard in his hands along with the same young blonde woman who had handed to Michelle her Boston Marathon medal.

Michelle and everyone turned around to face the man as Michelle said, "Yes?"

"I didn't mean to intrude on such a wonderful moment, completing the Boston Marathon, but I just wanted to confirm, are you Michelle Wong?" he asked

Michelle looked at her parents and turned back to the man, "That's me."

"Ah, great. Lydia here told me that you had picked up your medal for completing the Boston Marathon. My name is James, and I'm with the Boston Athletic Association, which manages the marathon. We understand from your application that you're not only running for yourself, but also your late fiancé. Very sad news, and you have our heartfelt condolences. But what makes your story so much more extraordinary is that you have his heart inside of you."

Michelle instinctively brought her hand closer to her chest to feel the steady beat of Michael's heart. She wasn't sure where James was going as she continued to look at him.

"Well, your story is so extraordinary, and I know you ran this marathon, but on behalf of the Boston Athletic Association, we would like for you to accept this second Boston Marathon medal for your late fiancé, whose heart was also in the race," said James as he dangled another medal in front of Michelle.

A wave of happiness crested over Michelle as she happily reached out for Michael's medal. The rest of the family was in awe and soon, Mr. Kim extended his hand to James, who received it with a big smile. Lydia also said congratulations to everyone before she and James went about their way.

Everyone was so overwhelmed with joy as Julie suggested with glee, "Put it on!"

Michelle smiled, and she looked at the second medal with deep thought. She looked up and smiled at Michael's parents, took a step toward them while extending the medal to Michael's father.

A befuddled expression came over Mr. Kim as he slowly grasped the medal by the ribbon.

"You should have this. Michael would have wanted it that way," said a grateful Michelle.

As Mr. Kim held the ribbon, Mrs. Kim held the medal gently in the palm of her hand, taking in what it meant to them. "Our son," said Mr. Kim somberly as a tear came from Mrs. Kim's eye. She then looked up at her husband in a silent moment, and he nodded.

Mr. Kim took a step toward Michelle, who was ready to receive a hug when suddenly Mr. Kim raised the ribbon over her head. Michelle was caught off guard as Michael's medal soon settled next to her own.

Before Michelle was able to protest, Mrs. Kim stepped forward reassuringly. She clasped the two medals together where the ribbon connected to them at the top and gently pressed the palm of her hand against Michelle's chest. With fondness, Michelle placed both of her hands on top of Mrs. Kim's hand and pressed it firmly against her chest.

Mrs. Kim closed her eyes and felt the steady thump of her son's heart, then another. She opened her eyes and looked at Michelle's eyes.

"Michael wanted to finish with you. But he couldn't. But you made it possible. His medal belongs here, where his heart is. With you," said an emotional Mrs. Kim.

Michelle's lips trembled and her eyes glistened at Mrs. Kim's words.

Mrs. Kim looked at Michelle's chest and spoke to Michael's heart, *"sa rang hae adeul,"* Korean for "love you, son." She then looked up affectionately at Michelle, *"sa rang hae taeul,"* Korean for, "Love you, daughter."

Michelle was touched by Mrs. Kim's words, and from the jump in Michael's heart, she was certain he felt it as well. She looked fondly back at his mother. Mr. Kim came forward and placed his hand gently on Michelle's shoulder as Michelle's parents closed in from behind. The heartwarming moment was soon interrupted when Julie burst between them and exclaimed, "Selfie!" This elicited a laugh all around.

* * *

About a month later on a Saturday morning, Michelle was leaving her bedroom and adjusting her running gear. She was pulling her ponytail through the back of her Red Sox baseball cap when she heard a knock at the door. She opened the door to Julie, who stepped through in her own running gear.

"The weather is great out there *Unni*!" said Julie as she hugged Michelle warmly.

"I'm ready for a marathon," teased Michelle.

"Noooo, just five miles," pleaded Julie.

"OK, just five miles," teased Michelle. "Wait, let me grab my phone."

Michelle approached the coffee table, and in the center was a collage of her and Michael in a loving pose. Another picture was of Michael crossing the finish line of his 10K. The other was her holding both medals on the day of the Boston marathon. A small assortment of the selfies that Julie had taken that day rounded out the collection. To the right, nestled gently inside the frame, were the two Boston Marathon medals.

Michelle grabbed her phone, paused, looked at the collage and then at the two medals side-by-side and thought, "We are a perfect match."

THAT KISS

There she sat, in the middle of my couch, with her legs gracefully gathered together and a bit off to her left. Her left hand rested along her knees while the elbow of her right arm rested on the cushion to provide her support. She sat there motionless as the images from the TV reflected in her eyes.

I would often find her like that in my comfortable one-bedroom condominium. I've been dating Judy for almost 3 months now, and she spends quite a lot of time at my place. I don't blame her; the roommate that she found through Craigslist wasn't exactly the most likeable person in the world, with her messy ways. Judy would go back every now and then when she's mad at me. Luckily, her lover's quarrel exodus never lasted too long, and we always eventually made up, though for whatever reason, I end up apologizing.

From the dining room table, I spied her by peeking over the screen of my Mac Air. I admit, I'm distracted from my work as I give furtive glances in her direction. Her flowing black hair gently draped along her back, a bit past her shoulders. Her hair was definitely one of her most seductive traits. She's as beautiful as can be, but I couldn't help this sinking feeling that I'm slowly falling out of love with her.

My mind wandered then as I ran a mental audit of our journey together in an attempt to find that missing piece in our relationship. Everything felt so right when I first met her, even though she was Thai American and I was Vietnamese American. Our mutual love for food gave me the confidence to ask her out. Our first date was at the chef's table of a fancy restaurant, and it was amazing. It was the third date, however, that was the most memorable. I invited her over for dinner because I wanted to impress her with my humble Vietnamese-inspired culinary skills. Although I was nervous, since it had been only a week since that first date of an amazing nine-course meal by a renowned local celebrity French chef.

I wasn't sure how my meal would even compare. But I confidently muddled through, and created a four-course Vietnamese-French inspired meal from scratch. The deconstructed Vietnamese spring roll was what left Judy with an indelible impression on her taste buds. While Mother would have given me grief for the French inspiration, detesting France's imperialistic history in our motherland, French cooking was the latest culinary craze.

Judy and I were already beginning to feel affection for each another prior. A stroke of our fingers here and there, the delicate stroke of my hand on her shoulder, the coy nudging of our shoulders, the hand-holding as I walked her back to her apartment on that second date. But we had not yet kissed.

She was special, and I didn't want to rush it. But I really wanted to kiss her. She had the most amazing lips, alluring and soft, and her lip-gloss made them glisten in the light. Every time she talked to me, I was mesmerized by her lips, and during my homemade dinner for her, it was no exception. I have to admit to possibly only hearing only every third word she said, but my saving grace was that I had to leave the dining room table to get the next course.

While I placed the dishes into the dishwasher, she had just come back from the bathroom after freshening up, and though she wanted to help, I insisted that she make herself comfortable on the couch. She reluctantly and playfully obliged, and that's when she found herself in the middle of my couch. She quietly watched me as I finished putting the final dishes away and got the dishwasher started.

The anticipation was building as I felt confident that I would finally get to kiss her. At the same time, I didn't want to come off as too aggressive, but my desire began to grow intensely. As she smiled at me, I excused myself to the bathroom as well as I needed a moment to ponder my move.

"Sure," Judy responded.

I smiled and nodded in her direction and cut through the kitchen to reach the bathroom. After splashing some cold water on my face, making sure there was nothing in my teeth, and taking a quick swig of mouthwash, I was ready. I looked into the mirror and looked at myself, making sure that I conveyed a confident self, knowing full well that there was a bit of nervousness about the unknown gnawing at my insides.

I then spent a moment thinking about my possible moves. Should I get us a glass of wine, sit beside her, and lean in for that first kiss? But wouldn't it be awkward to kiss if we both had a wine glass in our hands? It would be worse if in that awkward moment, some of the wine spilt onto my white couch.

Perhaps I could come into the living room, suavely put on some slow music, ask her to dance and then lean in for that kiss? But what happens if she didn't like to dance—would that create an awkward moment and destroy the mood?

Or maybe, I could come into the living room and with a running start, jump over the couch, and land right next to her. Possibly elicit a surprise laugh from her, and then I could move in for a playful kiss. But what if I slipped during the jump, slid off the couch, and desperately grabbed onto her only to drag her on top of me as she hit her head on the coffee table? I should definitely not do that.

By now, I was utterly confused and frustrated. I didn't want to ruin this first kiss and I had no plan! I had already been in the bathroom too long, and I didn't want her to think I was doing a number two. I exited the bathroom and saw that Judy was still on the couch, and it appeared that she was flipping through one of the magazines on the coffee table.

She was distracted. That was good, and I slowly approached her from behind. My mind started to race with the three scenarios that I had just previously envisioned. I looked at the half-bottle of wine that was still on the dining room table. I glanced at the TV remote, and thought of a music station to turn to. I then looked at the height of the couch, which now seemed higher than what I had visualized in my mind, and knew that clearing the height of the couch wasn't going to be a suave thing to do. Only a few steps separated me from her, and I still had no plan!

When her profile came into view, I saw those satiny red lips of hers. As if I suffered amnesia, I only remember quickly leaning in and placing my lips onto hers. I could tell that she was surprised, and instinctively, I cupped the side of her face in my hand and tilted her head slightly upward to seal the kiss, and it was amazing. She reciprocated fully, and her lips were soft, warm, and moist. I kissed her for a few seconds and then slowly delved my tongue into her mouth and met her tongue in a warm twirling embrace. I could feel my body temperature boiling, and I could feel the warmth of her cheek in my hand, but kissing her was just amazing. It was the best kiss ever, and one that I would never be able to reproduce.

I let out an audible sigh, and for a moment, my entire world was blurry and when my vision cleared up, I saw that Judy was staring at me with a smile.

I don't know how long she had been looking at me as I snapped out of my reverie, but I clumsily cleared my throat and looked back down at my Mac Air. A scarf-like warmth suddenly coiled itself around my neck as I tried to remember what I was doing. I glanced up, and Judy had gone back to watching TV.

Though we kissed often and we were intimate, that most amazing first kiss with its flood of emotions never came back. Hence, my doubt about our relationship started to take hold. It frustrated me to no end that I could not reproduce that kiss, which was so full of consuming passion.

I peered over the Mac Air screen once more and looked at Judy. Beautiful though she was, she was starting to become a stranger in my own home, and for a moment, my frustration turned to emptiness. But I couldn't give up hope. If we were meant to be, I needed to recapture that kiss.

I came home late one evening; way past dinnertime and just as the prime time shows had started. I had already eaten, and Judy had texted that she would make a quick bite to eat. As I opened the door, I noticed that Judy was on the couch in that same position, distracted by the TV.

I knew I had to act and quietly set my bag onto the floor as I eased the door closed, along with slipping off my shoes. The blood started to pick up pace as my heart started to throb. If I could not find that kiss soon, I feared it would be the end of our relationship, and I hated having "the talk."

As each footstep approached her, she was still unaware of my presence. The memory of that first kiss came rushing back, and I just needed that kiss. I was within a footstep of the couch when I suddenly leaned in. My lips found hers, and they were warm. In an instant, the kiss was broken and my necktie was forcibly yanked forward, throwing me off balance as I fell forward as my entire body landed on the floor between the couch and the coffee table.

"Tommy!" yelled Judy in alarm.

I laid there on the floor and looked up, momentarily dazed. For a moment I saw two images of Judy, and when the two images merged, I saw her looking down at me.

"Oh my God, are you OK?" asked Judy as she reached out for me.

"I think so," I replied as I reached up for her hand.

"Oh my God, don't sneak up on me like again! I thought I was being attacked!" said Judy as she pulled me to a sitting position on the couch.

"I'm sorry, I was trying to surprise you and..." I couldn't finish my sentence because I was distracted by something strange on her nose. I shook my head again, thinking that I may still be dazed, and I still saw what looked like a white strip across Judy's nose.

"What's that?" I asked.

"What's what?"

I pointed to her nose with my finger, and for a moment, Judy looked confused until her eyes gleamed and she said, "Oh, it's a Bioré strip."

Still confused, I asked, "What's a Bioré strip?"

"It's for removing blackheads," she said.

Still utterly confused, I asked flatly, "What's a blackhead?"

That's when Judy giggled, and her wondrous eyes looked down at me as if I was child, as she began to explain what a blackhead was and how Bioré strips were meant to remove them. I sat there listening to this amazing lecture on the virtues of deep-pore cleansing methods, and she even encouraged me to do it. When she removed it and showed me the blackheads that had stuck to the paper mache-like strip, all hopes of finding that kiss were lost for the remainder of that night.

On another evening, coming home late once more, my mind was still wrestling with my confusion about whether or not I still loved Judy and why I could not find that kiss. It was maddening. That magical moment sealed in a spontaneous kiss continued to elude me. I could not believe that I had allowed my thoughts to be so focused on that kiss and thought that only women were so obsessed about these kinds of things. But there I was, thinking about the missing kiss in the rising elevator of my condo building. How frustrating.

The elevator emitted its lonely ding, and the doors opened. I walked out and toward my condo. I opened the door and I saw Judy sitting on my couch once more. The urge to try to find that kiss suddenly came back but not wanting to be thrown over the couch in some jujitsu move, I said, "Hey, Judy."

Judy didn't turn around but gave a quick wave. She was watching something on TV, probably a good scene that she didn't want to miss, as the volume was up a bit louder than usual.

I placed my bag on the floor, hung up my jacket, and took off my shoes. But my eyes were fixated on her, as she had put her hair into a ponytail. There was something strangely attractive about that, and the urge to find that kiss reared its insatiable head. This time, there was no need to sneak up behind her. She knew I was home, and so if I came in behind her and kissed her, she would kiss back, and maybe I'd finally find that kiss.

I took a deep breath and simply walked over. When her cheek and nose came into view, I leaned in with my eyes closed for the kiss. My lips pressed onto hers, and they were soft and warm. My cheeks flushed with warmth as I pressed harder onto her lips despite her attempts to break the kiss. I inhaled deeply and a strong floral scent filled my nostrils, seeming to tickle my nose hairs. Judy struggled to turn her head for whatever reason, but I needed to feel that kiss once again despite the floral scent. I placed my hand onto her cheek just as I had done the first time, but my hand was met with something warm and slick, like oil. In that moment of bewilderment, Judy broke the kiss as she turned her head and suddenly, the slick, oil-like substance smeared all over my lips. Some of it even got onto my tongue, and that's when my eyes squinted in revulsion. I pulled back to an upright position. Instinctively, my hand went to my mouth to wipe the stuff off my mouth.

Judy was lying on the couch giggling. That kiss that I thought would happen simply vanished as my senses came back. I still couldn't get the floral taste out of my mouth as Judy just leaned upward, propped up by both of her elbows. She just looked at me as my face must have looked contorted. She laughed once more as I had to turn and spit out what was left of that oily floral residue on my tongue.

"What was that?" I mumbled to her.

"What's left of a perfectly good Korean face mask," she said. She propped herself into a seated position and with the tips of her right fingers, felt around the area of her lips and cheek.

"You use that stuff?" I asked.

"Yes, it's a clear face mask. A girl has to do what she needs to do to stay young, you know."

"Oh, I just assumed you were a natural beauty and didn't need any of that stuff."

Judy's eyes glistened and a smile came over her face. "That's the nicest thing I've heard!" she said as she reached out to me with her puckered lips.

I held her at arm's length, warding off her attempt as a perturbed look came over her shiny face. I quickly said, "Maybe after you take off your face mask? I think I can still taste it."

She smiled as her eyes lit up and she pulled herself back. Her response came in the form of a giggle while she added, "That's probably a good idea."

Judy gently pulled away, hopped off the couch, and headed to the bathroom. As I watched her, all anticipation of that kiss was gone for the remainder of the night, and the taste of a floral facemask lingered in my mouth.

Another week had passed since the second failed attempt at that kiss. Though we had kissed and made love since then, I was still missing that kiss. It was gnawing at me like a starved rat in a trap. That magical moment, spawned by that unplanned kiss and those emotions that came with it, needed to show itself for me to know if I really had feelings for Judy. Otherwise, she was just becoming more and more of a stranger in our relationship.

It was the middle of the following week when again, I came home late and entered my apartment. This time, I was hoping that she would be on the couch once again. I was longing for that momentous sensual feeling, and was desperate for those circumstances to re-occur so I could recapture that moment. But those circumstances were becoming harder to come by. A few other nights, she had gone out with friends or was working at the dining room table. But that night, she was sitting on the couch with the television on. Her head was bowed down slightly, and she must have been flipping through a magazine.

I closed the door and heard the distinctive audible click of the self-locking doorknob. I kept my eyes on Judy as I removed by jacket.

"Hey," I uttered.

Judy turned her head slightly as her eyes met mine. With a slight grin, she replied with a, "Mmmm" before turning away.

She saw me, so there would be no surprise femme fatale throw. There was no Bioré strip on her nose, and her beautiful face was devoid of that facemask glean. The moment was ripe for another attempt. The third time is the charm, as they say. I took in a deep breath as I stepped out of my shoes.

This had to be it. I could feel it. Any and all doubt that I had about Judy being my girlfriend, the girl that I cared about, the girl that I would cherish for the rest of my life would come down to this one momentous kiss.

I was right behind her, and she was engrossed in her magazine. I snuck in from behind and quickly cupped my hand around her cheek. My lips were firmly on her lips, and they were warm and moist. A bit more moist that usual, but that didn't stop me from having that kiss. She struggled, but I smothered her kiss with my own. I was starting to feel the sensuousness of the kiss, and I parted her lips with my tongue. That's when she tried to jerk free, but my hand was firmly around her cheek, and I placed my other hand on the back of head. But instead of finding her warm tongue, I was met with an acrid taste in her mouth. Suddenly my mouth was entangled in an unknown gelatinous web. I pulled back immediately, breaking that kiss as every hope within me deflated.

But there was something in my mouth, pasted to my tongue. As Judy was on her side uncontrollably laughing, I reached in with my index finger and pulled out a strip of dimpled plastic with a clear gelatinous foamy film. It was a tooth-whitening strip, the upper part at least.

Judy pulled out the mangled white strip from her mouth and reached out for a tissue to wipe away the drool from around her mouth. All the while, she was giggling.

My third attempt was thus foiled because my girlfriend was whitening her teeth. I felt totally entirely dejected, as if the forces of love were all conspiring against me. Maybe these were all signs confirming the hollowness in my heart, that Judy was not the one.

"What were you thinking?" asked Judy jovially.

I sighed as I looked at Judy's eyes, her hair flowing, though a bit tousled from before. "I was just trying to kiss you," was all I could say.

"I guess you didn't expect to whiten your teeth either!" she said playfully as she wiped away the residue from the teeth whitener from her tongue.

With remnants of the teeth whitener still on my tongue, which had now turned decidedly bitter, I said, "No, I didn't."

"Ugh, I need to rinse out my mouth, it's all over the inside of my mouth because of you!" she said, getting up, as she gave me playful but annoyed look as she headed to the bathroom.

All temptations to find that kiss that night faded away, as I went to the kitchen to rinse out my mouth.

We're about to hit the fourth month anniversary of our first date, and I knew that my feelings for Judy were no longer there. It would be unfair to her to continue this relationship. As before, I had always initiated something to celebrate the monthly anniversary of our first date. She thought it was cute and she was probably expecting something similar for this upcoming month, except this time, there would be none.

One of the most difficult things about breaking up was choosing the timing. You try not to break up too close around the holidays. Like Thanksgiving, for example: Do you break up well in advance so that she doesn't invite you over to her parents' place, only to break up with her right after? Christmas or her birthday are even worse because you don't want to buy her a present and then break up; in addition, she'll have a horrible Christmas or birthday. Valentine's is by far the worst. After meeting her parents over Thanksgiving, then giving her a Christmas gift, then having that New Year's Day kiss, breaking up with her in January before Valentine's would only fuel her anger. Thank goodness it was May and she's a fall baby, but it still didn't make it any easier.

I had rehearsed several scenarios in my head about how to break up with her. Each one had a disturbing ending in which I would have to dodge certain things in my condo being thrown at me. It makes it even tougher when your girlfriend has pretty much moved in with you and she has stuff in your place. It wasn't going to be a clean breakup, and I dreaded it. Obviously, she would not want to stay after I had broken up with her, and then there was the business of the box. That box that would contain all her belongings, and somehow I would have to get that box to her. And with girlfriends, there was never just one box.

As I pondered all these things on the ride up in that elevator, I was also mad at myself for being so fixated on that elusive kiss—that magical moment that lit up my senses and that I took as a sign that Judy was the one. If it wasn't for that, I think we could have had a relationship. We were getting along well, we both loved the same kind of food, she was very easygoing, her smile was always refreshing, and her silky black hair was amazing to the touch.

My reverie was interrupted by the ding of the elevator, and the doors opened. I sighed, stepped through them, and started to walk to my condo. A sense of dread started to weigh on me, making the relatively short walk to my condo longer than usual. What would I find upon entering my condo? Would I find her on the couch again, and should I attempt at finding that kiss one more time? Or perhaps, she'll be in my condo with another man, cheating on me in my very own condo. That would give me the right to break up with her and throw her out without the guilt of breaking up with her. But Judy wouldn't do that. She was absolutely loyal, and I trusted her and my mind was going crazy with outlandish scenarios.

I slipped the key into the lock and turned it along with the polished steel door handle. The television was on, but there was no Judy. I stepped into my condo, locked the door behind me, took off my jacket, and was in the midst of stepping out of my shoes when I heard the water running in the bathroom.

"Judy?" I blurted out?

"I'm in the bathroom," she answered.

"OK," was all I could say.

It was another long night, and the breakup scenarios started to race in my head once more. With my head drooping, I headed to the couch and just sat in the middle of it. I had to break up tonight, I thought. If she was expecting an anniversary dinner, it would be this following weekend, and if I chickened out, I would have to pay for an elaborate meal and have to break up with her shortly thereafter. This would surely engender all types of awful conversations among her friends that I had strung her along and how insensitive I was.

I clasped my hands together, rubbing my palms together in an effort to squeeze out the frustration that I felt while at the same time calming myself down for the talk. I would just be honest with her. She deserved that at the very least. I would hold her hands while having the talk, as I would say more or less to her that I still cared about her. But in actuality, it was to prevent her from grabbing something to throw at me, like a kitchen knife.

I let out another sigh, and I could feel my heart racing. I shuffled my feet a bit and straightened up when my sight was abruptly obscured. Warmth enveloped my face and I couldn't breathe. My lips were pressed up against by something soft and warm, and it was soothing. My feelings of doubt were suddenly suspended as my tongue was met with another, twirling about mine. It was sensational and magical all at the same time. Time seemed to have stopped as I indulged in the moment, and suddenly it was gone.

A second passed before my eyes opened, and I blinked a few times. I'm pretty sure my mouth was still slightly ajar as I let out a breath. I then looked to my right, and there was Judy. She had her forearms folded underneath her as she rested her head on top of them. She looked at me with cat-like curiosity, her eyes staring at me with a certain sense of wonderment and serenity.

She smiled playfully at me and simply said, "What?"

I looked back at her, noticed how beautiful she was from her black silky hair to her brown eyes, and finally to those lips. They were amazing lips. The softest and most sensual lips I ever laid my own lips on. With unbound eagerness, I twisted my body toward her and hoisted Judy over the couch with strength unseen, which elicited a playful squeal from her as I cradled her in my arms.

She looked up at me as lovingly held her. I parted a stray hair and looked at her eyes and I simply replied confidently, "Nothing."

I then leaned in and kissed her sensually without any further doubt about our relationship. I realized that I never lost that kiss—it had found me.

TAKE OUT

Like the strings of a violin being plucked, each tendril of his leg muscles twitched with each footfall as he was finishing his run. Gordon had just exited the north side of Central Park through Malcolm X. Blvd when he turned right along Central Park North. His tall frame swiftly dodged a few pedestrians, all of who were winding down the workday to get home for dinner.

He slowed down at the first intersection and jogged in place. His dark navy jogging pants hugged each of his flexing thigh muscles as his performance hoodie showed his athletic frame. He donned his New York Yankees baseball cap with pride along with his blue lens sports sunglasses, which gave him the demeanor of a determined athlete.

The traffic signal turned red at the intersection, and Gordon crossed diagonally to the other corner. He continued on before he stopped in front of the Chinese restaurant that his parents had owned since he was a boy. It brought back so many memories for him each time he entered. It was a local favorite, with a Yelp review of 4.5 stars.

He pulled on the metal handle of the glass door as the bell clanged a couple of times. A woman, along with her young son, was just exiting, and she smiled as he held the door open for her. Upon entering, he could feel the familiar warmth of the restaurant, and already he saw that the waiting area was full with people quietly talking amongst themselves.

His father, who was the host and cashier and answered the phone, was just finishing up a take-out order when he looked up. His grayish hair was neatly combed, and he always wore a jovial expression. He urgently waved his son over, and Gordon hurried over just as he placed the phone down.

"I need you to deliver a take-out order," he said.

"A hi to you too, Ba-ba," said Gordon mischievously.

His father's eyes winced in resignation, and he dismissed his son's need for pleasantries. He continued, "*Aiyah*, stop being so needy. It's dinner rush hour, and Johnny and Ronnie are slow to get back. Make your Ba-ba happy and run this delivery. It's very close."

Gordon smiled and was always happy to help his parents, even with such an unexpected request. He was about to ask where the food was when his mother appeared from the kitchen with a brown bag with the white-and-green order ticket stapled at the top.

His mother's eyes lit up, and she headed toward Gordon. She was a slim woman in a red blouse with black slacks. She was the queen expediter of the kitchen whose organizational skills always ensured that the customers got their delicious Chinese food hot and on time.

"Gordon is going to deliver it," said Gordon's father, and his mother promptly shoved the brown bag into Gordon's hands.

"Sheesh, a hi to you too, Mom," said Gordon as he took the bag from her.

"Oh, don't make a big fuss," said his mother coyly. "You may be a lawyer now but this restaurant is the family's…"

"Responsibility," echoed Gordon as it was the family motto grilled into his and his siblings' heads ever since they were young. Each one of them had a hand in working the restaurant, especially memorable times such as when seemingly every single Jewish family would visit their restaurant during Christmas. Christmas was very different for the Chin family.

"See, we taught him well," snickered his father as he winked at his wife.

"OK, where is this going?" asked Gordon as he looked down at the order ticket.

"Upper East Side, a couple of blocks from here. Go now, and it'll still be hot for her," said Gordon's father.

Gordon saw the address and the name "Erin" scribbled at the bottom and nodded, "Got it. I'll take care of it. Have a good night!" he said as he exited the restaurant.

"Are you coming back for dinner?" asked his mother, but it fell on deaf ears as the door closed behind him.

"Gone in a flash," said Gordon's father with a smirk.

After being let in by the doorman and shown upstairs by the concierge, he approached the customer's door, which was slightly ajar. He could hear a woman's voice from within speaking Cantonese. He quickly straightened up, a bit conscious that he was in his running gear and hoped he didn't smell like sweat. He checked the brown bag to ensure there were no leaks before he knocked gently on the door, which slowly swung open. She suddenly came into view as she leaned over with her cell phone in her left hand and with a smile, waved gently with the other hand.

Her slim fit jeans showed off her slenderness, and her casual dressy gray shirt flattered her. Her black shoulder length hair twisted slightly each time she turned her head, and Gordon simply couldn't ignore how graceful she was. He was a bit caught off guard as he smirked in kind. While still talking on the phone, she gestured at the desk with a friendly smile.

Gordon snapped out of his awe at her beauty and nodded. But he suddenly realized he had his sneakers on and noticed that she had on white socks. In a split second, he took one big stride over to the desk, stretched out his arms and gently dropped the brown paper bag onto the desk. Then he recoiled back by the door.

The awkward drop off did not go unnoticed by Erin, who gave Gordon a quizzical look. Gordon sheepishly pointed toward his sneakers and the hardwood floors. A glint of mutual cultural understanding resonated with her as she gave him a smirk and continued talking on the phone.

Gordon could only surmise that it was one of her parents, most likely her mother, as Erin continued to reassure the person on the phone that everything was OK. As Erin strode quickly over to the desk, Gordon took a quick look around her apartment and saw that she was still unboxing from a recent move, and the furniture looked like it had been plopped down wantonly.

Erin glanced at the order ticket and scooped up two twenties she had ready on the desk for a total that would have only amounted to $30 with a reasonable tip.

Gordon saw this as she approached him and he heard her tell her mother, *"One second,"* in Cantonese.

In Cantonese, Gordon stated embarrassingly, *"Oh, I don't have change."*

"It's OK, for all your trouble," she responded in her melodious Cantonese.

"Are you sure?" he asked.

"I'm sure," she said as Gordon could hear her mother's loud voice from the cell phone.

"I'll let you get back to talking to your mother," said Gordon humorously.

With a playful eye roll, she said in a shush, *"Thank you."*

Gordon backed out of her apartment into the hallway as he watched her friendly eyes twinkle at him along with her grin as the door gently closed. The deadbolt clicked and Gordon gave out a heavy sigh and suddenly, all he could think about was the beautiful woman in apartment 8B.

* * *

The next morning, Gordon was quiet as he rode the elevator up the skyscraper to his law firm's well-adorned offices. His crisp suit clung to his tall athletic frame, and he was ready for the day's work. The elevator's "ding" broke him out of his reverie about Erin. He collected himself, stepped off the elevator, and walked through the glass doors.

"Good morning, Gordon," said the cute blonde receptionist, who glanced up at him.

Gordon stopped in his tracks and glanced over at the receptionist with a smile. "A good morning to you too, Julia."

"Great suit, Gordon," said Julia with admiration.

Gordon walked over to the high-top counter as Julia turned toward Gordon. He put his arm out so that the sleeve could catch the light better as it glanced off the grayish blue hues of the fabric, "The color is quite striking. Kind of like your own ensemble," said Gordon, referring to Julia's cream-colored, ruffled trimmed short sleeve blouse tucked neatly into her just-above-the-knee black pencil skirt.

Julia blushed, but played coy, "Why thank you, Gordon, always nice of you notice," she said, giving off a giggle as he returned a flirtatious smile. "So hey, the big boss wanted to see you first thing this morning. Wanted me to let you know as soon as I saw you."

The senior partner wanted to see him, thought Gordon? He stood at attention and said, "Thanks for the heads-up, I'll head on in to see him."

"In a flash," said Julia teasingly.

Gordon chuckled, "Of course."

After leaving the receptionist desk, he dropped his messenger bag onto the guest chair in his windowed office. He quickly straightened up, and smoothed down his suit front before heading down to the senior partner's office. He approached the glass office, whose door was left ajar, and he could see the senior partner, an older distinguished white man with neatly combed thick silverish hair, peering over a document as he leaned back in his chair.

Gordon gently knocked on the glass wall, which caught his attention. "Geoffrey?"

"Gordon! Please come on in, have a seat," Geoffrey warmly said as he put down the document that he was inspecting. "How goes it?"

"Not too bad," said Gordon. "Just wrapping up that Montgomery case, which brought in some hefty billings for the office, if you don't mind me saying so. And now, I'm just gearing up for the Gaines estate."

"Right, right. You handled that Montgomery case very well. Gerald spoke highly of the efficacy that you brought to his case," said Geoffrey.

"Thanks, I did do my best," replied Gordon.

"Oh, stop being so modest, Gordon, a fine damn good job you did there," said Geoffrey graciously. "When one of my rich friends goes through a tough divorce, they are always grateful that they come out without losing their pants," he said with a chuckle.

"Which is why I wanted to speak to you this morning. I have a new one for you. Have you been following the very public Harold and Meredith Weintraub divorce?"

Gordon's interest perked up. The Weintraubs were an older couple who were among New York's well-known but exclusive philanthropic socialites.

They were charismatic billionaires who made their money in retail and real estate in New York and New Jersey. Everything was going well with them until they mysteriously decided to divorce after close to 35 years of marriage, and the New York news have been keeping tabs on them since.

"Definitely. There's at least one news item per week on them about their divorce, and the lack of details just makes it that much more intriguing," replied Gordon.

"You know, back in the day, people wouldn't care about a divorce proceeding that didn't have some drama, but now with this social media stuff, people are all gaga about nothing. Well Harold called me today, he and I go way back. He's firing his lawyer and wants me to bring it to the finish line for him. From what it sounds like, it's close to wrapping up, but he and Meredith are stuck on one asset, some old apartment building in Queens. I want you to take it on, OK?"

Gordon looked astonished, but he was eager to take on the case for its high-profile status, but his mind went back his other client, "Sure, that would be OK with me, but what about Gaines?"

"Don't worry about Gaines, I'll give it to one of the other attorneys in the office. He'll be well taken off. It's time you step into the big leagues now. You bring this home, and that partnership that you've been working hard for may potentially be fast tracked," said Geoffrey with a wink.

As a junior partner and having worked hard for the better part of 10 years at the firm, this was welcomed news for Gordon. This was his break. "Well then, I better get started. I need to meet with Harold to get caught up and…" added Gordon before he was interrupted by Geoffrey.

"You'll need to do that as you get yourself over to the courthouse, because you'll need to request a continuance from the judge," said Geoffrey. "He's expecting you at 11AM this morning."

"Like this morning?" asked Gordon incredulously.

"Yes, like in a flash," said Geoffrey smilingly.

Gordon's smile went from cheek to cheek, "You'll never let that one go, will you?"

"Hell no! It's too much fun," Geoffrey said jokingly. "Oh, one other thing to add to the drama. It looks like Meredith also got herself a new attorney. So it's a clean slate, but I have faith in you. Now go!"

"I got this," said Gordon as he got up and extended his hand, which Geoffrey shook wholeheartedly.

He spent the better part of an hour reading up on Harold and Meredith in order to get a better sense of who they were and got the latest legal updates from social media. After exiting his Lyft, he walked up the Parthenon-like steps to the Supreme Courthouse and entered the courtroom about 15 minutes before 11 o'clock. There were a smattering of journalist and photographers, most of whom were just idling, and the occasional click of a camera shutter could be heard.

To his right, he saw the back of Harold's crowning head ringed by curly dark brown hair. As Gordon walked up the aisle, he took a glance to the left and saw Meredith from the side. One couldn't miss Meredith's poof of curly red hair, and despite her age, she wore her makeup well. She donned a white business skirt suit that hugged her pudgy sides.

A photographer, then two, aimed their camera at Gordon and took a few shots as he made his way up the aisle to Harold. This caught Harold's attention. He turned to see Gordon approaching him and got up. He was a shorter fellow, probably the same height as his wife with her heels on and a bit frumpy around the middle. But he boasted a hearty presence.

"Mr. Weintraub, I'm Gordon Chin. I'll be your attorney for the rest of the case," said Gordon as he extended his hand out.

Mr. Weintraub looked at Gordon, who stood considerably taller than him for a moment before extending out his pudgy listless hand. For the first time, Gordon could see how time had weighed on him from his saggy cheeks and the dark eye bags.

Gordon motioned him to sit down and explained that he would seek a continuance. He also inferred that the opposing attorney was also new, and that he had not had the chance to introduce himself to that attorney just yet. That's when he heard the courtroom doors creak open and the sounds of high heels tapping along the marble floors of the courtroom aisle. The recognizable sounds of camera shutters buzzed through the air, and Gordon nodded to Harold and gave a reassuring nod.

Gordon straightened up in his chair, quickly pressed his tie against his shirt, and turned to his left to lay his eyes on his presumptive opposing attorney. She gently pushed the wooden gate forward and walked past it as it slowly swung back into place. She wore a navy business suit that exuded a sense of confidence and poise. She carried a slim attaché case with her left hand and quickly glanced over at Gordon expressionlessly before her slender legs pivoted left along with her twirling shoulder-length hair as she approached Meredith.

It was Erin. The same beautiful woman that Gordon had delivered Chinese food to the night before, while he was in his running gear. Embarrassment shot down his chest, and he felt his insides cringe before he turned to face forward. Did she recognize him as well, he thought? He took a glance to his left and saw Erin was busily talking with Meredith who clutched her oversized name-brand purse.

Gordon returned to staring ahead as he mulled the sudden distracting thoughts in his head. What a coincidence that the same beautiful woman that he had delivered Chinese food to was also his opposing attorney. Would he even be able to perform his fiduciary duties to his client if he had a romantic interest in the opposing counsel? Would he be breaking any laws if he asked her out? Was she even single? What was he even thinking? he realized.

The court officer suddenly rose and asked everyone to stand as he announced that the Honorable Judge Marshall was entering the courtroom. Gordon felt a nudge from Harold and realized that his distractions had kept him in his seat. Gordon scrambled upward, straight as an arrow, just as the door to the judge's chamber opened. The always serious and stern judge walked in, tall and regal in her flowing black robe, made more dramatic with her grayish-black hair that framed her black complexion, climbed the steps to her perch where she sat down. She adjusted her glasses and then looked about her courtroom, first from the left and then to the right and stated, "You may be seated."

She flipped open the manila folder that contained the contents of the case and then spoke, "It is my understanding that each party has retained new counsel to disposition their case?"

Gordon then stood up and respectfully announced, "Yes your honor, Gordon Chin from Winslow & Herbert, will now be Mr. Harold Weintraub's legal counsel."

Erin then chimed in, "And your honor, Erin Chung of Spade & Willard will now be representing Ms. Meredith Weintraub."

Damn, she sounded beautiful, Gordon said to himself.

"Very well," acknowledged Judge Marshall. "As you are both new, I'm assuming you'll both be requesting a continuance, so let me cut to the chase. Why don't we say, Thursday, two days from now, same time and let's see where we're at?"

Gordon looked over at Erin as she turned to him and they both turned to the judge with a nod. "Continuance granted, we'll resume on Thursday," said Judge Marshall who stood up, along with everyone else before she left the courtroom.

A few furtive whispers, and Meredith briskly walked away from the table and out of the courtroom without once looking at Harold. Gordon turned to Harold, "Let's meet tomorrow at your office for us to strategize. Sounds good?"

"Sounds like a plan," said Harold, who also got up and left the courthouse.

Gordon suddenly saw his chance as Erin busily gathered a few documents into her bag. He reached into his wallet and smiled as he pulled out a ten-dollar bill. He pulled on its edges, and it gave off taut snap as he walked over to Erin.

She looked up as Gordon approached and straightened up. Her opposing counsel had an imposing frame, which his grayish blue suit framed quite nicely. He was probably into some sport she thought. She was about to extend out her hand when he handed her the ten-dollar bill, which she received with confusion.

"Here's your change, ten dollars," said Gordon.

With dumbfoundedness, she looked down at the ten-dollar bill and thought maybe, it was some reference to the Hamilton performance on Broadway. "Excuse me?"

"For last night," said Gordon with a smile. He could still see that Erin was confused, so he added, "For the Chinese food that you had last night."

Erin suddenly crossed her arms defensively and asked, "Wait, how did you know that I had Chinese food last night?"

Gordon realized that she didn't recognize him, and he simply blurted out, "Um, because I delivered it to you? I'm the guy that delivered your Chinese food."

Erin's posture suddenly relaxed as her expression changed to that of lightheartedness when she blurted out, "You're the Chinese food delivery guy? And you're also a lawyer?" giggled Erin.

Gordon smiled and feigned straightening his tie and with smug look. "Yes, guilty as charged. Consummate divorce attorney by day, but delivery guy for the best Chinese food by night," to which they both shared a laugh.

Gordon extended his hand, "Hi, I'm Gordon Chin."

"Erin Chung, but I think you already know that," said Erin with friendly chuckle. "But wait, you spoke Chinese yesterday."

"Well so did you."

"Oh, I was speaking with my mom. Oh, so you heard me speaking Chinese so you…"

"Wanted to impress you with my Chinese!" blurted out Gordon with immediate regret as he may have implied that he was trying to impress her. Thinking quickly on his feet, he slipped in, "I wanted you to know that you ordered from a great Chinese restaurant, and what better way than having its own delivery guy talking in Chinese!"

"Um, I guess you're right. The food was delicious by the way!" said Erin.

"I'll be sure to tell my parents," answered Gordon.

"Thank you. This is so funny! Who would have thought that I would order Chinese food only to have the delivery guy turn out to be my opposing attorney? What a coincidence!" exclaimed Erin.

"Absolutely," said Gordon. "Anyhow, seeing that we're both new to this case, we both probably need to catch up with our clients."

"Your client can pony up more money and it'll be a done deal," said Erin teasingly.

"Oh really? What's makes you think it's about the money?" asked Gordon.

Erin smiled, snapped the ten-dollar bill and simply said, "It's always about the money."

* * *

Later that afternoon, Erin found herself in Meredith's penthouse home, which sat atop a coveted view of Central Park. Meredith was seated comfortably on her supple white leather couch as she doted on her bichon frise, who playfully took a small piece of doggy kibble each time Meredith offered it to her.

Erin found it distracting that she had to fight for Meredith's attention as she ran down the list of the most-salient points of the proposed settlement, but she was patient. She wanted to earn Meredith's trust, considering she was brought in to finalize this divorce. Although she would always be a Bostonian, she had always wanted to try to live in New York just to experience the hustle and bustle of the city. So when the New York office had an opening, she took it and suddenly found herself being handed this case. Life in New York did move fast, but she was up to the task.

"OK, Meredith, so that leaves us with only one asset…" but before Erin could finish, Meredith spoke up.

"I'm not selling it. Harold can offer all the money in the world, but I'm not selling it," said Meredith as she dangled a piece of doggy kibble above her little dog's mouth before letting her have it.

Erin paused. She knew that this one last asset, an apartment building in Queens, had been an impasse for the last attorney, and they couldn't break through. She couldn't find herself in the same situation.

"But why do you want to keep it?" asked Erin as she shifted her legs along the edge of the couch opposite of the one that Meredith was sitting on.

"Just cause. You need to convince Harold that he needs to let it go," said Meredith sternly.

"I see," said Erin despondently, but she needed to give off a sense that she was in control. "Let me talk to your husband's…"

"Soon to be ex-husband! That ungrateful man," stammered Meredith.

"Yes, I'm sorry, soon to be ex-husband," replied Erin.

Meredith looked at Erin and sighed. "There's nothing to be sorry about, it's Harold. It's all his fault."

Erin saw an opening and offered, "Isn't it always?"

Meredith relaxed a bit into the side of the couch and sighed. "Men, they never know how good they have it, and they can't have everything."

"Woman to woman, I know how you feel. We give so much and what do we ask for in return?" asked Erin.

"Love," said Meredith and Erin in unison as they looked at each other and laughed.

"I have everything that I need for now, I'll see you in the courthouse on Thursday," said Erin as she gathered up her things.

"Yes, the courthouse," said Meredith as her voice trailed off.

* * *

On Wednesday afternoon, Gordon found himself cornered in Harold's posh but stodgy office in midtown. A large Oriental rug stretched out, covering most of the room's center. The dark wood paneling combined with halogen lighting that diffused the air gave off a dingy atmosphere. Two large brown leather chairs were up against the wall, separated by a round wooden table that contained an ashtray for the cigar that Harold was smoking, along with a glass of whiskey. Hanging on the wall above the table was an oil painting of Harold looking regal as a game hunter while holding a shotgun.

"Where are we at?" asked Harold as he brought the cigar to his lips as the excited embers of the lit end swirled.

"My quick review of where the last attorney left off, was there is one last property to be settled, the apartment building in Queens," said Gordon.

"Has anyone called you Gordy?" asked Harold abruptly.

Gordon looked stupefied but answered awkwardly, "Um, no."

"Yah, you don't strike me as a Gordy type. You're not stocky enough," said Harold. "But yes, I'm getting that property back one way or another. She can't take that away from me!"

"I see. But the property is currently held under an LLC that she controls..." said Gordon before Harold interjected.

"For tax purposes! But before, I was its sole owner. Good-for-nothing accountant," grumbled Harold as he took another puff on his cigar. "And I've been making the payments on the mortgage we took out on it!"

"OK, so you just want to buy it back, and the last offer you gave her was seven-point five million dollars..."

"And she shot it down like a goose during hunting season," exclaimed Harold. "I only paid one-point-five million dollars for it."

"Are you willing to sweeten the offer? Say an additional five hundred thousand?" asked Gordon.

Harold leaned back in his chair as the supple leather squeezed in around him. He looked up at the ceiling and took another puff of his cigar and let out a smooth smoky stream. He cast his eyes in resignation toward the opposite corner of the room and begrudgingly said, "Throw in another five hundred thousand and let's see if she'll take it."

As the end of the day drew near, Gordon attempted to organize the paperwork for Harold's divorce along his desk, but he found himself constantly distracted by Erin. In a fit of frustration, he sat straight up and placed his palms flat on the desk and stretched out his arms. He let out an audible grunt and then relaxed.

Though Erin was his opposing counsel and he was supposed to see her only as a peer, he kept on reminiscing on how her business suit hugged her slim figure, the way her legs gracefully moved across the courtroom, the sound her high heels made when they tapped onto the marble floor, and how her hair would sway with each bob of her head. But it was her eyes that were the most beautiful, and the flash of her smile held him spellbound

The growl from his stomach was quite audible, and he placed his left hand on his stomach to temper it. He gathered up the paperwork and tucked it into this messenger bag, donned his suit jacket and slung the messenger back across his chest for the commute home. But first, he had an urge to stop by his parents' restaurant.

After leaving the taxi that dropped him off, he entered the restaurant as the familiar sound of the bell clanged above him. The dinner rush was just starting and his mother was bringing out the take-out orders. His father looked up and waved to his son.

"Hey, Ba-ba," said Gordon.

"Hey, son, what brings you here tonight? Need something to go?"

Gordon casually made his way over to the back counter where his mother was organizing the take-out orders, each one with its ticket stapled neatly at the top.

"Hey, Mom," said Gordon. "And no, Ba-ba, I just came by… to say hi."

"You should go home; you're working tomorrow," advised his mother.

Gordon squeezed by his mother so that he could get a better view of the tickets and started to read off the names to himself, "Nancy, Owen, Tommy, Henry, Ingrid, Noel, George," but when he got to the last name, "Barron," he realized there wasn't a ticket for Erin.

"*Aiyah*, what are you doing back here if you're not going to help out?" asked his mother as she went back into kitchen.

"I better get going," said Gordon as his father picked up the phone and waved to his son goodbye.

Gordon stepped out of the restaurant and instinctively found himself headed east. He navigated the throngs of people along the sidewalk who were focused on getting home or to the nearest bar for drinks or dinner with friends. Time seemed to blur around him despite him glancing down at his Apple watch at roughly 5-minute intervals. But once he crossed Madison Ave., a snakelike nervousness started to unwind itself from within his gut as he neared Erin's apartment building.

In his mind, he hoped that he would just casually bump into her on the street and a natural conversation would just begin from there. But being the lawyer that he was, he questioned his intent, the seemingly random chance meeting. What he feared most, was that she might find the meeting creepy and awkward. And the optics didn't look good for two opposing attorneys to meet up in a non-professional manner either. But despite that, he found that he wasn't slowing down his pace. He had intent, and for better or worse, he was going to follow it.

As he crossed Lexington Ave, he froze mid-stride and quickly tucked himself behind the corner of the building. He slowly peered around the corner and saw her. Erin was standing in front of her apartment building, under the dark green awning with overhead lights that illuminated the red carpet below.

Erin's little black dress accentuated her body even from afar. Her posture was classy as she stood there waiting in her black high heels, with her hands gently clasped together as a tan raincoat covered them.

Every few seconds, she would look left and straight ahead again. She was waiting for someone, surmised Gordon, but from his distance, he felt confident that he was concealed enough from her to not be spotted. A flurry of thoughts raced through his mind about how he could use the situation. He could simply appear from out of the corner and as he approached her, he would wave should she look at him. But that would look too rehearsed. Perhaps, if he just walked toward her while pretending to be preoccupied with this phone and unintentionally bump into her? Yes, he liked that idea. He took out his iPhone, took a deep breath, smiled, and turned the corner, but suddenly froze.

A black sedan with a lit Lyft logo in the back windshield pulled up that piqued Erin's interest just as the driver side rear passenger door opened. A white man with swept-back dark brown hair emerged, and while he buttoned up his suit jacket, he confidently rounded the rear of the car and stepped up onto the sidewalk and greeted Erin with open arms. Erin smiled and took a couple of steps forward before she was suddenly in his full embrace. He took a couple of steps back to admire her beauty as he glanced at her eyes, to her toes and back to her eyes. A few pleasantries were exchanged before he led her to the car and opened the rear door for her. When she was comfortably seated inside, he closed the door and with a sneer, quickly rounded the rear of the car and entered the backseat. The rear lights flashed bright red for a moment before the car sped off.

Gordon stood there and as his shoulders slumped. He felt a sudden void within him in the waning shadows of the early evening.

* * *

The table candlelight flickered in its glass enclosure. It shook a bit as Richard gave one final nudge to the chair as Erin adjusted herself into it. She smiled at his chivalry as he quickly settled into his chair and unbuttoned his suit jacket. He quickly unfurled the cloth napkin and draped it across his lap and looked up at Erin to admire her beauty. She was how she looked in the Tinder profile, and he was not disappointed.

The host handed to Erin the large, fancy one-page menu, which she took with one hand as she gently swept her hair back with the other. Richard happily took the menu along with the wine list with a snarling smile. The host took leave as a young waiter came to their table.

"Good evening. My name is Antoine, and I'll be serving you tonight. May I get you any drinks to start you of with?" he asked politely.

Erin looked up, "Yes, I'd like to have a glass of chardonnay…"

"If I may," interjected Richard as Erin looked at him curiously. To the waiter he asked, "Would you bring a bottle of the Louise Jadot Chablis 2015? It's a great white to start off with and depending on how the night goes, we could move onto a full-bodied red wine," he added with a wink.

The waiter paused, looked at Erin and grinned as he replied, "Certainly sir. Right away."

The exchange between the two men didn't go unnoticed by Erin, but she could tell that Richard was confident in himself. After she matched with him on Tinder, through a few texts with him and her own sleuthing on LinkedIn, she found his credentials to be quite impressive. An Ivy League graduate and an investment banker with a million-dollar smile.

"So you're new to New York, from Boston," said Richard as he stared into her eyes.

Erin felt his piercing eyes, and she wasn't sure if she should be flattered. But she'd handled worse in the courtroom and returned the stare. "Yes, and thank you for coming out to show me around New York. I've always wanted to live…"

Richard interrupted her, "Not at all! How often does a guy like me get to take out an Asian beauty like yourself?"

Erin glanced down at the plate hiding her smile while instinctively pulling the soles of her high heels inward just a bit along the carpet. She looked back and nodded silently just as the waiter came back. He gently held the bottle of the Chablis and angled the label at Richard, who glanced it off with a nod. The waiter promptly dispensed with the opening of the wine and carefully placed the cork on the table with the label facing Richard. He then poured a small amount and with the twirl of the spout, brought it back to its upright position in front of him.

Richard looked at the glass with its glistening elixir and took it by the stem, giving it a quick swirl before taking half of it into his mouth. He swished it a couple of times as the chilled citrusy taste of the Chablis tickled his taste buds to his liking. He looked at the waiter approvingly and placed the glass back on the table. The waiter took his cue and poured a copious amount into both glasses and informed them that he would be right back to take their order.

Richard raised his glass toward Erin, and with a slight whip of her hair, she did the same.

"To new beginnings," said Richard with a smile.

"To new beginnings," Erin replied as their glasses clinked as she sipped on the Chablis. The acidity was a bit more than her liking, but the citrusy notes did balance out the overall wine, and she placed the glass down on the table. She carefully pushed herself away from the table as Richard looked up. "I'm just going to use the restroom, I'll be right back. Oh please, don't get up," she smiled as Richard stopped midway before settling back into his seat.

As she pulled away from the table and straightened up, Richard's eyes followed the lines of her backside and made his way down to her calves before he looked back up just as she turned to him. She then brought her clutch to waist level and asked a passing waiter the whereabouts of the ladies rooms. He indicated that it was at the end of the hall behind and around their table. She thanked him and was soon out of sight.

Richard finished off the Chablis and didn't hesitate to pour himself another copious glass of it. He took another gulp when his cell phone sounded. He sat upright, reached into this pant pocket for his cell and took the call.

"Dan, my man! How are you doing? Me? Oh you know me, just on another Tinder date. Of course! It's another one of these Asian chicks, man.

They are so easy! This one is fresh too! She's from Boston. I betcha I'm going to score with this one tonight and by tomorrow, I'll match up with more hot and easy Asian chicks. It's like a white guy's dream! Who needs prostitutes when you got so many Asian chicks ready to be plucked. You know what I mean?" Richard then let out a hearty laugh. "OK, I'll give you a play-by-play tomorrow man. Later."

Richard placed his cell phone on vibrate and set it aside on the table. He took another drink of the wine and noticed a couple across the way from him looking at him disapprovingly. But he didn't care that they overheard. In his mind, he was going to score that night. He raised his glass toward them and gulped the wine smugly just as Erin rounded the corner.

She looked ravishing as she smiled at him, and he could tell she was into him. She shimmied herself into the seat and placed both of her elbows onto the table while starring wondrously at him.

The waiter came back and asked if they had decided on what they would like to order. Before Richard could respond, Erin spoke, "We haven't just yet, as I had to excuse myself to the ladies room, but I've been craving oysters. You do have oysters, right?"

"Certainly," he replied.

"Well then, I'll take two dozen. How I love oysters," Erin said as she smiled at Richard.

Richard smiled back as he raised his glass up toward her and took another sip.

"And you know, it looks like we're almost done with our first bottle of Chablis. How about we move onto that full-bodied red wine?" asked Erin seductively.

Richard looked up at the waiter with a nod and then continued starring at Erin.

"Very well. I'll put the oysters in and be back with an excellent red wine. I'll look forward to take your entrée order at that time," said the waiter who then finished pouring the remainder of the wine into Richard's glass.

"That sounds delightful," said Erin.

"Well, you've certainly gotten quite feisty," remarked Richard.

"Oh, you can blame it on the wine. I get happy even with a little sip," said Erin coyly.

The waiter came back and skillfully repeated the uncorking process and poured out two new glasses of the red wine and placed the bottle onto the table.

With the waiter gone, Richard picked up his glass, leaned in and raised it toward Erin. If a little wine was already loosening her up, what would a full glass or two do to her? he wondered. In his many conquests, he found that wine and Asian women were a good pairing, and it was one that he was going to put Erin through. Erin raised her glass as well, smiled, and brought the curve of the glass close to his.

"To a night to remember," said Richard confidently.

"Actually, to a night that you'll definitely not want to remember," said Erin and she withdrew her glass.

Richard looked puzzled and smiled, "Hey gorgeous, you forgot to clink your glass."

Erin's smile suddenly went away as she straightened up, her elbow on the table while holding the glass in her right hand. "No I didn't, because I'm no easy Asian chick," Erin said firmly.

Richard realized that she must have overheard him, as he could be boisterous sometimes. He attempted to temper the situation and leaned back into the chair in a disarming posture. He looked down and back into her brown stern eyes.

"Hey, I was just joking…" said Richard.

"What? That I'm just an easy Asian chick for you… how did you say it, to pluck for tonight?" asked Erin as her voice rose.

"Hey, hey gorgeous, no need to raise…"

"And don't call me gorgeous!" Erin stammered as she rose from the table. "And like your name, you're nothing more than a dick!" she said as she tossed her wine into Richard's face as his eyes closed.

As Erin rounded the table, she grabbed his full glass of wine and tossed it into his lap and walked off as quickly as she could.

Richard raised himself from the table to the delight of the couple that had stared at him earlier and to the shock of the other customers. Richard left let out a bellicose laugh and yelled at her, "You bitch! You think you're special! You're nothing! All you Asian women are nothing! You just prostitute yourself to us white men for free and we white men are just loving it! I don't need you. There a lot more Asian chicks and they keep on matching me on Tinder! You are just another long line of easy Asian pussy!"

Erin cringed as she quickly handed the coat tag number to the host, but he already had her coat ready. She looked up at him with embarrassment and nodded as she took her coat from him.

She could hear Richard's incredulous exclamations from inside the dining area, "Look at what that Asian bitch did to my clothes!"

Erin turned away and exited the restaurant in disgust.

* * *

The slow tap of his pen as it hit the legal pad was numbing as a low thud rippled throughout the courtroom. Gordon was slightly hunched over the table as he zoned out. Harold sat next to him, and with his bifocals at the tip of his nose, he immersed himself in the newspaper. He was leaning back in his chair with his suit jacket unbuttoned, adorned with a flashy pocket square that gently wrapped itself around a cigar.

The opening of the large courtroom doors echoed through the room as a pair of high-heeled footsteps were heard. They were getting louder, and Gordon straightened up while keeping his gaze forward. He cleared his throat as he heard the gate's spring moan as it opened. Soon, it swung back into place with a flutter. The sound of the wooden chairs scraping across the marble floor was soon dulled as Erin and Meredith settled into them.

Gordon looked to his right, and Harold's face was still behind the newspaper with only the top of his head appearing above it. He then glanced over to his left and Erin's back was turned to him as she consulted with Meredith in hushed tones. At that moment, the court officer stood up and asked everyone to rise.

With everyone standing, the back door opened, and Judge Marshall came in with her billowing robe and sat down in her seat. As she adjusted herself, she waved for everyone to sit down.

"Good afternoon everyone," said Judge Marshall. "Well, we've had a couple of days, where are we?" she asked as she looked to Erin and Gordon.

Gordon rose from his chair with Harold looking on and addressed the judge. "Your Honor, my client would like to raise his offer to buy the property in question by adding an additional five-hundred thousand to the offer. That's now eight million dollars."

Erin then stood up and spoke, "Your Honor, while I appreciate opposing counsel's offer, it's simply not enough." Gordon then cast a glance in her direction. "My client feels that an offer of fifteen million dollars would be sufficient to start the conversation."

"Fifteen million dollars!" exclaimed Harold as he twisted his body with both hands planted on the table while facing in the direction of his soon to be ex-wife. "I only paid one-point-five million for it, and you want ten times that amount? Outrageous!"

"Not outrageous, Harold!" Meredith screamed back. "You know it's worth every dollar!"

Harold's crimson face suddenly swelled up, and he looked like he was about to explode in anger as he stood up from his chair. Meredith looked ready to march right on over to Harold, and suddenly both Erin and Gordon had to play linebackers and hold back their agitated clients as the sound of the gavel thundered through the air.

"Order! Order in my court!" said Judge Marshall sternly as the court officer moved to the center of the courtroom, looking at both parties. The clerk was unfazed by the commotion and silent typing.

Gordon managed to settle Harold back down into his chair, and despite Harold's stocky bulldog frame, Gordon's athletic build gave him the strength to control him.

Erin, on the other hand, being slim and trim in high heels, had to push with all her might to hold Meredith, a scorned woman who had become a bit top-heavy over time.

With both clients back in their seats and casting sinister glances at each other as their lawyers calmed them, Judge Marshall addressed the participants in the courtroom. "I will not tolerate such outbreaks in my courtroom ever again. Do I make myself clear?"

Both Erin and Gordon replied in unison, "Yes, Your Honor."

"I didn't hear it from your clients," said Judge Marshall.

Meredith nodded and Harold begrudgingly muttered "yes "underneath his breath.

"OK, well… it looks like we are far apart on this last property. You're offering eight million dollars, and you want fifteen million dollars. Maybe you two need more time to consult with each other to come to a reasonable agreement."

"That would be a good idea," said Gordon as Erin nodded.

"Well then, our next hearing will be next Tuesday. Perhaps the weekend will let cooler heads prevail and come to an agreement soon, or I will," said Judge Marshall sternly.

"Thank you, Your Honor," said Erin as Gordon nodded.

Everyone stood as Judge Marshall left the courtroom, and as the back door closed, Harold abruptly got up and without hesitation, left the courtroom giving his wife a disgruntled glance.

Meredith exchanged a few words with Erin, and soon, she also shuffled out of the courtroom.

As Erin turned, she bumped the table causing her legal pad to fall onto the floor and her pen rolled in the direction of Gordon, who noticed the noise.

"Uh, really?" she muttered underneath her breath. She pivoted on her heels bringing them together, with a brush of her hair, she gently knelt down in a graceful manner to pick up the legal pad.

This did not go unnoticed by Gordon, who walked over to the pen and bent down to pick it up. He then strode over to Erin, who looked up at him. He held out the pen to her, "Here you go."

Erin looked up into his stern eyes and sheepishly took the pen. "Thanks."

"Are you OK?" asked Gordon.

"Oh, I guess so. I've never had to hold back a client before," said Erin as she brushed her hair back once again with her eyes glancing downward.

"You're sure, you just seem a bit distracted," pressed Gordon.

She gave off a laugh, "Oh let's say on top of a passionate client, a bad Tinder date doesn't help."

Suddenly Gordon's senses perked up as he realized the Tinder date that she was referring to was probably the man that he saw last night. "It didn't go well," he thought elatedly and realized that she was single!

Gordon then loosened up with Erin and with a smile said, "Tinder? You're much classier than that."

Erin felt her cheeks blush a bit and covered her sudden embarrassment with a beautiful smile, "Well, I was really using it to meet new people who could maybe show me around as I'm new and well…"

"Well you don't need Tinder, there are many MeetUp groups for that," offered Gordon.

"You're probably right," said Erin with resignation. "Hey, what do you make of our clients?"

Gordon chuckled. "They really love that building. What's your angle?"

Suddenly, Erin's lawyer instincts went up and with a coy smile, "Well Mr. Attorney, you know I can't tell you that."

Gordon sensing the perky tone played along, "Are you sure? You tell me, and maybe we can compromise."

"I never compromise. My client has a price, as does everyone," Erin responded.

"Then my office, let's talk and I'll tell you about this great city that we call New York," offered Gordon.

Erin was caught off guard by the offer, but she recovered quickly and responded, "Sure, we can do that. Your office then, say 3PM?" she asked.

"3PM sounds great," said Gordon as he handed her his white linen embossed business card.

* * *

Later that afternoon, a few minutes before his meeting with Erin, Gordon found himself preoccupied with tidying up his office. On the shelf where he kept his personal items, he angled his Columbia Law School Degree more prominently. He adjusted the pictures of him crossing the finish line at the Boston Marathon. He then angled his pictures of when he tried out for American Ninja, and finally felt everything was perfect to show him in the best light.

The buzzer on his desk phone rang, and he strode over to it. "Hello Gordon, an Erin Chung here to see you," Julia announced.

Gordon's heart skipped a beat in anticipation, "Please send her in."

He quickly got behind his desk and tried a pose of him hunched over his desk working, but that made him look too studious. He quickly got into a pose by leaning back in his chair propping his legs up, but realized that looked too arrogant. Then he caught a glance of Julia through his glass wall and leaned back in his chair, picked up his phone pretending to look at it only to realize it was upside down.

A light knock sounded, and Julia pushed the glass door open, allowing Erin to enter. She had her sunglasses propped up on her head and gave a wonderful smile to Gordon, who smiled back as he placed the phone down as he got up. He adjusted his suit jacket and walked around his desk and warmly greeted her with a handshake.

"Nice to see you once again, counselor," said Gordon playfully. "Why don't you place your bag on the chair."

Erin smiled and did as she was asked. She was about to sit down in the other chair when Gordon motioned her to follow him to the window. "Oh, a man trying to impress a girl by showing him the view from his office," she thought.

As she stood next to him, he took a furtive glance at her to admire her before turning back to the view. "And there is the famous Central Park."

Erin looked down at the lush green expanse that was perfectly nestled into a city of rising skyscrapers. She had to admit to herself that she was genuinely impressed by the view.

"I'm not sure if you know much about Central Park but it was designed by Olmsted…"

"Olmsted, he also designed the Emerald Necklace in Boston," interrupted Erin. "Sorry, didn't mean to interrupt, go on."

Gordon smiled, "No problem. I didn't know that Olmsted also designed the park in Boston. Is that the Boston Common?"

"Not really. He designed a number of parks around Boston. If you colored them all green and view them from above, it looks like an emerald necklace. I think it's beautiful."

Gordon stared at Erin and remarked, "Beautiful." Erin looked up and he suddenly caught himself by adding, "Central Park, it's just as beautiful. Looks like Olmsted had a way of connecting New York and Boston."

"I guess so," Erin responded. "Columbia, is that where you went for law?"

Gordon was inwardly elated that she caught sight of his big diploma and nonchalantly walked over to it as she followed.

He looked up at it with humble pride and said, "Yep, that's me. A lot of countless, sleepless nights studying up on cases. How about you?"

"I can relate. It was like that for me at Boston College Law… Hey what's that?" asked Erin as she pointed to one of his pictures.

Gordon picked up one of the pictures and displayed it for her, "That's me crossing the Boston Marathon last year!"

"Oh wow, you ran the Boston Marathon! That's really impressive," said Erin with a smile. "But what's with the lightning bolt on the red shirt?" she asked bewilderedly.

"What? You don't know the Flash? That's the really fast superhero from DC comics. That's why people call me Flash Gordon," said Gordon with a smirk.

Erin looked puzzled. "Wait a second, aren't Flash Gordon and the Flash two totally different characters?"

Gordon looked stupefied, "Um, yah, that's a technicality," said Gordon as Erin let out a laugh. "But growing up with the name Gordon, everyone always called me Flash Gordon, and since I liked the Flash, when I ran, I kind of adopted the superhero too."

"How adorable!" exclaimed Erin as she looked up at him and then back down at the shelf. "What about those?"

Gordon took the marathon photo and placed it back on the shelf and picked up one of the other photos. "This is my failed attempt at American Ninja Warrior," said Gordon.

Erin's mouth gaped open in stunned belief, "No way, you did American Ninja? Whoa, look at your muscles!"

Gordon suddenly straightened up proudly to put his physique in the best light just as Erin look up at him. She quickly cast her eyes across his broad shoulders and chest. She suddenly looked down in embarrassment, shuffled her feet a bit to distract herself and looked back at the photo.

"So that's me right at the start. I was playing to the crowd…" explained Gordon when Erin interjected.

"The same red Flash T-Shirt from the marathon?" asked Erin.

Gordon chuckled, "Yep, same shirt, kind of like a good-luck charm. Here's the photo where I was on the hang climb," he said as he swapped the photo that she was holding.

Erin looked down as the photo caught him dangling precariously upside down and holding onto rock climbing-like hand holds. She pursed her lips as she noticed his triceps in action and deliberately didn't glance toward him. He then swapped in another photo in which he was dangling from the doorknob obstacle, which really showed his upper body strength.

Erin looked up at Gordon with a sheepish grin and handed back the photo. "Very impressive," Erin said with a smile. "How far did you make it?"

"Well, I made it all the way to stage 3, and on the last obstacle, I went in like the Flash but came through with a splash instead."

Erin chuckled, "Did you just come up with that right now?"

"I guess I did," said Gordon.

"Clever," she said.

"Well…" continued Gordon before he was interrupted.

"What obstacle did you make a splash in?" asked Erin.

"I'm not going to tell you that…"

"What? Why not?"

"Because it's somewhat embarrassing…"

"Wait, are you on YouTube?"

Gordon paused when he realized that he was.

"You are on YouTube!" said Erin excitedly.

Gordon brought his hand to his bowed head in shame and pulled it away. With a smile he said, "Let's get back to this case."

Erin let out a laugh, "I'm going to look you up once I get home."

"Please don't," he jokingly pleaded.

"The Flash makes a splash," said Erin in a melodious taunt.

Gordon pointed to a chair by the table along the window, which she took. Gordon hovered over the table as he poured out two glasses of water and offered one to her. He then sat down across from her.

"Crazy clients we have, don't we?" asked Gordon.

"Oh my God. I thought they were going to fight right there in the courtroom!" said Erin.

They both let out a laugh and knew that they were thinking the same thing.

"What's up with this property? An old apartment building in Queens?" asked Erin.

"I'm not sure. It's not exactly an investment area, especially for two wealthy people like them. What's with the fifteen million dollar bombshell?" asked Gordon.

She swayed her head a bit and responded, "It's her price. She said if Harold really wants it, he'd pay it. Can he?"

"It's not a matter of can't, I think it's he won't," said Gordon firmly.

"Well that's her price, what more can I say?"

"You know, if we can't get our clients to agree, the judge is going decide for us," said Gordon.

"Yes, that's true, and it's not going to look great for my first case here in New York," said Erin despondently.

"Well maybe it's not about the money…" said Gordon before he was interrupted.

"It's always about the money," said Erin with a smirk.

"Hear me out. Maybe there is something about the property that we don't know about, which is why they both want it so badly. She seems intent on keeping it, while he seems intent on getting it back. There's got to be something with the property," said Gordon.

Erin thought for a moment, "Maybe. Should we just start asking them?"

"I can do that if you ask Meredith," offered Gordon.

"Deal," said Erin as she raised her glass.

Gordon looked at her and didn't raise his glass. He then started, "You know, it's bad luck to toast to water. How about a handshake instead?" he asked as he extended his hand.

Erin liked his attention to etiquette and put down the glass. She placed her hand into his and shook it firmly.

"And maybe, after this case is done, I can take you out for drinks and show you New York."

Erin wasn't sure if he was flirting or asking her out on a date. It was just drinks, but she really didn't know his intentions. Then, she felt her hand in his was getting a bit warm with embarrassment. She smiled and simply said, "Sure, I'd like a tour guide."

Behind the smile she thought to herself, did she just call the Flash Asian American Ninja Warrior a tour guide? Why did she make it sound so awkward? she thought. Soon she felt his hand loosening, and to her relief, she gently pulled away.

Suddenly, she heard the all-too -familiar muffled double tone of her iPhone in her bag. She rose up and walked toward her bag to retrieve it. Gordon followed her, and he suddenly saw her cheery expression drop.

"What's wrong?" he asked.

Erin looked up as she fidgeted with her phone, "Oh it's nothing."

"Well it can't be nothing. You were cheery one moment, and now you're not. What's wrong?" he asked again soothingly.

After letting out a heavy sigh, "Ugh, remember how I mentioned I had a bad Tinder date? Well, he texted me again. God, why did I give him my number? Now I can't get rid of him," she said with a tone of regret.

Gordon could see Erin's distraught expression and extended his hand outward towards the phone.

"Huh?" asked Erin.

"Your phone," asked Gordon gently.

"No, I don't want you text him back," replied Erin.

"I promise I won't do that, but let me show you how to block him,"

Gordon suggested, and after a few seconds of hesitation, Erin reluctantly gave him her phone.

"Please don't read his text, it's pretty ugly," beseeched Erin.

Gordon nodded, and though he tried to obey her request, he couldn't help but glance at the text already on the screen, which was littered with profanity directed at Erin. Gordon tried not to let it faze him, but from within, anger started to stir.

He took the phone and pivoted toward her so that she could see what he was doing. From the text, he clicked on the info icon, then the right arrow, which brought up Richard's contact profile. He then scrolled to the very bottom and showed her the feature "Block this caller."

Erin's eyes lit up as she exclaimed, "I didn't know you could do that!" as she took the phone back, and her happiness brought a smile to Gordon's face.

Erin, who was still smiling looked back up at Gordon and said, "Thank you. I'm such a noob at technology sometimes."

"You're welcome, and before you block him, just be sure that he will ultimately leave you alone if you ignore him. If he becomes a problem, you may want to document his text for the police."

"God, I've been in New York for less than two weeks, and I've already attracted a creep," said Erin resignedly.

"I have some friends in NYPD if you ever need help with this creep," offered Gordon.

"Aww, that's sweet that you offered. I'll let you know if I need your help," said Erin appreciatively.

"But you know, you don't deserve that, and you deserve better," said Gordon.

"Thanks. I appreciate that," smiled Erin as she started to feel her cheeks flush and for a moment, she didn't see Gordon as the lawyer but rather the Flash Asian American Ninja Warrior.

Gordon shifted his feet a bit and felt that the silence was getting awkwardly long, though it was only a second in reality. "Um, now that you know how to submit a text injunction on the creep…"

"Text injunction!" said Erin as she let out a light laugh, "Did you just make that up?"

"Yes, I guess I did," said Gordon with a smile as his ears perked up to her lovely laugh.

"That's so adorable," said Erin.

"I'm glad you think so," Gordon replied. "Any ways, about the case, we'll both try to find out what's up with this apartment complex and maybe find an agreement?"

With a smile, Erin extended her hand, to which Gordon took as she said, "Deal!"

* * *

"Are you going to get her to come down?" asked Harold as he clipped the end of his cigar before he began to light it with a wooden match. The flame undulated as he drew back on the cigar while giving it a quarter turn with each puff that he took. Soon the cigar was lit as red embers snaked along its end

Gordon clipped both ends of his Monte Cristo Eagle Master cigar and performed a similar ritual as he spoke. "Harold, I will definitely try. The fifteen million dollars is totally above market price…"

"It's not about the money," said Harold in between puffs as he stared off from Gordon toward a corner in his office. "She just doesn't want me to have that building."

Gordon saw an opening and asked, "Well if it isn't about the money, then what is it about that building?"

"I can pay the fifteen million if I have to!" said Harold bluntly. "If she won't come back to me, then she will definitely not have that building!"

Gordon paused as he sensed the frustration in Harold's tone. He put his cigar arm down along the armrest, since he had about half an inch of ash on his fine Cuban cigar. He looked at Harold and pressed him, "But what's so special about the building that you just have to keep it away from her?"

Harold's shoulder's slouched a bit as he settled back into the plush leather seat and took another puff of his cigar. "You know kid, I was young once like you. I was just starting my business, and I started it all from my apartment, in that very building."

"Oh, you had an apartment in that building and it brings back good memories?" asked Gordon.

"Well, that too," said Gordon when his tone turned slyly and he added, "It's where I met Meredith."

* * *

Across town, in her penthouse suite, Meredith dangled a treat over her dog's nose, letting the dog beg before letting it nibble the treat away from her hand. As she grabbed another treat, Erin, who sat in the couch across from her smiled at the affection between Meredith and the dog.

"Do you think Harold will pay the fifteen million dollars?" asked Erin?

"He probably will. He's got the money, that son of a bitch," exclaimed Meredith. "And then I'll raise the price again."

"Meredith, you can't do that..."

"I sure can, it's my property! And he will not get his grubby fingers on it as long as I'm alive," said an agitated Meredith.

"Help me understand, Meredith. Why is it so important that he can't have that property? What's so special about it?"

Seeing that she had frightened her dog, Meredith put away the bag of treats and pulled the dog in closer, soothingly caressing its fear away.

"Meredith, why can't you let go of the apartment building?" Erin asked gently.

As Meredith caressed her dog, she simply muttered underneath her breath, "It's where we first met."

* * *

"Let me tell you, kid. It was just me with this crazy idea to sell women's blazers with shoulder pads. Dolly Parton, this bombshell blonde who had a pair, I tell ya, a real sexy gal way before your time, kid, showed up in this movie called *9 to 5*. You should look it up when you get a chance. It was about working women in the office trying to be more than secretaries, and I saw the future fashion trend! Working women in the workplace, but they couldn't compete with the boys, and I thought, they need a suit that would make them look more authoritative but feminine too. A woman in a dress may not be taken seriously in the workplace. But if they put on a jacket with shoulder pads, they would look more serious. You know what I mean?" asked Harold.

Gordon nodded in agreement but really had no idea what Harold was talking about. However he made a mental note to stream *9 to 5*.

"I'll be the first to admit, I wasn't a seamstress. I bought the smallest men's jacket that I could find and stuffed it with this padding that I made from sandwich bags, toilet paper, and duct tape. I thought if I could present my concept to the good folks at Macy's, they would get it right? No, they didn't get it, and I was laughed at. I have to admit, the working concept using a men's blazer wasn't very feminine, you know. But I believed in my idea, so get this, I bought a sewing machine and read that manual inside and out. I tried to tailor the men's jacket, but it looked horrible, and I knew I had to take it to the next level. I bought fabric and patterns for suit jackets. But the problem was, there were only men's patterns! It was frustrating."

Harold's eyes lit up. It was obvious to Gordon that Harold enjoyed telling this story. He placed the cigar down in the ashtray and with animated hands, he continued.

"I was trying to make these feminine jackets, and it wasn't working out. They were horrible, and I was at my wits end. And I remember that hopeless night like it was yesterday. I was down in the laundry room and down on my luck. I was short on quarters, and I bent over onto the washer, just trying to take a break from life's misery. Then I hear this voice saying, 'Are you OK?' I looked up, and there she was, this beautiful young thing. Let me tell you, I know she's a little frumpy now, but boy, when she was in her 20s, she was this beautiful woman, slender and best pair of gams I ever laid eyes on!"

Gordon had never seen this side of Harold, excited and jovial. Then Harold looked Gordon straight in the eyes and continued, "Kid, you'll know when you meet the right woman. When she asked if I was OK, I must have looked like a total loser. But I recomposed myself, and I looked at her and I said, 'I'm all out of quarters, and if you know your way around a sewing machine, then you'd be an angel sent from heaven.'"

Then she said the damndest thing, "Quarters I don't got, but I do know my way around a sewing machine."

* * *

An incredulous Erin pressed forward, "You met Harold in that apartment building?"

Meredith's face lit up as she responded, "I sure did! I didn't tell you this story? Of course not, Heaven's to Betsy! It was in the laundry room, and I come in to pick up my clothes from the dryer and I see this bloke hugging the washing machine. But he was quite the handsome fellow. I asked him if he was OK. He looked at me and said he had no quarters, and he asked the strangest thing. He asked if I could sew. It just happened that I was a seamstress for a textile company not too far away."

"He began to tell me about his idea, and I have to be honest, I thought it was dumbest thing ever. It's not every day that you meet a man interested in women's clothing, let alone making it. But I loved his passion and him wanting to make women look more successful. Back then, I was a simple girl with a simple job. Being a secretary was what most women could hope for in those days. When I was young and naïve, I could only dream of being one of those women. That would not be my destiny, but after I heard his story, I thought, wouldn't it be nice to sew these new blazers for women who would be ready to be part of the office in some big ole' company?"

Erin was engrossed with how her client met her first love and asked, "You and Harold started dating then?"

Meredith gave out a laugh, "Oh no, dear, Harold wasn't my type. He was jobless and was just scraping by. I was looking for an office man, but what Harold was working on sounded like fun. When he asked if I could help, I said sure. And thank goodness I came in. He had no experience designing women's clothing, so I had to help him make custom patterns. I will say though, he had an eye for how the blazer should look on a woman. Men, you know, they are so much more visual," she said with a wink.

"We also had no mannequins to fit the dresses, so I was the fitting model too!" Meredith let out a laugh. "I was so slim back then, just like you! Oh how

I missed those days, being young and beautiful."

"You look great, Meredith!" reassured Erin as Meredith continued, "Oh you're so sweet. After a week, I had sewn a few concepts together. They were strong but also feminine, for the new 9 to 5 girl, as Harold would say."

* * *

"She was a sewing angel! She had sewn these stunning feminine blazer suit jackets that looked great! Back then, I didn't have a mannequin, so she was the model too. And let me tell you, she can definitely model! They looked so great on her, I knew they would looked great on the next generation of 9 to 5 girls!"

"You must have had your first big break," asked Gordon.

"Yeah, I'm getting to that. I made my usual round, and you said it, a regional clothing retailer liked the concept and put in an order for a hundred units! It was an amazing feeling! I rushed back to my apartment and burst through the door. Meredith was just trying on a new blazer that she had just sewn together. I was so excited that I didn't notice her pulling the suit jacket together. I had this big grin across my face and showed her the order for a hundred units!"

"I could see that she was excited because she grabbed the order with both of her hands, and the jacket split open and I could see her bra."

Gordon's eyes widened as he asked, "And what did you do next?"

* * *

"Then he kissed me!" exclaimed Meredith!

Erin was so enamored with the story that she blurted out, "He kissed you?"

"Oh, he did more than that, honey!" said an excited Meredith. "At first, I was so taken aback by his kiss, but there was so much passion. I kissed him right back. He grabbed the order out of my hand and threw it onto the table. I must have blushed so hard, but right then and there, I knew he was the man for me. He pulled me back into him and we kissed and fooled around like teenagers on his couch for the rest of the night."

Meredith slid her right side into the couch as she cuddled one of the throw pillows. A smile swept across her face as her reddish hair flowed along the curve of her face.

"Then with every new big order he got, we were that much more passionate together," said Meredith as her voice trailed away.

* * *

"It was the best sex ever!" proclaimed Harold. "Those were the best days of my life. My business was growing, and I found the love of my life. So I bought the entire building when I could afford to do so."

"You wanted to preserve it," said Gordon. "It was where everything began for you and her."

"Yah, and if she wants me out of her life, she's not going to get the building where I gave her the best loving that any man could do!" hollered Harold as he took another puff of his cigar.

* * *

"And if he thinks he can divorce me and forget me, I'm not going to give him the one place where we fell in love!" exclaimed Meredith.

Erin interjected, "You want to keep the building…"

"Because it's where I fell in love, and I don't want him to have it!"

Just then, both Gordon and Erin realized together and separately, "They still love each other."

* * *

Gordon was steadily tapping his pen on the legal pad. He was scheming about how he could get his client and his soon to be ex-wife, whom he still loved, to make up while still serving the needs of his client. He wondered if Meredith still thought the same way about Harold. They may have been passionately in love then, but they'd been estranged for the past year. Just then, he heard the familiar sounds of high heels coming down the marble aisle and turned around to see Erin, followed by Meredith.

Erin cast a quick glance over at Gordon before bringing her attention back to Meredith by holding the gate open for her. Soon they settled into their seats.

A tap came upon Gordon's shoulder and he turned around. Harold leaned in a bit and simply said, "Pay her the fifteen million. That building is mine."

Gordon nodded in acknowledgement when a devilish smile crept across his face. He had an idea as he looked over at Erin. He let out a sigh as he admired her, her grace, and the way she had twisted her body away from him toward Meredith in consultation. He wanted the case to be over so that they were no longer opposing attorneys, which would allow him to ask her out.

The court officer stood at attention and asked everyone to rise. He then let in Judge Marshall, who looked stern and ready to continue with the divorce proceedings. She sat down and then motioned for everyone to sit down with a quick wave of her hand.

"Good afternoon, everyone," said Judge Marshall. "So, here we are again. At our last meeting, you were willing to offer eight million and you want fifteen million. Who's going to blink first?"

"Fifteen million, your honor. My client is willing to pay what is being asked," stated Gordon as he finished buttoning his suit jacket as he rose up on both feet.

"Well that sounds..." began Judge Marshall before she was interrupted.

"Excuse me, your Honor, my client had a change of mind, she now wants twenty million." Harold gaped just as Gordon cast an incredulous look towards Erin.

"Excuse me?" asked the judge.

Erin pulled out a folder and walked over to the court officer, handed him a sheet of paper, then came toward Gordon. She was distracted by his tall frame and couldn't help but see the Flash Asian American Ninja Warrior that he was. But she held her composure and handed him a copy of the sheet.

As Erin walked back to her table, Gordon once again couldn't help noticing just how graceful she was, and her confident poise was melting him on the inside. A sudden warmth snaked itself around his neck and he had to abruptly immerse himself in looking down at the paper full of numbers.

"As you can see in this budget forecast that I will enter in as Exhibit A, many of the apartments are below market rates," stated Erin.

"They're low because it's for our more modestly paid employees," said Meredith.

"Mrs. Weintraub, please don't disturb the proceedings," admonished Judge Marshall.

"For example, apartment 1A on the first floor could go for 2-3 times what it is going for now," said Erin.

Meredith's and Harold's ears perked up when Erin mentioned apartment 1A. It was their beloved apartment.

Erin continued, "If all the apartments were brought up to market rate within a year, this last property in question would be worth the twenty million that Meredith is now asking. As her attorney, I'm just looking out for her best interests."

Judge Marshall turned to Gordon, "Well counselor, what say you?"

Gordon should have consulted with Harold, but he didn't blink. Instead, he produced a sheet of his own from a folder and handed it to the court officer who then handed it to the judge. He turned and walked toward Erin, who had her eyes fixed on him as he handed to her his sheet with a smile.

From his table, Gordon began, "As you can see Your Honor, all forecast aside, I wanted to see the actual fair market value of the apartment building, and it became clear that the building is in dire need of renovations. But renovations would also mean that many things would need to be brought up to code, and that can get very expensive. The apartment building is not worth twenty million. As is, it's not even fifteen million. It's eight million at best, but I doubt that we can reach an agreement on eight million dollars."

A silence hovered over the courtroom before Judge Marshall said, "What do you recommend?"

Gordon looked over at Erin, who was also waiting for his answer, "I would let you dictate a price where the profits would be split evenly, but given everything I've seen, I think it would be best to have an investor buy it, demolish the building and rebuild it."

"No!" exclaimed both Harold and Meredith.

Judge Marshall looked at them both and asked, "Why 'no?' Gordon's proposal sounds very reasonable, and from what I've seen, I don't think you two will come to a mutually satisfactory number. And with the building being in such a state of disrepair, demolishing and rebuilding anew may be a good investment."

"You can't demolish that building!" uttered Harold as he stood up with both of his fists on the table.

"And why not, Mr. Weintraub? Even as a businessman, you can see that the numbers don't add up, even though you're willing to pay twenty million insane dollars for it," said Judge Marshall.

"It's not about the money!" uttered a very agitated Mr. Weintraub.

"Then what is it that it's worth twenty million dollars?"

"Memories," said a defeated Mr. Weintraub as he cast his eyes downward. The answer drew a startled stare from Meredith.

"Please explain," asked Judge Marshall.

"Apartment 1A. It's where it all began, my business, but most importantly, it's where I met Meredith. I'm an older man now, but those memories keep me smiling and without them, I don't know what I'll do."

"Oh Harold!" exclaimed as Meredith bumped Erin aside and walked past the table's edge. "You didn't want just the building, but you wanted it because it reminded you of us?"

Harold looked over and walked past Gordon and stood face-to-face with his wife. "If you were going to leave me, I wasn't going to let the best part of us go. Call me selfish."

"I don't think it's selfish, I think it's romantic," said a blushing Meredith. "Because I wanted the same thing, and I wasn't going to let you have it if you were going to leave me."

A humbled Harold then asked questioningly, "You don't want to leave me?"

"Of course not, silly! And you don't want to leave me?" asked Meredith.

"Why would you think that?" asked a puzzled Harold.

Meredith's expression collapsed into happiness with a tear from one eye as she walked toward Harold with open arms. Harold's grumpy face was overcome with a smile, and he walked toward Meredith and grasped both her hands.

"What happened to us, Harold?" asked Meredith.

"I don't know. The business? The charities? Life? Old age?" offered Harold.

"Oh Harold, I have a crazy idea. No more of this Central Park ritzy lifestyle, let's both move back into the apartment!" said Meredith!

Harold's eyes lit up, "That's a wonderful idea! We can renovate it!" Harold exclaimed as he leaned in to touch his nose to Meredith's and their lips just barely touched when the sound of the gavel interrupted their courtroom rekindling.

"Ahem," interjected Judge Marshall. "I can see that a mutual settlement may be underway. Am I to assume that there is no longer a need for a divorce?"

Both Gordon and Erin looked at their embracing clients who quickly smiled. They looked at each other as they both said together, "No divorce."

"Well, that's good to hear. Then with that, let me dismiss this case and let you get busy... with the renovations," said Judge Marshall sneakily as the gavel came down.

"You heard the judge, we got some renovations!" said Harold.

Meredith smiled and as if Erin anticipated her, she grabbed her bag from Erin's hands. "Thank you! You did a wonderful job!"

Harold also turned quickly to Gordon, "I'm going to put in a good word to Geoffrey for you! Good work!" He then moved the gate to let Meredith through as they both trotted down the aisle together like giddy schoolchildren.

Gordon and Erin exchanged smiles and went about getting their belongings. As Erin approached the gate, Gordon was there and with a smile, pushed it open for her. Erin smiled and nodded gently, and they too walked down the aisle out of the courtroom.

As they found themselves outside of the courtroom, Erin exclaimed with her portfolio held across her chest, "That was amazing!" as she turned to Gordon.

He looked just as relieved. "It was! Wait, did you know it wasn't about the money too?"

Erin nodded with a brimming smile. "I did. And when you suggested the demolition—that was brilliant!"

Gordon deflected the compliment but replied, "Thanks, and with your forecast, it was a perfect segue into the demolition idea. You like anticipated my move."

Erin graciously took credit, "I did, didn't I?" she boasted as she flashed her beautiful smile.

Gordon couldn't contain himself any longer and leaned in for a kiss. But his anxious lips were suddenly met by her portfolio. He pulled back immediately and saw the stunned look on Erin's face.

He quickly stood up and could feel the embarrassment on his face but quickly apologized, "I'm sorry, I didn't mean to be so fast..."

"Like the Flash?" asked Erin.

A chuckle was ready to emerge, but he didn't as Erin pulled him in by his tie and placed her lips onto his. Gordon then leaned in and gently placed his hand behind the small of her back and pulled her in for a more sensual kiss.

Back in the courtroom, the court officer then took out some folded bills from his front pocket and pulled out a single. He walked over to the judge and with a sigh, handed over the one-dollar bill to her waiting hand.

"Hmph, and you thought I was wrong on this one," said Judge Marshall smugly.

"You got me on this one," said the court officer. "I for sure thought they were going to divorce."

"It's not always about the money," said the judge. "But I'll tell you what, I'll wager a dollar that there's something between those two as well."

"You sure about that? She fine, and you know Asian women, they usually don't go for their own kind," he said.

The judge gave him a dirty look and added, "I've got a feeling about this one. He's playing the long game. So, one dollar?"

The court officer smiled and said, "You're on."

* * *

Later that evening, Erin was talking on her phone with her senior partner as she was unpacking some things in her apartment, which was still strewn with boxes and packing material.

"Thank you! Yes. I think they found a new purpose in life," said Erin with a smile. "Oh, that's nice to hear that she said nice things about me. I'm still settling into New York. A lot of places to explore. Oh tonight?" she asked questioningly just as a knock came upon her door.

Dressed in her slim jeans, a cute Boston College T-Shirt, and white socks, she strode over to the door as she replied, "Oh, I can't tonight."

Erin opened the door to see a beaming Gordon leaning up against the door jam. He was still dressed in his suit with his tie loosened as he cradled in his hands, a brown paper bag with a green-and-white order ticket stapled to the top.

Erin looked teasingly downward at the floor and then back into his eyes and said to her senior partner, "Not tonight, I ordered take out."

IT'S ABOUT TIME

The time had come. After five grueling years of research, in which Brandon Lu sacrificed probably more than he was willing to admit, he was on the brink of a discovery of a lifetime. He closed his eyes to relieve the stress that had built up behind them, but he was also deeply excited. When the results from the simulation came back positive for the first time, he excitedly ran a second and a third simulation. When the third set of results came back positive, he let out an excited holler that echoed throughout the steel-lined room to no one's attention other than his own.

Pentagon funding for his project was cut due to what the government termed, "a lack of credible evidence to achieve the stated objective." His staff was laid off and scurried away under the shroud of an intimidating federal non-disclosure agreement. Even his once-ardent believers, the university itself that had sponsored his project and the technicians who worked night and day for his dream, ultimately gave up on what had been at first such an exciting idea. But Brandon insisted they needed to be patient, and that they were foolish to rush something that could change the world.

But in the end, Brandon was the only person who believed in the project. With hundreds of millions spent that left a hulking, circular steel contraption that resembled a large centrifuge that could fit into a small hangar, he was the only one furthering the project, and Brandon would have been fine with that. But the reality was, in two short weeks, the Pentagon would mothball the top-secret facility hidden within a university's physics department, powered by a secret nuclear reactor.

Time was running out for Brandon's dream, but if his experiment was successful that night, time would no longer matter. For Brandon had discovered the power of time travel.

His cell phone rang suddenly, and his head jerked in its direction as it rang again on a table not far away. He straightened up from his chair, stretching out his six-foot frame, and walked toward the cell phone. It was his wife, and for a moment, despite his wariness, he let out a smile. She was the only person who had stood by him, but even he admitted that his work came between him and his seven-year marriage. They still had no children, and he knew she was getting anxious, as she was about to turn 32. He himself was almost 38,but like many men, he felt he had the luxury of time to ponder kids.

On the third ring, he answered, and using the usual Korean greeting, he said, "*Yo bo se oh?*" Though he wasn't Korean himself, he had learned many things from his wife, and his wife learned a lot from him, as he was Chinese American. He was an advanced quantum physics professor, and she was a graduate student in his quantum mechanics class. Catherine Kim was an exceptionally bright student and she amazed him intellectually. But it was her dazzling smile that really captivated him. He never thought he would become romantically involved with one of his students, fearing what others may think. However, fate intervened and they wed one year later.

"Are you going to be late again?" Catherine asked.

After a hesitation he replied, "Yes, but I'll be home shortly."

There was a pause, and Catherine simply said, "I left dinner for you in the fridge. You can just reheat it."

There was a sense of distance in her tone. It was the same story over and over again. Brandon had not been on time for dinner over the last year, and though he knew it disturbed her deeply, it could not be helped. But each time she called him, he promised that he would be home, only to break that promise. Eventually, Catherine resigned herself to calling him only out of routine, knowing that each time it would end in a broken promise.

Brandon wanted to tell her he had just achieved the breakthrough that he had pursued for so long, but his time travel project was another sore point in their marriage. It was the reason for his absence from his marriage, and Catherine bitterly resented it. She once supported Brandon unconditionally, but as time wore on, she too lost hope, especially when their marriage was affected.

"Thank you, honey. Everything will change after tonight."

"Good night," she simply said and the call ended before he could wish her the same.

The phone's display faded away until the time appeared in its place. It was 10:25 PM.

"Everything will be different from this night onward," he thought. He would make it up to her once he could prove that time travel was possible. He would show the Pentagon brass how wrong they were when they did not extend him the funding that he needed. Without it, he was forced to toil away on the project for the past year alone.

He walked back to the large flat-panel display that showed the status of the time machine. It would take two hours alone to prepare the machine. He maneuvered the mouse to the button that said "Import." With a click of the mouse, the newly working destination algorithm was fed from the simulator and into the actual time matrix and soon, he would be the first person to travel through time.

With a bit of nervousness that clung to him, he looked up to survey the round contraption with its steel-grated floor. At the center was a seemingly solid black circle, which in fact would open up to unleash the temporal vortex.

With recent temporal discoveries and hundreds of millions of dollars from the Pentagon, the temporal chamber was built to exacting standards to spin around without any friction using new state-of-the-art magnetic super conductors to achieve phenomenal speeds. With the chamber built, the temporal vortex became a reality. But the Pentagon lacked the one key element to make it work: the destination algorithm. In a sense, they lacked the GPS system for time travel. That's where Brandon stepped in as he tackled the complex and elusive mathematical algorithm. But only that night, after months of toiling, had the simulations finally worked. He had his destination algorithm but there was one catch: each journey through time could only last six hours. Like a boomerang, his corporeal matter would eventually return to its original time and place.

Brandon let out a sigh, and with his mouse, he clicked on the button labeled, "Engage." The lights from within the monstrous temporal chamber turned on, the hum of mechanics from underneath began to rumble to life. Jets of super-cooled gases shot out in spurts from underneath the platform, and a soft hum soon filled the air.

Brandon stood tall and proud as he marveled at his work through his soulful brown eyes. He took off the long white lab coat that hung from his slender athletic frame and ran his hand through his black hair, which was a bit longer than usual.

After a couple of hours with the time machine in its optimal state, he peered down at his computer display. All the diagnostics read green. He only had to choose when and where. Conceivably he could simply return to the point of origin in a different time, but he was afraid of who might be there to greet him, since his project was scrapped. He also needed to be sure that the space in which he would appear in would also be empty, free of any matter that he had no desire to materialize into. But he already had that alternate location, something that he had planned a few months back: the basement in his home. He had cordoned off a part of the basement as his own work area.

Using the temporal chamber as the point of origin, he programmed his home's coordinates into the time machine. His next decision was when. Though he thought about the past, he decided against it. The future is where the excitement would be, and he decided that his first trip would be a personal trip.

He would go exactly one year into the future to see how his life had been affected by his achievement. He would see how happy the future him would be with his wife. In the end, time heals all wounds, and he so desperately wanted to see himself and his wife happy. He was sure that would be the case.

He entered the date for exactly one year in the future into the time machine, with the hope of surreptitiously appearing in his own basement. He found himself excited once more as he stared down at the display. The future time was 12:30 AM of May 1, 2008, and at the time of his return from the future, it would be May 1, 2007, 6:30 AM.

The GoPro camera was activated to capture the entire event for posterity. He locked down the facility and denied all access to the computers except for his own account. Though no one had been in the facility in the past year, he thought it prudent to be absolutely sure.

Finally, he set the timer to start the time machine in one minute. As the minute began to count down, he briskly walked toward the time machine and up the cold steel stairs into the circular temporal chamber that measured some fifty feet in diameter. The door to the chamber sealed automatically upon his entry, and he calmly stepped into the middle of the temporal vortex. His heart started to race when he realized that there was no override button within the chamber—it was outside. For a moment, Brandon thought that perhaps he had made a fatal mistake. He looked up to see that there was only 10 seconds remaining on the countdown clock. He tried to calm himself down by exhaling while clenching his fists. Then the countdown reached zero, and the room began to spin.

The circular walls quickly picked up speed, and soon a large hum was heard from beneath his feet. The power that would be needed to propel him into the future was about to be released through the temporal vortex and accelerated instantaneously into the spinning temporal chamber. A feeling of warmth began to travel upward and through Brandon's body as he clenched his teeth in preparation for the inevitable. The black circle beneath Brandon's feet suddenly opened up and he looked down to see a bright light flare upward. Brandon had just shut his eyes in time and the last thing he remembered was letting out an audible grunt as a tingling pain shot through his body.

When Brandon opened his eyes, he was momentarily blinded. They soon adjusted, and he realized he was in a dark space. The floor was no longer metallic, but concrete. He took a couple of steps forward and when he could make out the shape of his basement, he smiled uncontrollably.

He had done it! He had succeeded in moving instantly from one point to another but did he really travel one year into the future, he wondered? He needed proof. Being mindful that it should be a bit after 12:30 AM, he didn't want to wake up his wife, but knowing himself, his future self may be waiting to surprise him. As he pondered the temporal humor of that scenario, Brandon decided that seeing himself was not something he had ever envisioned. But if temporal mechanics were to hold true, his future self would have known of his maiden trip, since it would now be part of his past.

There was a row of storage boxes along the wall, but otherwise, everything seemed in order. He made his way to the bottom of the stairs and grasped the rail. As he placed his right foot onto the first step, he hesitated and nervously thought that maybe the trip wasn't a great idea after all. A ton of questions about temporal discipline rushed into his head, but in the end, curiosity won out.

With each step he climbed upward, he kept saying to himself, "Please be asleep." He reached the top of the stairs and grasped the doorknob. He turned it and opened the door a crack. The hallway was empty and quiet. He took a moment to take off his shoes and quietly pushed the door open. He stepped lightly into the hallway and placed his back against the wall. His sigh was soft as he felt his heart pounding. Again, the nervous feeling came back, rumbling in the pit of his stomach. He turned to the right and then to the left toward the kitchen. "All he needed to see was the iPad," he thought. He just needed to see the date, and then he would silently creep back into the basement until he was returned to his own time, six hours later.

As he approached the kitchen, the moonbeams sliced through the darkness and landed on top of the island counter. As expected, the iPad that was used for recipes was at the end of the counter. He walked over to the counter and gently tapped on the iPad until his eyes settled on the date at the top, "May 1, 2008."

It had worked! It was exactly one year into the future. He had done it, and though he felt like jumping for joy and exclaiming "Yes! Yes! Yes!" the kitchen lights turned on abruptly. He spun around suddenly to meet Catherine, who also seemed surprised to see him. Surprised because she must have just left him upstairs in the bedroom to only find him in the kitchen.

Brandon was caught off guard, almost to the point of feeling embarrassed. He was about to sheepishly greet her when suddenly her eyes widened and she let out a piercing scream before she fainted onto the floor.

Brandon carried Catherine to the sofa in the living room, and seeing that his future self was not rushing downstairs, he made the assumption that his future self was probably in the lab. As he cradled her in his arms, he admired her soft black hair draped about her face and her skin was still smooth to the touch. It had been a while since he had held her, and he realized then that he missed her.

He parted away a stray strand of hair from her face and looked down at her. She seemed so at peace, despite just letting out a bloodcurdling scream. He whispered her name, softly at first. Then he said to her, "I love you." She stirred, and he let out a smile. "See, I don't have to say it in Korean."

It was a private matter between him and Catherine. His Chinese was passable at best but she was fluent in her Korean. Though they were both born in Boston, Massachusetts, his parents weren't very strict about him learning Chinese, but for Catherine, her parents were insistent that she learn Korean.

As he and Catherine had gotten to know each other, she had taught him a few words and phrases in Korean, and though he was able to pick up most of it, he totally embarrassed himself on some. The most notable one was the phrase for, "I love you" in Korean. He had thought it would be a nice gesture on his part to learn to say, "I love you" in Korean, which he recited phonetically as "*sah rang hap nee dah*," but for some reason, he was never able to say it perfectly. So with all his loving emotions wound up in that moment, when he said it for the first time to Catherine, it instead made her laugh.

Though she had no intent on being mean, he was thoroughly embarrassed and never felt inclined to ever say it again to her. Ultimately, his stubbornness held steadfast, and it had become a sore point between them, for she had learned how to say, "I love you" in Chinese, but he never attempted to say, "I love you" in Korean ever again.

Finally, Catherine began to come to, and Brandon looked down at his wife. Her eyes opened, and she blinked a few times until finally her eyes simply met his. He looked at her and smiled when suddenly, she kicked herself off the couch and out of his arms. She landed on the floor on all fours with a thud, bolted toward the hallway and the stairs that lay just beyond it.

Brandon was entirely taken aback by her reaction, but he yelled out, "Catherine!"

She stopped and turned around. Her terrified gaze met his, and she simply stared up at Brandon. He took a step toward her, but she turned onto her bottom and with a stern finger pointed at him, yelled, "Stay where you are! Don't come any closer!" Before Brandon could utter another word, she blurted out, "Who are you!"

Brandon was entirely confused but he replied, "It's me, Brandon."

There was a pause and without breaking her bewildered stare, she said, "You can't be Brandon! Brandon is dead!"

The startling words sliced through his very being. He couldn't believe the words he had just heard. As he took another step forward, Catherine edged backwards and he stopped. He brought his hands together in a pleading manner and said once more, "It's me, Brandon, your husband."

At those words, Catherine turned and jumped to her feet, readying to race up the stairs. He had to stop her and in a moment of complete loss, he uttered, "The time machine worked!"

The words stopped her in her tracks. For a moment, some sort of recognition or reason resonated in her mind, and she turned back to Brandon. "It worked?" was all she said.

As Catherine sat on the bottom step with Brandon on the living room's hardwood floor, Brandon explained to her that he had just overcome the last obstacle to time travel and in an attempt to prove that it worked, he traveled exactly one year into the future to see how his life would be changed.

Catherine sat there, muted by the story from her dead husband who traveled from the past into her present. After Brandon finished his story, there was only silence as Catherine stared down at the base of the staircase.

In a low tone, Brandon called out to her, "Catherine?"

"I don't remember you telling me about the time machine ever working," said Catherine.

"That's because I haven't told you yet," said Brandon. "Upon my return, if I tell you in a few hours, you'll remember. Temporal mechanics honey."

Catherine nodded in understanding, and Brandon knew she understood.

"Honey?" asked Brandon as the tough question crept forth.

Catherine looked up, as if she had already anticipated the question.

"What happened? How did… how did I die?"

There was a pause. "It was cancer. We were both at a loss to explain it, since you were always so healthy. When it was discovered, it was already terminal and you passed away soon thereafter. The doctors said they've never seen such an aggressive cancer. It was so hard on me to lose you."

Brandon sat in silence to absorb the dreadful words. To hear of his demise from his future wife was not what he had anticipated, and a heavy sense of guilt suddenly fell upon him. He had never expected a life without his wife. He thought he had all the time in the world. His wife's head dropped into her crossed arms, and he could tell she was crying. Instinctively, he got up to console her, but she suddenly raised her head and with tearful laden eyes, she stammered, "No! Stay back! I can't handle this now!"

"But Catherine…"

"No stay back! I can't accept this! I don't know if I have gotten over you yet, and you being here and really not is something I can't handle right now!"

Brandon reached out to her as the morning's first rays suddenly surfed across his arm. He suddenly remembered that his six hours were almost up. At that moment, the alarm on his watch went off and his expression turned to worry.

"What's that?" she asked.

With only 10 seconds left, he said, "I lost track of time, but I can only stay in one temporal point in time for 6 hours before I am brought back to my own time. I can't stay any longer but I'll re…"

At that moment, in a blink of an eye, the surprised and fearful look on Catherine's face vanished and Brandon was simply staring at the spinning wall of the time machine that had begun to slow down. He had returned to his own time within the temporal chamber. He dropped to his knees as a tear slowly seeped from his eye, as he finished his sentence, "…turn. I'll return to you."

Later that night, he returned to the lab. After having gone home earlier in the morning to find that his present-day Catherine had already left for work. He could only think about the future day Catherine. He was disappointed that he left her in such a state of confusion with his untimely arrival. At first, he deliberated not going back into the future, but in the end, the guilt he had for the future Catherine won out. He had to at least go back and make things right with her. Future wife or not, she was still his wife.

The time machine came to life once more, and like the night before, in a blink of an eye, Brandon appeared in the basement, exactly one day after his first future visit. He had closed his eyes on the second trip so that the bright flash of the temporal vortex wouldn't blind them. However, this time, there was something different. Catherine was waiting for him.

Brandon's eyes focused on Catherine, who was seated in a chair in front of him. She caught him off guard until she said, "It really does work."

"Catherine," whispered Brandon. He was so excited to see her. She was dressed casually in a pair of jeans and a black long sleeve top. But she sat there guardedly, not immediately replying to him.

"Catherine," but before Brandon could continue, Catherine responded, "I almost didn't believe what happened last night. I wanted to believe, but at the same time, I wanted to think that I must have been delusional. Please, don't come any closer, just listen. I mean, who would believe that my dead husband from the past had come to visit me, but didn't know that he died? But when you simply vanished, I really thought that maybe I was seeing a ghost, but you had mentioned that the time machine worked. And I remembered the basement, so I waited for you here, and now, here you are."

"I didn't want to leave things the way they were when I left last night. I came back for you."

"Don't say that," said Catherine with a hint of resignation in her tone. "I only started to let you go. You don't know how painful it was for me to lose you. And now to see you alive is just all too confusing."

Brandon took a step forward. He wanted to hold her, but she stood up from her chair and took a step backward. "Don't come a step closer!"

But Brandon ignored her as he rushed toward her. She tried to run away from him, but he was too fast for her and caught her around her mid-section. After struggling hopelessly, she began to scream for him to let her go, but he wouldn't. He had never seen her so agitated, but he wanted to calm her and soothe her. For whatever reason, her struggle eventually subsided as she sank into his arms. There was a familiarity there that she longed for, and his scent brought back cherished memories. Finally the tears began to stream from her eyes as she choked back on the tears.

Soon, they sank to the floor together, and he simply held her as she sobbed into his chest. He found an overwhelming sense of sadness that he never felt before. The immense guilt was eating away at him, and the thought of him leaving her made the guilt grow even more. Under her sobs, Catherine uttered, "I missed you." She conceded that she was ready to let him go, but seeing him, having him hold her again, and being in his embrace were all too comforting, and she allowed the moment to overtake her doubts.

Eventually, Catherine cried herself to sleep. Brandon figured she had not slept at all, since the experience was probably more traumatic for her. After a few hours, when she couldn't be coaxed out of her deep sleep, he carried her to the bedroom and placed her gently into bed. After pulling up the covers against her chin and parting her hair from her face, he placed a soft kiss on her lips to which she gently stirred.

He watched her for the remainder of his time, but he found that his heart ached, as he would be gone again and she'd have to wonder if he'd ever return. He couldn't do that to Catherine, to let her second guess his commitment to her. He would be there for her no matter what. Then like the night before, in an instant, he was back, staring at the time machine.

On the third night, he had prepared for his journey. He was not prepared to tell the world of his great scientific achievement, not just yet. His future wife was all that he could think about. At the usual time, his present-day

Catherine called him to ask if he was coming home for dinner, to which he replied, "No." She didn't expect anything more of him, and she simply said once more, "I'll leave dinner in the fridge for you." But before she could hang up, he said to her, "I love you." There was silence on the other end but she responded, "*sah rang hap nee dah.*" He could sense that she was waiting for him to repeat it to her. He wanted to respond in his mediocre Korean, but his voice couldn't wrap around the phrase before she hung up.

On his third trip, he found his future wife waiting for him. He hesitated, but this time she stood up and she smiled. She was absolutely beautiful, he thought, and this time, he walked over to her. He reached for her, and she stepped into his arms as the warmth of her body pressed up against his body.

"I don't know if this is wrong or right, but right now, I don't care. You're here with me," she said.

"I'm so worried for you," replied Brandon. Soon, they embraced in a longing kiss. His lips pressed onto her supple lips and it was like kissing her for the first time all over again. Her hands feverishly began to untuck his shirt and Brandon broke the kiss to look at the devilish smile on Catherine's face. With a primal yearning urge, he grabbed the ends of Catherine's sweater and smoothly lifted it over her head as she giggled teasingly. As he took off his shirt, Catherine quickly slipped out of her jeans to reveal her slender legs. With Brandon bare-chested, she lunged at him as her silky legs wrapped around his waist as her arms went around his neck. As Brandon held onto her smooth butt, they pressed their hot steamy lips together as he walked over to the basement sofa. Still locked in a passionate kiss as their tongues intertwined longingly, he slipped off her underwear, which she was more than eager to get off. With some help from her, he worked his pants off and soon plunged deep into her. To her delight, he made love to her for seemingly hours on end.

For the remainder of the night, as she lay on top of him on the sofa under the blanket, they just talked. He had learned that she was still working, and that she had kept mainly to herself after his death. She told him where he was buried and who had attended. It was a morbid thought, but at the same time, Brandon found himself intrigued to hear of his own funeral and what was said about him. Brandon diverted the conversation about him and asked Catherine what she remembered about a year ago. Catherine simply said that she did not remember him saying anything about the time machine ever being successful, even on his deathbed. It made sense to Brandon because in his timeline, he simply had not told her just yet. Then the alarm on his watch went off. They held each other tightly and under her breath, she said, "Take me with you."

He wished he could, but he knew it would not be possible. He attempted to part from the embrace but she wouldn't let go. Suddenly, Brandon became alarmed. He didn't know what would happen if she didn't let go when he would be whisked away through time and space back to his own time. But he didn't have the chance to find out when he suddenly found himself back in the time machine, alone and naked.

For the remainder of the day, he was worried about his future Catherine. He wasn't sure if being in such close proximity to the temporal vortex would have harmed her. He was confident that she was fine, but he couldn't be absolutely sure until he went back to the future to see for himself.

On the fourth night, anxious to see his wife, he started up the time machine a couple of hours early. Like clockwork, at 10:30 PM, his present-day Catherine called him and asked the same question about dinner. He replied to her once more with the usual answer, "No, I won't be home, but thank you for asking."

"Sure. I'll leave dinner in the fridge for you," said Catherine.

Again, Brandon felt his tongue wrestling with the Korean syllables, and his lack of confidence added only another constraint until he finally just said, "I love you."

"Sure," replied Catherine before she hung up.

Brandon prepared the fourth visit and when all the lights went green, he clicked on "Engage." But unlike previous nights, the display flickered and the lights in the lab fluttered wildly. Suddenly, power to the time machine was interrupted and it shook violently as it began shutting down. An eerie silence invaded the entire laboratory. Then it appeared on the screen, a dialogue box with a request.

"Enter the date of your first time travel."

Brandon hesitated. "Someone else knew of his time travel," he thought. The only clue that he had to understand what had just happened was on the computer display. He carefully typed into the computer, "05/01/07," and then he hit "Enter."

The dialogue box disappeared, and a video started to load. It was black at first until the current date, "05/03/07" appeared in white. His eyes widened as his wife suddenly appeared on screen. He was a bit taken aback by her unexpected appearance. Though it was Catherine, she was about two decades older. Her hair was still black as ever but her face had aged. However, she was still beautiful in his eyes. Before he could comprehend what was happening, she began to speak.

"Hello Brandon. You're probably wondering what's going on right now, and let me assure you that nothing is wrong. In fact, everything should be better from this day onward. Let me explain. When you first traveled into the future and arrived on that fateful day, May 1, 2008, it changed my life forever. And yours as well. Losing you and living without you were so hard, and seeing you again was very traumatic. But I didn't let it bother me because in the end, I wanted to have you, even if it was the man from my past. And you were so good to me. All in all, you made about 40 trips to see me, in a span of four weeks. Then the cancer erupted and ravaged your body in your timeline, and you never came back after that. I endured losing you a second time because I knew what it meant when you no longer traveled back from the past to see me. I spent the next few years thinking about the past and your time travel until I realized what had brought on the cancer: It was the time machine. Somehow, the numerous visits through the time machine caused the cancer, and your last trips accelerated its growth. My own selfishness, along with your immense guilt for me, only made your cancer worse. Soon after, I decided that I needed to do something, and for two decades, I continued your work. I first studied day after day, and earned two doctoral degrees in temporal quantum mechanics. I reviewed all your notes. I had a lot of catching up to you in understanding temporal quantum mechanics, but soon, I got a grant to continue your work with only one intent: to travel back in time to the laboratory where you had discovered time travel, to end your work, and to tell you why. So yes, I sat where you are probably sitting right now and reprogrammed your time matrix so that it would never work again. I filmed myself with that old camera that's in front of you and password-protected this video with something that only you would know. But I also did it for the former me, who's at home worrying about you and our marriage. The former me who always wondered if you still loved me. The former me who felt so empty when you finally left this world."

Tears welled up in her eyes, but she continued on. "If you listen to me, you'll stop visiting the future me because the present me needs you more, and if you love me, you will stop spending time for me and instead, spend time with me. I can't say how much I love you, but I can only say that my love is timeless. I miss you, please come home."

Brandon's eyes were transfixed on the very future Catherine who had traveled back into the past to help him when all this time, he thought he was helping her. She stared back at him and gently, he placed his fingertips along her face and in her soothing voice she said, "*sah rang hap nee dah.*"

A flood of emotions suddenly washed over him as he choked back on his own tears and though it was guttural sounding, he uttered the words, "*sah rang hap nee dah.*"

Then in a moment of realization, he knew what he needed to do.

He had wanted to save the video of his distant wife, but she built in a program that effectively deleted it. She was true to her temporal discipline, he thought. He rushed home that night because there was nothing for him at work, all that he ever had to look forward to was already waiting for him at home.

As he entered his home, his wife was taking off her apron. She was surprised to see him, but for Brandon, seeing Catherine, just as she was, was like seeing her for the first time all over again. Without so much as a hello, he rushed over to her and embraced her so hard that she was startled. But the warmth of the hug was overwhelming and she welcomed it and hugged him back, fully absorbed into his arms.

"I didn't expect you to come home," she said to him, but he didn't respond.

He almost didn't want to ever let go of her. A sudden sense of calm elation settled over him until finally he just simply and perfectly said, "*sah rang hap nee dah.*"

Catherine's eyes widened in genuine surprise and she simply said back to him, "It's about time."

TAMAGO LEFT YOU HUNGRY FOR MORE?

The 8 stories known collectively as "The Tamago Stories," is my Asian American short story collection in addition to my first novel, "The Purple Heart"

If you like my work, please spread the word by doing the following:

1) Go to the following Facebook Page and please LIKE:
    a. **fb.com/thetamagostories**

2) Go to your favorite Japanese restaurant and take a picture of an order of delicious tamago along with the book or your e-reader. Post your picture to **fb.com/thetamagostories** and check into the restaurant

3) On your **Facebook** or **Instagram**, post the same tamago picture with the book or your e-reader and link to **@thetamagostories** and the following **#thetamagostories and #readeattamago**

4) Feel free to tag as many of your friends who are yearning for Asian American stories to read

5) Please write a review on **Amazon** and **Goodreads.com**

6) Are you part of a book club, please consider recommending this book

7) Go to **www.thetamagostories.com** to keep up to date

8) Feel free to check out "The Purple Heart Book" buy going to www.thepurpleheartbook.com or simply purchase the paperback or Kindle from Amazon

SPLIT THE TAMAGO!

Did you like one story in particular? In time for the 2018 holiday season, the following stories may be available as standalone paperback novellas.

Ba-Ba
Green Light
Perfect Match
Take Out
It's About Time

Gift it to your Asian Americans friends!

Before 2018, all the short stories will be available in Kindle format giving you more ways to gift amazing Asian American short stories to your friends. Or just gift the entire Tamago collection.

Thank you for your support!

ABOUT THE AUTHOR

Vincent Yee was born in Boston, Massachusetts. For most of his career, he has worked for a number of Fortune 100 companies in various managerial roles. At all other times, he has a vision...

> *"To use the power of fiction to portray Asian American men and women positively in the media."*

His first novel, "The Purple Heart," is a story about love and courage. Vincent Yee was a former National President for the National Association of Asian American Professionals (NAAAP). He's also been known to create artistic culinary dishes for friends. He now lives in Cambridge, Massachusetts and planning his third book project.

Made in the USA
Middletown, DE
06 September 2018